DEATH
(AND APPLE STRUDEL)

(A European Voyage Cozy Mystery —Book Two)

BLAKE PIERCE

Blake Pierce

Blake Pierce is the USA Today bestselling author of the RILEY PAGE mystery series, which includes seventeen books. Blake Pierce is also the author of the MACKENZIE WHITE mystery series, comprising fourteen books; of the AVERY BLACK mystery series, comprising six books; of the KERI LOCKE mystery series, comprising five books; of the MAKING OF RILEY PAIGE mystery series, comprising six books; of the KATE WISE mystery series, comprising seven books; of the CHLOE FINE psychological suspense mystery, comprising six books; of the JESSE HUNT psychological suspense thriller series, comprising fourteen books (and counting); of the AU PAIR psychological suspense thriller series, comprising three books; of the ZOE PRIME mystery series, comprising four books (and counting); of the new ADELE SHARP mystery series, comprising six books (and counting); of the new EUROPEAN VOYAGE cozy mystery series, comprising six books (and counting); and of the new LAURA FROST FBI suspense thriller.

An avid reader and lifelong fan of the mystery and thriller genres, Blake loves to hear from you, so please feel free to visit www.blakepierceauthor.com to learn more and stay in touch.

FACE OF DARKNESS (Book #6)

A JESSIE HUNT PSYCHOLOGICAL SUSPENSE SERIES
THE PERFECT WIFE (Book #1)
THE PERFECT BLOCK (Book #2)
THE PERFECT HOUSE (Book #3)
THE PERFECT SMILE (Book #4)
THE PERFECT LIE (Book #5)
THE PERFECT LOOK (Book #6)
THE PERFECT AFFAIR (Book #7)
THE PERFECT ALIBI (Book #8)
THE PERFECT NEIGHBOR (Book #9)
THE PERFECT DISGUISE (Book #10)
THE PERFECT SECRET (Book #11)
THE PERFECT FAÇADE (Book #12)
THE PERFECT IMPRESSION (Book #13)
THE PERFECT DECEIT (Book #14)
THE PERFECT MISTRESS (Book #15)

CHLOE FINE PSYCHOLOGICAL SUSPENSE SERIES
NEXT DOOR (Book #1)
A NEIGHBOR'S LIE (Book #2)
CUL DE SAC (Book #3)
SILENT NEIGHBOR (Book #4)
HOMECOMING (Book #5)
TINTED WINDOWS (Book #6)

KATE WISE MYSTERY SERIES
IF SHE KNEW (Book #1)
IF SHE SAW (Book #2)
IF SHE RAN (Book #3)
IF SHE HID (Book #4)
IF SHE FLED (Book #5)
IF SHE FEARED (Book #6)
IF SHE HEARD (Book #7)

THE MAKING OF RILEY PAIGE SERIES
WATCHING (Book #1)
WAITING (Book #2)
LURING (Book #3)

TAKING (Book #4)
STALKING (Book #5)
KILLING (Book #6)

RILEY PAIGE MYSTERY SERIES
ONCE GONE (Book #1)
ONCE TAKEN (Book #2)
ONCE CRAVED (Book #3)
ONCE LURED (Book #4)
ONCE HUNTED (Book #5)
ONCE PINED (Book #6)
ONCE FORSAKEN (Book #7)
ONCE COLD (Book #8)
ONCE STALKED (Book #9)
ONCE LOST (Book #10)
ONCE BURIED (Book #11)
ONCE BOUND (Book #12)
ONCE TRAPPED (Book #13)
ONCE DORMANT (Book #14)
ONCE SHUNNED (Book #15)
ONCE MISSED (Book #16)
ONCE CHOSEN (Book #17)

MACKENZIE WHITE MYSTERY SERIES
BEFORE HE KILLS (Book #1)
BEFORE HE SEES (Book #2)
BEFORE HE COVETS (Book #3)
BEFORE HE TAKES (Book #4)
BEFORE HE NEEDS (Book #5)
BEFORE HE FEELS (Book #6)
BEFORE HE SINS (Book #7)
BEFORE HE HUNTS (Book #8)
BEFORE HE PREYS (Book #9)
BEFORE HE LONGS (Book #10)
BEFORE HE LAPSES (Book #11)
BEFORE HE ENVIES (Book #12)
BEFORE HE STALKS (Book #13)
BEFORE HE HARMS (Book #14)

AVERY BLACK MYSTERY SERIES

CAUSE TO KILL (Book #1)
CAUSE TO RUN (Book #2)
CAUSE TO HIDE (Book #3)
CAUSE TO FEAR (Book #4)
CAUSE TO SAVE (Book #5)
CAUSE TO DREAD (Book #6)

KERI LOCKE MYSTERY SERIES
A TRACE OF DEATH (Book #1)
A TRACE OF MUDER (Book #2)
A TRACE OF VICE (Book #3)
A TRACE OF CRIME (Book #4)
A TRACE OF HOPE (Book #5)

CHAPTER ONE

London Rose was jarred by a shouting voice.

"London!"

She knew that particular voice always meant trouble.

She'd just been enjoying a nice feeling of success, watching Amir, the ship's fitness instructor, lead water aerobics on the sleek riverboat's open-air Rondo deck. The passengers were obviously enjoying themselves, and more than one had thanked London for organizing the class this morning.

The blue-tiled pool raised above the deck was too small for any serious water activity like lap swimming, but it was perfect for cooling plunges, games, and this sort of small-scale exercise class. The fresh air, warm sunlight, and happy passengers had gotten the *Nachtmusik*'s trip from Gyor to Vienna off to a great start.

But again came that sharp noise.

"London! We've got a problem!"

It was Amy Blassingame, the concierge here aboard the yacht-like river tour ship called the *Nachtmusik*.

And she just loves to bring me problems, London thought.

She turned and looked apprehensively at her colleague. Amy was a couple of inches shorter than London's five-foot-six, and her figure was more robust. With her smooth helmet of short dark hair, she could appear almost militant when she wanted to take charge of an issue.

The concierge scarcely bothered to conceal a trace of a smirk.

"You're going to have to get rid of that dog," Amy announced.

London felt a jolt of alarm.

"No," she said. "I'm sure that issue has been settled."

Or at least she thought it had been settled. She'd gotten permission for Sir Reggie to stay with her after his owner had died.

"I'm afraid you're wrong," Amy said. "Because a passenger has complained. He's in stateroom 108—the one right next to yours. Your dog has been yapping and disturbing him."

Amy crossed her arms and shook her head.

"Oh, London," she said. "You should have known it wouldn't work

1

out. You can't keep a dog aboard this ship, I told you so. You should have listened."

London stifled an urge to say, *"You told me no such thing."*

In fact, the two of them hadn't talked about the issue at all.

But it was hardly surprising that Amy was gloating over London's predicament. Just yesterday, London had pretty much single-handedly solved the mystery of a passenger's death and the disappearance of a precious antique snuffbox. Her impromptu amateur detective work had led to the culprit's arrest by the police back in Gyor.

Amy was still stinging from embarrassment over the way she'd developed a crush on the man who had done the deed—or at least with one of the many personas he'd assumed—and had even invited him on board. Amy had fallen for one of the villain's disguises hook, line, and sinker.

And London had exposed that mistake when she'd solved the crime.

Not that Amy and I were on great terms from the start of this trip.

"What are you going to do about it?" Amy demanded.

"I don't know," London said.

"Do you want my help?"

That's the last thing I need, London almost said.

"No. I'm sure you've got other things to do," she said instead.

"You'll have to get rid of the dog, of course," Amy repeated.

"We'll see," London told her, struggling to think of some alternative.

As Amy headed away, London glanced back at the pool. The guests in the water aerobics class were obviously having a good time. So were a few other passengers who stood at the railing looking out over the beautiful blue Danube, which was flanked on either side by lush, forested hills.

She was glad to see their contentment. There had been far too much trauma during the last couple of days, starting with Mrs. Klimowski's mysterious death. Then the boat had filled with police, and the investigation had led to a full day's delay in setting sail to Vienna. The whole episode had taken its toll on everybody's nerves. London knew she had a lot more work to do before this voyage felt like a happy, carefree European river tour again.

But what am I going to do about Sir Reggie? London wondered as she turned and hurried to the elevator. She supposed she could turn him

2

over to animal services when they arrived in Vienna, but …

No, I can't do that, she realized.

I just can't.

There has to be another way.

London got off the elevator on the ship's lowest passenger level, the Allegro deck. The "classic" staterooms here were the least expensive on the ship. Nevertheless, they were very comfortable and the décor was delightful. London had been surprised and charmed to be assigned ones of these rooms for herself. When she was first offered this job, she hadn't realized that her position as social director would carry a certain status.

But of course, the entire ship was much more elegant than any of the huge ocean cruisers that London had worked on in her previous jobs. The *Nachtmusik* was built low like other riverboats, but it was smaller, more advanced in design, and able to travel some rivers where others couldn't go. In fact, it felt very much like a large yacht.

All was silent at first as she walked down the passageway. But as soon as she neared her own room, she could hear the yapping sounds. She opened the door to her room and found herself facing the tiny, teddy bear–like dog.

Reggie stopped yapping and sat looking up at her. Like most Yorkshire Terriers, he was less than eight inches tall at the shoulder, but he had a giant-sized personality.

"Reggie, you've got to stop making that noise," London whispered. "You're going to get into serious trouble."

Wagging his tail excitedly, Reggie trotted out the door into the passageway. London picked him up and wagged her finger at him.

"I get it," she said. "You don't like being left in the room alone. You'd like to go with me everywhere. And the truth is, I'd like that too, because I really enjoy your company, but …"

She felt a lump form in her throat as she continued.

"But I've got a job to do. And I can't have you around all the time, everywhere I go. And this is where your food and potty is. I can't always be running back here to let you in or out of the room."

Reggie let out a whine of resignation as London set him back down in her room. She stood looking at him, and he looked back at her with an almost human expression of longing.

London felt a deep pang of pity.

He deserves better than this, she thought.

He hadn't had a very good life under Mrs. Klimowski's care. Since he weighed less than ten pounds, the woman had carried him around everywhere she went in a tight, uncomfortable leather handbag. Now that he was liberated from that bag, he naturally wanted more freedom—and more human company.

The lump in London's throat tightened.

Aside from being adorable and smart, Sir Reggie had proven himself a hero—and scarcely less of a detective than London herself had unexpectedly turned out to be. He'd identified the killer with a sharp yap, then pursued him bravely when he tried to get away.

His courage had almost gotten him killed. He'd grabbed the escaping man by the pants leg on the ship's gangway, tripping him up so the police could apprehend him. But in doing so, he'd been thrown into the river, and London had plunged in to rescue him.

She'd very nearly lost him. And now her eyes watered as she remembered how pathetic and lifeless he'd looked on the shore, his then-untrimmed coat soaked with water and mud, his little feet sticking up in the air. She also remembered her own gasp of relief when he'd coughed up some water and started to breathe again.

"I'll fix this somehow," London told him. "Meanwhile, please be quiet."

She shut him back up in her quarters, and at least he didn't start yapping right away. But she knew better than to suppose the silence could possibly last.

Meanwhile, she had to talk to her angry neighbor.

She knew his name from her passenger list, Stanley Tedrow, stateroom 108. But she couldn't remember what he looked like. He certainly hadn't been on any of the tours in Budapest or Gyor or any other activity she'd seen. She wondered what he'd been doing on the trip so far.

In an effort to look as dignified as possible, London straightened her uniform and ran her fingers through her short unruly auburn hair.

Then she walked over to room 108 and knocked on the door.

But what am I going to say to him? she wondered.

4

CHAPTER TWO

"Who is it?" growled a rough, raspy voice at the sound of London's knock.

"This is London Rose, the social director," she said.

She heard some grumbling, and then the door opened. A short, stooped, elderly man with a hawklike nose and squinty eyes stood there, glaring at London. He was wearing pajamas, a bathrobe, and slippers.

"You're here about that dog next door, I take it," Tedrow said.

London nodded.

"Have you talked to its owners about the racket it's making?" he asked.

London gulped hard.

"Um, Mr. Tedrow—*I'm* the one taking care of the dog."

"You?" Tedrow said.

"Yes, you see, I ... well, my own stateroom is next door, and since Mrs. Klimowski died, there's no one else to take care of the dog."

"Somebody died?" Tedrow said with surprise.

London was startled. Had the man been so isolated here in his room that he had no idea what had happened during the last few days? Hadn't he even read the letter she'd written to inform the passengers Mrs. Klimowski's death—the one she'd put in all the passengers' mailboxes?

Apparently not, she realized.

And he didn't seem to be at all curious about it, either.

"Well, it's none of my business, I suppose," he said with a shrug. "What matters right now is that you do something about that dog."

"Mr. Tedrow, Sir Reggie's just a little dog. Is he really too noisy for you? Once he gets used to things, surely he won't complain so much. I'll bring you over and introduce him to you. I'm sure you'll like him."

"I need peace and quiet," Tedrow insisted. "What is he barking about anyway?"

"He likes human company. And he likes to run around. But I can't take him wherever I go. I have to leave him in my room sometimes."

5

"Why?"

London was startled by the question's abruptness.

"Can you blame him for not wanting to be shut up like that?" Tedrow added. "Why don't you just give him the run of the ship?"

London was about to explain about how Sir Reggie needed access to the food and dog potty when she suddenly wondered something.

Why not *give him the run of the ship?*

Maybe there was actually a way she could do that.

"I'll see what I can do," she said.

"You do that," Tedrow said. "As long as the dog shuts up, I'll be happy. I don't care who lives next door."

He sat down at an out-of-date-looking computer on his table, apparently anxious to get back to work at something.

London took a look around at the room. Like most of the other staterooms on the Allegro deck, this one was almost identical to hers.

It was hardly as luxurious and spacious as the rooms on the upper levels, but it was much, much nicer than the cramped, windowless quarters she'd shared with other employees while working as a hostess on oceangoing cruise ships. While hers was pleasantly decorated in shades of soft gray and blue, Mr. Tedrow's room décor was a range of earth tones. His little table was mostly taken up by the computer and a small printer, and a few books were scattered on his queen-size bed.

It was a perfectly nice room. But she was worried by the solitude of its occupant.

"Um, Mr. Tedrow—is everything else OK? Aside from my dog, I mean?"

"Why do you ask?" he asked without looking away from the computer screen.

London swallowed uncomfortably.

"Well, as the ship's social director, it's my duty to make sure that everybody aboard the *Nachtmusik* is perfectly happy."

"Don't worry, I'm perfectly happy," Tedrow growled. "Or at least I will be after you do something about that dog."

London peered at him curiously as he kept staring at the computer screen.

He sure doesn't sound perfectly happy, she thought.

She figured it was her job to draw him out, get him to talk to her a little.

"What did you think of Gyor?" she asked.

6

"Why, did we stop there?"

London's eyes widened with surprise.

"Yes, we did," she said. "We just left there last night."

"Well, I knew the ship has been sitting still most of the time since we left Budapest, but I'd sort of forgotten all about the itinerary. I don't much care about it, if you want to know the truth."

What do *you care about?* London wondered.

She tried to hide her worry behind her best professional smile.

"I hope you've at least enjoyed some of the amenities aboard the *Nachtmusik.*"

"Amenities?" he asked, as if he didn't understand the word.

"You know—features, luxuries, activities."

"Such as?"

London peered at him with growing concern—and growing curiosity.

"Well, surely you've checked out the Habsburg Restaurant up on the Romanze deck. Or the swimming pool and outdoor activities up on the Rondo deck. Or the Amadeus Lounge on the Menuetto deck. You know, we've been adding some casino features to the lounge—"

"Sorry, not interested," Tedrow said with a dismissive wave of his hand, still staring at his computer screen.

London was baffled. Surely Mr. Tedrow had explored the ship at least once since the beginning of the journey. But since then ...

Has he been outside this room at all?

She noticed a tray of mostly eaten breakfast also on the table where he worked. Perhaps he'd had all his meals delivered here since they'd left Bucharest. It suddenly occurred to London that a passenger *could* spend the entire Danube tour cooped up in one's own stateroom.

But why would anyone do that?

And wasn't it up to her to coax such a passenger to get out and around?

But Mr. Tedrow was obviously a prickly character, so she knew she'd better be careful how she went about drawing him out.

"Mr. Tedrow, if you don't mind my asking ..."

Tedrow growled as if he did mind.

London continued, "What have you enjoyed most about your trip so far?"

"The privacy," he said, scowling at her. "At least most of the time. And the quiet—at least when I've been able to get it."

7

"And?"

He pointed to the high window, which was open.

"The fresh sea air," he said.

London squinted with perplexity. She had no doubt that Mr. Tedrow knew perfectly well that the *Nachtmusik* was on a river tour, and that the ship hadn't been at sea since they'd left Budapest.

Now he's just trying to annoy me, she thought.

She was determined not to let him succeed.

"Mr. Tedrow—" she began.

"If you don't mind, Miss Sociality, I'd like to get back to enjoying myself."

He kept his eyes glued to the computer screen.

"Just do something about that dog, OK?" he grumbled, drumming his fingers on the table.

"OK, Mr. Tedrow," London said, then left the room.

When she closed the door behind her, she stood in the passageway trying to process the strange visit. She remembered something he'd said.

"Don't worry, I'm perfectly happy."

Might he have really meant it, despite his grouchy tone? Was it possible that Mr. Tedrow really was enjoying the river tour in his own peculiar way? Maybe so, London thought, but she wondered whether he couldn't have had just as good a time by staying home.

She quickly reminded herself of her own professional motto.

"The customer may not always be right, but the customer is always the customer."

It surely wasn't up to her to change Mr. Tedrow's solitary ways. It was his choice, after all. She couldn't exactly drag him kicking and screaming into all the entertainments, pastimes, and diversions of a luxury tour boat.

Besides, London had another pressing concern at the moment. She went back into her room, where Reggie welcomed her eagerly.

"I've got an idea," she said. "You and I have an errand to run."

As she attached a leash to his collar, she added, "I'm going to try to fix things for both of us. But you've got to be a perfect little gentleman, as adorable as you can possibly be. You can do that, can't you?"

Sir Reggie let out a little yap of what sounded like agreement. She led him out into the passageway, where he trotted toward the elevator in front of her. They took the elevator back up to the open-air Rondo deck.

As soon as they stepped off the elevator, London was surprised to hear a small burst of applause. The people playing on the shuffleboard court had stopped playing and were expressing their delight at seeing Sir Reggie.

As if daunted by this warm reception, Sir Reggie jumped up into London's arms.

"There he is—our hero!" shouted a woman.

"The fearless Sir Reggie!" exclaimed a man.

Another woman laughed. "We can all breathe easier, knowing that Sir Reggie is always here to save the day!"

As passengers started to cluster around him, poor Reggie didn't seem to quite get what the fuss was about. But London understood. Word had gotten around the ship about Sir Reggie's courageous behavior yesterday, and he was now rather famous aboard the *Nachtmusik*.

"Get used to it, kid," she murmured to him, scratching his head. "You're now a celebrity."

She couldn't help feeling amused that she herself wasn't getting the same kind of acclaim after having solved the mystery of Mrs. Klimowski's death.

Maybe if I was just little and cute ...

But she decided it was just as well that people still seemed to still regard her as London Rose the social director, and not as London Rose the intrepid sleuth. It made her job a little easier.

Meanwhile, London took comfort in the reception Sir Reggie was getting. Whatever else might happen, he wasn't going to get evicted from *Nachtmusik*. With his popularity, any attempt to get rid of him would result in a scandalous ship-wide uproar.

Also, if it turned out that she *couldn't* keep Reggie in her own room, there would be other people who would be thrilled to take care of him ...

London felt a sudden alarm at that idea.

No, she thought.

He's my dog now.

He's no one else's.

My plan has to work, she thought. *It just has to.*

CHAPTER THREE

Although Sir Reggie was obviously enjoying all the attention, London knew that she needed to keep moving. The demands of her job left little time for taking care of personal issues. She had to solve this problem right now so she could stop worrying about losing her dog.

Carrying Reggie away from his fans, she headed for the ship's glass-enclosed bridge, which towered over the Rondo deck. She climbed the steps to the bridge and knocked on the door.

As she expected, she was greeted by the portly Captain Spencer Hays, an Englishman whose walrus-style mustache couldn't begin to hide his smile of delight at her arrival.

"Why, London Rose! What an unexpected pleasure! Come in, come in!"

London realized she'd never actually been on the *Nachtmusik*'s bridge before. It was an awe-inspiring sight, with the Afro-French First Officer Jean-Louis Berville overseeing the three crew members who manned a vast bank of computerized controls while overlooking the river ahead.

And as it happened, London was in for a bit of luck. The captain had another visitor—the ship's lanky maintenance chief, Archie Behnke. The young blond mechanic was adept at fixing anything with moving parts.

Just who I need to see, she thought.

The captain's eyes widened at the sight of Sir Reggie.

"But—good lord! What's this? Do we have another animal aboard?"

London laughed at the captain's confusion.

"No, this is still Sir Reggie," she said.

"But what a transformation! Why, he scarcely looks like the same creature! What on earth has happened to him?"

Of course, Captain Hays had seen Sir Reginald Taft only one other time, and that was back when the little dog's hair had been long enough to drag on the ground. He'd looked to her like a weird wig with eyes and a little black nose. London thought that such glamour might have

10

been appropriate for a former show dog, but she hadn't liked it much, and even Reggie had never seemed especially comfortable that way. After his near-drowning, London had taken him to the *Nachtmusik*'s beautician for a shampoo and a serious do-over.

"We've given him a new look," London explained to the captain. "It's called a 'puppy cut.'"

"Jolly good!" Captain Hays said. "It suits him well."

"Now he looks just like one of the crew," Archie Behnke added.

London laughed, then carefully broached the subject she'd come to discuss.

"I've been keeping him in my room," she said. "But it's not working out very well."

"No?" the captain said.

"I can't spend every minute with him," London said. "And he doesn't like being shut up alone."

"Of course he doesn't," Captain Hays said with a stern nod. "He'd rather be out and about tracking down international jewel thieves. And it's a waste of his talents as far as the rest of us are concerned. He's got important work to do here on the *Nachtmusik*. We can't do without him."

London was relieved at the captain's sympathetic tone. Before she could make the request she had in mind, the maintenance chief spoke up.

"It sounds like you need a doggie door," Archie said.

London held her breath for a moment. A doggie door was exactly what she had planned to ask for. But would such a thing be allowed?

"Yes, I think that's exactly what I need," London agreed, a little shakily.

The captain wiggled his enormous eyebrows.

"A doggie door?" he asked. "Please explain."

Archie shrugged.

"Oh, I'm sure you've seen such a thing before," he said. "It's just a square hole in the door for the dog to come and go. It's got a flap on it that can be latched at night. And for a dog Sir Reggie's size, it can be very small."

"Capital idea!" the captain proclaimed.

London looked back and forth between Archie and the captain. This was sounding almost too good to be true.

"Do you think it will be OK with the passengers?" she asked.

11

Of course, London already felt as though she knew the answer to that question. She only hoped the captain would agree.

"The passengers?" he said. "They'll be thrilled to see him at large. Just the sight of his fearless visage will inspire them with a feeling of safety and confidence."

London was happy to hear this, but there was still another matter she felt obliged to mention.

"The thing is … how do I … I mean do I need to get permission from …?"

"From someone high on the corporate ladder?" the captain said with a scoff. "Oh, I hardly think so. We're just cutting a hole in a door, that's all. We're not talking about carving some gaping cavity in the boat's hull. Besides, you happen to be in very good stead with our CEO. I'm sure you have his tacit approval for pretty much any measures you think to be necessary. I can let him know the next time I talk to him. Of course it will be all right."

London smiled. She was sure the captain was right about that. Yesterday Jeremy Lapham, the CEO of Epoch World Cruise Lines, had called her from the U.S. after she'd solved the mystery of Mrs. Klimowski's death.

"Congratulations and cheers and kudos are definitely in order," he'd said.

Of course a simple doggie door would be all right with him.

London felt her eyes misting up. Everything was going to work out just fine. She could keep her dog! From now on, Sir Reggie would have a better life, and she would have a trusty companion.

Archie got up from his chair.

"My guys and I will get right to work on it," he said. "It's nice to have something simple and straightforward to do after some of the odder demands we're getting from the passengers."

"So you're getting some strange ones?" London asked.

Archie scoffed.

"Oh, most of them are reasonable. But your concierge told me about one guy who wants me to … well, never mind. It can't be done, and I told her so."

Something about Archie's words rang a bell with London, as if she'd heard something about that complainer before.

She gave Archie her keycard so he could get into her room and start working. Then she and Archie both left the bridge and headed off on

12

their respective ways.

With Sir Reginald trotting along with her, London took the stairs two flights down to the Habsburg Restaurant. The large room in the bow of the Romanze deck provided elegantly set tables of various sizes and arrangements for the passengers to choose as they pleased. The tables placed near the large windows almost created the feeling of eating outside.

As Sir Reggie entered the restaurant ahead of her, he got another round of applause from customers having a late breakfast. A few got up from their tables to come over and make over the little dog. This time Sir Reggie seemed unalarmed and didn't jump up into London's arms.

He's getting to like all this attention, London realized.

As London had hoped, her old friend Elsie Sloan was sitting at a table enjoying a cup of coffee. The tall blond woman was in charge of the Amadeus Lounge and was taking a break after setting up the bar with her staff. As London and Reggie each took a seat at her table, she was visibly amused at the fuss over the dog.

"You're getting upstaged, honey," Elsie said, laughing. "It's an old rule of show business—never go onstage with children or animals."

A familiar male voice said, "Sir Reggie is no animal. He's an elite security guard."

London turned and saw Bryce Yeaton approaching the table wearing his white chef's uniform. She was always happy to see his warm smile, and she found his gray eyes, dimpled chin, and stubble of beard quite attractive. Like many of the crew, the handsome Australian had more than one job, doubling as the ship's head chef and chief medic. He'd helped save both London and Reggie from drowning while the police had taken the escaping culprit into custody.

"My mistake, Reggie," Elsie said to the dog. "Let me know if you want to put in some extra hours as a bouncer."

"Are customers getting rowdy on you?" London asked wryly.

"Not yet, but it's only a matter of time."

London knew that Elsie was joking. So far, most of the passengers on this voyage seemed to be quite content. Of course, it was up to London to keep them that way.

At the moment, she felt pretty happy with the job she'd been doing. For example, yesterday she'd suggested that Elsie set up a roulette table in the Amadeus Lounge. And just this morning, she'd helped Elsie and her staff set up a blackjack table there. A section of the bar was getting transformed into a sort of makeshift casino that promised to be extremely popular.

"What can I get for you this morning?" Bryce asked London.

"Coffee, of course. I've already had breakfast, so maybe something sweet to go with the coffee."

Bryce smiled at her—a bit flirtatiously, London thought, or maybe hoped.

"May I suggest our apple strudel?" he said. "It seems fitting now that we're heading for Vienna."

"Apple strudel would be nice," London said.

"Coming right up," Bryce said. "What have you got planned for lunch?"

"I may have to skip that," London said. "I'm going to be on the run all day."

"How about a sandwich to go?"

"That would be nice."

Bryce took a small bag out of his pocket and took out what looked like a small cracker.

"I cooked up something just for you, Sir Reggie," he said, holding the treat in front of the dog. "Want it?"

Sir Reggie let out a yap, and Bryce tossed the treat to him. The dog caught the cracker in midair and gobbled it down.

Bryce smiled at London.

"I'm always prepared to please customers of all kinds," he said.

London felt her own smile broaden as he headed back to the kitchen.

Elsie leaned across the table and said to London, "Do I detect some romantic sparks in the air?"

London rolled her eyes.

"Elsie, when are you going to learn to mind your own business?"

"Never."

London stifled a sigh.

"It's too soon to tell. And besides …"

"Don't tell me, I already know. You've also got your eye on our ship's German historian."

London felt herself blushing. Yes, the suave, intelligent Emil Waldmüller had gotten her attention. He'd also done his own share to help solve the mystery. But he could be strangely off-putting as well as charming, and London hadn't yet decided what she really thought of

14

him.

"I'm not here for romance," she said to Elsie. "I've got a job to do."

"The two aren't mutually exclusive," Elsie replied.

Before London could comment, a man stepped up to the table. He was wearing a nautical cap and a colorful silk shirt with a broad collar that spread over his jacket lapel.

"Are you London Rose, our social director?" he said sharply.

"Yes, how can I help you?"

"My name is Kirby Oswinkle. And I've got a complaint to make."

London felt a tingle of apprehension. She could tell by his sour tone that this was going to be no ordinary complaint.

Just remember, she reminded herself. *The customer is always the customer.*

CHAPTER FOUR

Kirby Oswinkle, London thought, mulling over the name in her mind.

Something about the arrogant way the man said his own name suggested that she ought to know who he was already.

Of course, she realized.

She'd met him briefly when he'd boarded the *Nachtmusik* in Budapest, and although he hadn't made much of an impression at the time, she did remember that nautical cap.

And also that he hadn't been especially pleasant.

Since then, she'd memorized every name on the ship's manifest, and she knew that Kirby Oswinkle had a suite on the Menuetto deck—not a grand suite, but still very nice accommodations.

"What can I do to help, Mr. Oswinkle?" she asked.

"I think you know," Oswinkle said, crossing his arms. "I brought it up with your concierge on the second day of our voyage. Nothing has been done to take care of the problem."

London squinted with thought.

What problem?

Then she recalled Amy approaching her about a passenger with a "small complaint" the day before yesterday.

"Well, not a small complaint as far as he's concerned," Amy had added.

Now she remembered. And now she was also pretty sure she knew who the maintenance chief had meant when he'd mentioned a passenger with an impossible demand.

"Oh, yes," London said to Oswinkle. "You were anxious about the temperature in your room."

"Anxious?" Oswinkle scoffed. "I believe I put it in stronger terms than that."

London nodded.

"You want the temperature in your stateroom to stay at seventy-eight degrees," she said.

"*Constantly* at seventy-eight degrees," Oswinkle said. "And I do

16

mean *exactly*, not so much as a fraction of a degree higher or lower."

Bryce had come back from the kitchen. He placed a full to-go bag and a plate of apple strudel on the table in front of her, then stood listening quietly.

"I'm sure our concierge is doing her best to—" London began.

"No, she's *not* doing her best," he interrupted. "Your concierge came to my room and saw the problem for herself. But she hasn't done anything about it."

"But are you sure the temperature varies—?"

Interrupting, Oswinkle produced a digital thermometer from his pocket.

"I know it for a fact. I don't trust thermostats to tell me exactly what temperature it is. They're too approximate. That's what my personal gauge is for. It tells me when the temperature varies even the slightest. And it *does* vary—sometimes by as much as half a degree!"

Half a degree! London thought.

No wonder Archie Behnke had told Amy this particular task *"just can't be done."*

Then London noticed that Oswinkle's agitated manner was attracting the attention of people at nearby tables. Some were openly staring at him and others were smiling or even starting to giggle. Then she realized that Sir Reggie was also paying rapt attention to Oswinkle. Sitting on the chair next to London's, the little dog kept tilting his head sympathetically at everything Oswinkle said.

The other passengers were beginning to find the whole scene amusing, especially the dog.

London started to worry.

If Mr. Oswinkle notices …

London stood up to talk with him more confidentially. "Is this due to, uh, health concerns?" she asked in what she hoped was a soothing tone.

Mr. Oswinkle drew himself up and replied huffily and rather loudly.

"I don't see how my health is any business of yours, young lady. The fact that I'm *asking* for this temperature setting ought to be sufficient."

Still listening, Sir Reggie nodded emphatically, as if in complete agreement.

The nearby customers were chuckling now. A man at a nearby table spoke up.

"It looks like the dog is the only one here who takes you seriously, Mr. Oswinkle."

London was alarmed to see Oswinkle's face redden with anger.

Pointing at Sir Reggie, he snapped, "That animal is mocking me!"

Before she could protest, Sir Reggie drew back sharply, then buried his head in her forearm, acting exactly as if he were crying with shame.

Most of the surrounding people were laughing now.

Oh, no, London thought.

This isn't good.

Of course she was sure that Sir Reggie didn't intend actual mockery with his behavior. He'd probably learned these gestures as tricks at one time or another, presumably before he'd come under Mrs. Klimowski's tyrannical care.

Oswinkle let out a growl of anger, then turned to walk away.

London called after him, "Mr. Oswinkle ..."

Oswinkle turned toward her again.

"We'll do our best to solve your problem," London said.

Oswinkle took his cell phone out of his pocket.

"I'm calling your maintenance chief right this minute," he said. "It's about time I personally got him involved."

He turned away again and stalked out of the restaurant, tapping a number on his phone.

Relieved that the people around her didn't break out into applause again over Reggie's little performance, London sat down at the table again.

She leaned toward Sir Reggie and murmured, "You might be too cute for either of our good."

He looked back at her as if he couldn't understand how such a thing was possible.

Then London gave her attention to the apple strudel that Bryce had brought her. When she took a bite, the flavor vanquished her anxieties over the fussy passenger and his room temperature. The filling was a perfect mixture of cooked apple, cinnamon, and sugar—exactly as sweet as it ought to be, no more, no less. The pastry itself was made out of astonishingly delicate, tissue-thin layers of flawlessly kneaded dough. Like the baklava Bryce had made for London earlier, the whole concoction melted deliciously in her mouth.

"Um-m-m," she said.

"Take your time with it," Bryce advised her. "Never rush through something that good."

He took his bag of dog treats out of his pocket.

"I'll bet Sir Reginald has lots of tricks in his repertoire," he said, unsnapping the dog's leash from his collar and handing it to London.

As the other customers watched attentively, Bryce took four glasses off an unoccupied table and set them in a row in the aisle of the eating area, placing them about a foot and a half apart from one another. He coaxed Sir Reginald to sit at one end of the row of glasses, then stood himself at the other end.

He held out a treat in one hand and snapped his fingers with his other.

Sure enough, Sir Reginald deftly wove his way back and forth, snaking his way through the row of glasses, and receiving a treat from Bryce at the end. Then Bryce and Reggie switched places and repeated the trick again. This time several customers did applaud.

Then Bryce stood with his legs apart, and Sir Reginald wove back and forth between them.

"How did you teach him to do that so fast?" one of the customers asked.

"I didn't," Bryce said. "Those are pretty standard tricks, and somebody may have taught them to him already."

"Or maybe he's just smart," Elsie suggested.

"Maybe," London agreed.

She'd been struck by his uncanny intelligence during the last few days—especially how he'd led her along the path Mrs. Klimowski had walked through Gyor just before her death. He'd done more than his share to solve the mystery. If it weren't for him, maybe they'd still be stuck in Gyor while the police looked in vain for the killer.

"It looks like we've got a new ship's mascot," remarked Elsie.

"Yeah, and he'll have the run of the ship soon," London said. "The maintenance guys are installing a doggie door in my room."

"So he'll be able to come and go exactly as he pleases," Elsie said. "How does that make you feel?"

"What do you mean?" London asked, a little surprised at the question.

"Well, he's a high-spirited, independent little animal. He's not going to want to go following you around all the time anymore. He'll have things to do, places to explore, people to meet and entertain."

19

London felt an unexpected twinge of melancholy at the thought.

"I guess I won't be needing this," she said, putting the leash in her handbag.

Finally Bryce and Sir Reggie finished up their little impromptu performance, and they both took bows as the nearby customers applauded. Bryce headed back to the kitchen, and Sir Reggie hopped back onto the chair next to London.

"So how's your apple strudel?" Elsie asked London.

"Beyond perfect," London told her. "You should try it."

She offered Elsie a taste with her fork. At the taste, Elsie's eyes rolled back in ecstasy.

"Mmmm," she purred. "I wonder if we'll get strudel this good even in Vienna."

London wondered that too—although it seemed almost a blasphemous thought, considering Vienna's reputation as one of the pastry centers of Western civilization.

"I'm starting to see what you see in Bryce," Elsie added. "I mean, it's one thing that he's easy on the eyes. If he keeps making desserts like this, I'm liable to develop a crush on him too. I hope you don't mind having a rival."

London shook her head with an embarrassed smile.

"You're just impossible," she said.

"Yeah, I get that a lot," Elsie said, getting up from the table. "Well, I'd better get back to the lounge. What are you going to do about Mr. Oswinkle's temperature problem?"

London suppressed a sigh.

"Check in on him, of course. I guess he's already called Archie Behnke about it. But Archie told me there's nothing to be done. If Archie can't fix it, I sure can't."

"I hope you can work something out," Elsie said.

"Me too."

"Good luck."

"Thanks."

Elsie walked on out of the restaurant.

London quietly enjoyed the last bites of her strudel and finished her coffee before getting up from her chair. She looked down at Sir Reggie, who was still sitting in the chair next to her.

"I'm on my way to deal with a grumpy passenger," she said to the dog. "You can come along if you like, but I'm afraid it won't be much

20

fun. It's entirely up to you."

She was a bit relieved that Sir Reggie hopped down from his chair, apparently happy to join her on this errand.

As she and the dog walked out of the restaurant together, London said to him, "Maybe you can help me deal with Mr. Oswinkle. I sure don't know what to do about him. But still ..."

She paused for a moment, then said, "At least it's not like solving another murder."

Sir Reggie let out a little, uncertain-sounding yap.

"I know what you mean," London replied as they took the stairs down to the Menuetto deck. "At least a murder can be solved. Maybe there's no way to solve a problem like Mr. Oswinkle."

It irritated her more than she wanted to admit to herself. This seemed like such a mundane issue to have to handle after the excitement, mental challenges, and even danger of the last couple of days. Now that she'd gotten a taste of detective work, was it possible she actually missed "the chase"?

As London mulled that question over, she and Sir Reggie reached Oswinkle's room on the Menuetto deck. Oddly enough, the door to the suite was standing wide open.

Even stranger were the words she could hear from out in the hallway.

"What you want me to do is against the law."

CHAPTER FIVE

London recognized the voice as Archie Behnke's.

But what on earth does he mean by "against the law"? she wondered.

As she hurried to the doorway, Archie's voice went on, "You see, a stateroom can be thought of as a thermodynamic system. Which means we're up against the second law of thermodynamics ..."

London stopped and leaned against the doorway, trying not to laugh out loud.

Archie was standing inside the room pointing to the thermostat. He was delivering what sounded like some kind of scientific lecture to Kirby Oswinkle, whose eyes were glazed with perplexity.

"Are you following me so far?" Archie asked Mr. Oswinkle.

Oswinkle nodded uncertainly, and Archie continued.

"The second law tells us that entropy takes over any system sooner or later. That means that your room temperature is always going to get *cooler* if it's truly isolated from any other system—that is, if it doesn't interact with anything that changes its temperature one way or the other."

Oswinkle scratched his chin. He was beginning to look a bit like a trapped animal, but London didn't feel inclined to interrupt Archie's lecture.

Since neither man seemed to have noticed her, she took the opportunity to glance around the Bartok suite, which she'd never visited before. Like all the suites on the *Nachtmusik*, it was named and themed after a Danube-related composer. A large portrait of the twentieth-century composer Bela Bartok, looking serious and a bit sad, hung over the bed.

The walls featured pages from music scores and images from the composer's life, including photos of village scenes of when Bartok had toured Eastern Europe collecting and recording peasant folk songs. Although not as vast as the grand suite that the late Mrs. Klimowski had occupied, this one was twice as big as London's stateroom and quite luxurious.

London also noticed quite a lot of clutter. Scattered over almost every furniture surface were dozens of little souvenir gifts, presumably of places Oswinkle had visited at one time or another. There was a little brass Eiffel Tower, a figurine of a Beefeater at the Tower of London, a small plaster Rock of Gibraltar, a little Leaning Tower of Pisa, and many more such items.

He's a collector, London thought.

Or maybe more of a hoarder. And he brings it all along with him.

Meanwhile, Archie kept right on with his lecture.

"Now, you can try to maintain equilibrium in your thermodynamic system—your room temperature, that is—by having it interact with other systems, say by pumping in warm air or cool air. Even so, the temperature can't help but change just a little from its intended state, if only because of the law of entropy. Let me try to make that clearer ..."

Oswinkle waved his hands anxiously.

"No, no! I think I get it," he said.

"You do?" Archie said.

"Yes, I do."

"Are you sure? I'll be glad to go over it all again."

"You're saying it's impossible to maintain the exact temperature of my room."

"Well, our system gets you pretty close—less than a degree of variance either way. Which is pretty good, considering that ..."

Oswinkle looked positively desperate for Archie to not start talking again.

"No need to explain. Really, really, I get it."

"That's good," Archie said, shaking Oswinkle's hand. "It was nice visiting with you, Mr. Oswinkle."

"Uh, likewise."

Trying to conceal her amusement, London said, "Is there anything else we can do for you, Mr. Oswinkle?"

"No, no, everything's ... just fine for now."

"Well, be sure to let us know if you need anything," London added.

"I'll do that."

When she and Archie left the room and the door closed behind them, London couldn't help laughing.

"You handled that in a really interesting way, Archie," she said.

"I was just presenting him with the facts," Archie told her. "I've found that a little scientific information can go a long way when it comes to dealing with really stubborn problems—and stubborn passengers. They tend to listen to reason sooner or later. I could have gone on like that for another fifteen minutes or so."

"I'm glad you didn't have to," London said.

"Me too. I even bore myself sometimes." Then he added with an innocent expression, "But it is often effective."

London suddenly noticed that Sir Reggie wasn't trotting along with her.

"Where did Sir Reggie go?" she said.

Archie chuckled.

"My guess is he got tired of listening to me talk and took off on his own. Can you blame him?"

"Well, no, it's just that ..."

Her voice faded.

It's just that what? she asked herself.

"I wouldn't worry about that little hero," Archie said. "After all, you really want to give him the run of the ship. I'm sure he's able to take care of himself."

London didn't doubt it. It just felt a little odd to not know exactly where Sir Reggie was at the moment.

I'd better get used to it, she thought.

"Let's go down to your room and see how the guys are doing with your doggie door," Archie

Archie and London took the stairs to the Allegro deck, where they encountered a fierce racket as soon as they entered the passageway. Two of Archie's maintenance men had taken London's stateroom door off its hinges and laid it out across two sawhorses. Several power tools were scattered around, and one of the men was working with an electric sander.

London realized that she hadn't gotten word of any more noise complaints. She reminded herself that it was the middle of the day. The crew members or other passengers who lived here must be either relaxing or working on other levels.

Except, of course, her immediate neighbor, the mysterious Stanley Tedrow. Surely he must be still in that room he hadn't left during the whole trip.

Why wasn't he out here objecting to the clamor?

The workmen had just about finished fitting the doggie door together. It was a little square frame with a vinyl flap over it. They

24

were smoothing out the opening they'd cut into the stateroom door where the mini-door would fit.

"They're doing a good job," London said to Archie over the noise. "It's going to look like the little flap was always part of the big door."

Archie nodded.

"You can have this back," he said, handing her back her master keycard. Then he continued making suggestions to his workers.

Glancing into the room, London was surprised to see Sir Reggie stretched out on the bed, apparently sleeping quite soundly.

I guess Archie was right, London thought.

The dog had gotten bored up in Oswinkle's room and had come straight back here. He didn't seem to be bothered by the noise, and certainly wasn't making any noise himself.

But as the thunderous rumbling of the sander continued, London decided that she'd better check on Mr. Tedrow. This whole door project had come up in response to his complaint about the yapping dog. Why hadn't he been annoyed by the racket the workmen were making?

When she went to stateroom 108 and knocked, she could barely hear a voice inside but she couldn't tell what he was saying.

To her relief, the din of the sander finally stopped.

She leaned her ear closer to Tedrow's door and knocked again.

Then she heard the faint voice again. Was he telling her to come on in?

London tried the knob, but the door was obviously locked.

"Mr. Tedrow," she called.

She pressed her ear against the door. This time, she heard him call out anxiously.

"Unhand me, sir. You've got no right to treat me like this."

London's nerves quickened with alarm.

Something bad is happening in there, she thought.

She put her keycard into the latch and opened the door.

CHAPTER SIX

London pushed the door open and dashed into the suite. To her surprise, no one was attacking the occupant. In fact, nothing seemed to be happening at all. Although he had called out in apparent distress, Mr. Tedrow sat at his table staring at his computer screen, as if unaware of her arrival.

He spoke sharply as his fingers kept clacking away on the keys.

"You've got no business laying your hands on me! I'm an innocent woman!"

An innocent woman? London wondered.

Then she realized—he was writing dialogue. And as writers sometimes did, he was speaking the words aloud.

London stood there awkwardly. Stanley Tedrow was obviously hard at work on a book. What she'd mistaken for a cry for help was nothing more than a character's words.

"I'm sorry about the noise," she said.

"Huh?" Mr. Tedrow said.

Then he turned toward her and seemed to notice her for the first time.

"Oh, it's you," he said. "What do you want?"

"I said I'm sorry about the noise."

Mr. Tedrow's eyes moved back to the computer.

"Noise?" he said. "What noise?"

London was startled.

"Uh, there's a bit of work going on just outside," she said.

"I hadn't noticed."

Apparently not, London thought.

"They're installing a doggie door for my room," London explained. "My dog will be able to come and go as he pleases. Just like you suggested."

"Is that so?"

He sounded as though he had no idea what this could possibly have to do with him. London wondered if maybe she should just leave. Still, she felt that she owed him some sort of explanation.

26

"You were complaining about my dog barking," she said.

"Oh, yeah, that."

"Well, it won't happen now that he's not cooped up in the room alone."

"That's good."

For a moment, London didn't know what else to say. She half-wondered whether it had been a waste of effort to get the doggie door installed. Didn't Mr. Tedrow care about noise after all? But she figured installing the door had still been a good thing to do, if only for Sir Reggie's sake. Life aboard the *Nachtmusik* was going to be a lot better for him now—and surely more fun as well.

But again she felt concerned about this passenger.

How could this elderly gentleman possibly be enjoying himself, cooped up alone in his room like this?

Maybe he's *the one who really needs a doggie door,* she thought wryly.

"Mr. Tedrow, if you don't mind my asking …"

"Well?"

"What are you writing?"

"I can't talk about it."

"All right," London said.

But as she turned to go, he spoke again sharply.

"Jeez, you're not going to leave it alone, are you? You'll just keep nagging until you hear all about it. OK, if you insist, I'll tell you."

"You don't have to tell me," London said.

"I'm writing a book," he said.

"Oh," London said.

That was obvious, of course. But now London felt more than ready to leave the topic alone and to get out of the room.

"It's going to be a blockbuster," Tedrow said. "It's going to be a bestseller. It's going to make me rich and famous."

"That's great," London said, fidgeting a little.

"And now I guess you've just got to know what it's about," he said.

Not really, London thought.

But would it be rude to tell him otherwise?

"It's a murder mystery," he said.

London's eyes widened.

A murder mystery?

Was he writing a book about what had happened to Mrs.

Klimowski? But of course London knew that was impossible. He'd been so isolated here in his room, he didn't even know the ship had stopped in Gyor, much less that anyone had gotten killed there. The fact that he was working on a mystery of his own invention was just a bizarre coincidence.

He stared at her silently, then muttered, "You'd never understand how difficult this is, figuring out how a murder can take place. Leaving clues for my detective to discover, creating a group of plausible suspects, revealing the true culprit at the end …"

With a shake of his head, he turned his gaze away and started typing again.

"One of these days, you'll be able to tell your passengers that Stanley Tedrow wrote his first bestseller right here on the *Nachtmusik*. People will pay extra just to stay in this room where I did it."

"That's—that's really exciting."

"You bet it's exciting. But if you think I'm going to tell you the plot, you're wrong."

"OK."

"Plead and badger me all you want, I'm not going to tell you that."

"OK," she said again, worried that he was about to tell her the plot in agonizing detail. "I'll go now. Good luck with your writing."

"Thanks."

As she left the room, she saw that Archie and his workers had just finished putting her door on its hinges and were cleaning up the mess they'd made.

"We've got it done," Archie said. "Let me show you how it works."

He whistled, and sure enough, Sir Reginald himself popped out of the doggie door.

"Are you happy with our work, buddy?" Archie asked him.

Sir Reginald let out a yap of approval, then went through the door back into the room again.

London thanked Archie and his crew, who picked up their tools and left.

She realized that she was starting to feel hungry. Fortunately, she was still carrying around the to-go bag that Bryce had given her back in the restaurant. She had a long list of tasks to take care of today, but now seemed as good a time as any to take a lunch break.

She considered going into her stateroom and having her lunch in private, but she had spent much of the morning in and out of

28

staterooms. London realized she needed some fresh air. She was on a boat, after all, traveling one of the world's most beautiful rivers, so she decided to take the elevator up onto the Rondo deck.

When London stepped onto the outdoor deck, she was momentarily surprised by the sight that met her eyes. Instead of hills and forests, the *Nachtmusik* was flanked either side by a city with both very old and very modern buildings.

Bratislava, she realized.

This was the capital of Slovakia, a city that also straddled the border between Hungary and Austria.

A group of passengers was clustered near the bow, staring at a massive and peculiar-looking bridge that stretched out across the Danube. It appeared to be quite lopsided, with a single gigantic tower near one end that sprouted cables to support a long, broad span. As usual, London had done some studying and was prepared to explain what they were seeing.

"What do you think of the famous UFO Bridge?" she asked as she approached the group.

"The UFO Bridge?" one passenger asked.

"Is that really its name?" another asked.

London laughed.

"Well, its official name is the *Most SNP,* or the Bridge of the Slovak National Uprising. But you can see why people who live right here in Bratislava call it the 'UFO Bridge.'"

As she pointed, people let out exclamations of agreement. The round structure perched at the top of the tower, almost 300 feet above the Danube, did look like some sort of flying saucer.

London explained, "The 'UFO' structure has got both a restaurant and an observation deck."

"It certainly looks odd," one woman commented.

"Don't let it distract you from some of the city's nicer sights," London said, pointing to the shore. "Over there is St. Martin's Cathedral, where eleven Hungarian kings and queens were crowned between 1563 and 1830."

The tall cathedral stood out impressively, with its simple and severe Gothic lines. As the ship passed slowly under the bridge, four broad traffic lanes loomed high above the *Nachtmusik.* London pointed to the shore again as the boat emerged out from under the bridge.

"Over there you see Bratislava Castle," she said.

The dignified castle with pearly white walls and towers at its four corners looked down upon the city. Perched on a hilltop as high as the *Most SNP*, the castle was a commanding presence.

"There are lots of legends about that castle," London told the group. "For example, a long, long time ago, the inhabitants woke up one morning to find the entire castle had been turned upside-down! It seemed that a giant named Klingsor from Transylvania had stopped by and turned the castle over to use as a table. The queen of the castle summoned a witch for help, and the witch cast a spell that put everything back in its proper place."

Indicating the shape of the castle, London added, "Indeed, you might already have noticed that the castle looks like an upside-down table, with the four towers resembling table legs."

The passengers chuckled at the story.

"Anyway, welcome to Austria!" London told them all cheerfully. "We'll be leaving Hungary and entering a whole different world. I hope you enjoy the time we spend here."

After the group thanked London for her little lecture, she went to a table with a wide umbrella and sat down to eat her lunch. When she opened the bag Bryce had given her, she found a tuna salad sandwich served on a toasted English muffin.

No ordinary sandwich, she realized as she savored a single delicious bite.

But of course, nothing that came out of Bryce's kitchen was ever quite ordinary. She closed her eyes and tried to guess the combination of herbs and flavorings.

Basil, I think ... and parsley and tarragon leaves ... and grated lemon ...

She couldn't guess all the rest. She tasted mayonnaise, of course, but also sour cream, kosher salt, freshly ground pepper, and chopped shallot and garlic. She ate slowly, enjoying her break as the charming city of Bratislava slipped behind them, giving way to the beautiful hills and fields of the Austrian countryside.

London knew that she couldn't linger here for very long. She soon finished her sandwich, got up, and cleared off the table. Before she boarded the elevator, though, she turned and looked again at the lush scenery.

Austria, she thought with a surge of emotion.

She hadn't been here since she was a little girl. Even so, Austria had a special significance for her. It harbored personal secrets, and maybe personal ghosts. One of the great mysteries of her own life was rooted right here in Austria—a mystery she doubted she could ever solve.

Don't think about it, she told herself.

There's nothing you can do about it.

CHAPTER SEVEN

London held her breath in anticipation.

I hope this is good, she thought.

Everybody needed a little success right now. Some of the passengers were still quite disturbed by the death and the delay they had encountered in Gyor. London had been on the run ever since her lunch break, keeping them pleasantly occupied. She thought that most of them had put those shocking events behind them.

As for London herself, she'd made sure she was too busy to consider the mystery that she would face just ahead in Vienna. She'd helped Elsie finish turning a section of the Amadeus Lounge into a makeshift casino, organized a ship-wide trivia competition, and arranged for Emil Waldmüller to give a lecture about Austria in the ship's library.

Her most ambitious project had been recruiting a small choral ensemble to perform this evening at dinner. She'd sent word out through the ship that she was looking for a few experienced singers and a capable director who could perform unaccompanied by musical instruments. Once she'd put the group together, they'd gone off on their own to rehearse, and London had no idea how they would sound. They certainly hadn't had much time to prepare.

Now she was about to find out how well that had worked out. The Habsburg Restaurant was full of diners and the music director was raising her hands to start conducting the group of eight singers.

At the opening words of the song "Edelweiss," London breathed again. The lovely, harmonious voices singing the familiar song couldn't have sounded prettier. She broke into a wide smile, and saw that all the diners in the restaurant also appeared to be charmed.

It was a pleasant way to end a long, busy day. As she looked out over the happy faces in the restaurant, she really felt as though she'd succeeded at something quite important.

A woman sitting at a table next to London sighed with delight.

"How nice to hear the Austrian national anthem as we sail toward Vienna!" she said.

London cringed slightly at the woman's mistake.

For a moment, London wondered—*Should I tell her?*

She quickly decided that she'd better do so.

"Mrs. Cubbage, I'm afraid 'Edelweiss' isn't really Austria's national anthem."

The woman looked shocked, and so did the other people at her table.

"Oh, but it simply *must* be," another woman said.

London's heart sank a little. She didn't want to disappoint anybody. She also didn't want to come across as a know-it-all.

Fortunately, before she could say anything else, she heard a familiar, German-accented voice next to her.

"London is right, madam. Allow me to explain ..."

London breathed a sigh of relief. Emil Waldmüller, the ship's historian, had arrived at exactly the right moment to put matters straight.

"Have you seen the musical *The Sound of Music?*" Emil asked the people at the table.

They all said that they had.

"Well, then," Emil continued. "The composer Richard Rodgers and the lyricist Oscar Hammerstein the Third wrote 'Edelweiss' especially for that *American* musical. It became so popular that people mistakenly came to think it was a traditional *Austrian* song. Austria's actual national anthem is *'Land der Berge, Land am Strome,'* which means in English, 'Land of the Mountains, Land by the River.' It is set to a tune by Wolfgang Amadeus Mozart."

Chuckling a bit smugly, he added, "Of course, I doubt that you'll hear this group sing it this evening, because it is in German."

The people at the table laughed as well, although London suspected that part of their amusement could be at Emil's somewhat pedantic manner. She wondered whether he knew that he sometimes verged on self-parody.

Maybe he even laughs at himself some of the time.

Or maybe not. So far he hadn't struck her as having much of a sense of humor, although she thought his intelligence made up for that. It also didn't hurt that he was so good-looking in that Old World manner, with his long, serious face and thick dark hair.

I guess Elsie was right, she thought.

I do have a bit of a thing for him. But maybe also for ...

33

London cut short her wandering thoughts, reminding herself what she had told Elsie.

"I'm not here for romance. I've got a job to do."

She needed to keep that in mind. Still, it would easier if Emil was just a little less suave, sophisticated, and engaging.

He continued to hold forth to his listeners about *The Sound of Music*, and how none of the songs in it were ever really performed by the real Trapp Family Singers, and how the musical's story departed in many ways from what had really happened, and …

Rather surprisingly, the people at the table were clearly enjoying this little lecture. And London had to admit, Emil was being quite entertaining in his way. This was nothing at all like Archie Behnke's deliberately tortuous lecture about the Second Law of Thermodynamics.

Then the singers started into another song from *The Sound of Music*—"Climb Every Mountain."

London felt her throat catch with emotion. She knew that soaring, inspirational song from her childhood, and it also stirred up some of those emotions about sailing into Austria …

Don't cry, she told herself.

Don't even think about it.

She'd done a good day's work, and it was time to unwind, not to let her feelings run away with her. She decided stop by the Amadeus Lounge and see how Elsie was doing, and maybe have a drink.

London took the elevator one deck upward, then went to the large open room in the bow of the Menuetto deck. She wasn't surprised to find the lounge crowded and busy and rumbling with happy chatter. A long bar stretched across the far end of the room and various clusters of seating arrangements, tables, and potted plants offered a range of possibilities for socializing in small groups. The mini-casino that she and Elsie had set up was off to one side, and several cheerful passengers were hovering around the roulette table.

She heard Elsie's voice shout out from a table near the bar.

"Hey, London! Come over here! You'll want to see this!"

She made her way toward Elsie and a handful of people who were clustered around a small table that was pushed up against a wall.

Amy Blassingame was standing there with a drink in her hand, actually looking pleasant and relaxed. London recognized the others as passengers. Rudy and Tina Fiore were young newlyweds on their

34

honeymoon. Steve and Carol Weaver were a middle-aged couple whose daughter had just left for college. They had come on the cruise for what amounted to a second honeymoon. The stout, formally dressed woman was Letitia Hartzer.

"Look what we've got here," Elsie said, gesturing to some objects on the table. "Our own little musical ensemble."

London saw a group of small upright-standing dolls representing musicians. Dressed in picturesque and colorful embroidered costumes, they seemed to belong to a matching set. One was playing a violin, another a double-bass violin, another a clarinet, another a drum, and another a trumpet.

"How cute!" London said. "Where did these come from?"

Tina Fiore replied, "Rudy and I bought the violinist and the drummer at a little gift stand back in Gyor."

"It's a great place to shop," Letitia Hartzer added. "I bought the trumpeter there too."

Carol Weaver said, "And Steve and I bought the bass player and the clarinetist at the very same stand."

Elsie said with a grin, "The five of them were sitting together having drinks when they realized they'd all bought little dolls belonging to the same set. They ran back to their rooms and fetched them and came back and showed them to me. Well, naturally, I thought they'd make a cute little display. The whole group can stay together right here on this table for a while."

"Too bad there's no conductor," Amy commented.

"Oh, but there is!" Letitia Hartzer said. "When I bought my trumpeter at that gift stand, there was a gentleman from the boat there too. He bought the conductor."

Amy's eyes widened with interest.

"Oh! Do you remember who he was?"

"Yes, he introduced himself to me. His name was Kirby something ... I think his last name began with an O."

Amy and London exchanged startled glances.

"Kirby Oswinkle?" Amy asked Letitia.

"Why, yes! That was his name! I'm sure of it!"

"And look—there he is!" Letitia added. "Sitting right over there at the bar!"

Sure enough, Kirby Oswinkle was sitting there wearing his nautical cap, flanked on both sides by empty bar stools.

"Hey, I've got an idea," Steve Weaver said. "Why don't you ask him if he'll share his conductor for our display?"

London hesitated. It appeared that either Oswinkle had gone to a lot of trouble to sit alone, or else nobody wanted to sit next to him for very long.

"He doesn't strike me as the sharing type," Amy muttered.

London silently agreed. But remembering the trove of trinkets she'd seen in the man's room, London wasn't surprised that he'd bought one of the musical figures. That meant he had something in common with these other passengers. Maybe that would help with the job of making his trip enjoyable.

"Let's go over and give it a try," London said to Elsie and Amy.

Amy crossed her arms shook her head.

"Oh, no, not me," she said. "After all the trouble he gave me about his room temperature, you can count me out."

"I think that's been settled," London told her.

"Still, that man was pretty rude to me. You two go ahead if you feel like it."

London realized that she again needed to remind Amy of her role on the ship, and of who was boss.

"Amy, the three of us are all in the passenger satisfaction business—you as much as Elsie and me," she said. "So come along and be helpful."

Amy let out a grumble of discontentment, but she followed London and Elsie toward Oswinkle. Elsie went behind the bar and faced the man with a smile, while London and Amy stepped up beside him.

"So how are you this evening, Mr. Oswinkle?" London asked him cautiously.

"OK, I guess," he grumbled, stirring his drink with a swizzle stick. Gesturing toward Elsie he added, "Your bartender here makes an acceptable martini, anyway."

At least he's happy with something, London thought.

Elsie pointed at the group standing around the table with the musicians.

"Hey, we hear that you bought a little doll like one of those," she said.

"So what if I did?" Oswinkle replied.

London said, "Those people over there wondered if you'd like to share yours for their little display."

36

Oswinkle squinted at the group curiously.

London nudged Amy with her elbow

"I'm sure they'd like to meet you, Mr. Oswinkle," Amy chimed in.

"I don't know ..." Oswinkle muttered.

"How about a drink on the house?" Elsie added.

Oswinkle looked at her as if he wasn't sure she really meant it.

He's tempted, though, London thought.

Finally he spoke.

"It's only a loan, right? The figure, I mean. I'll get it back when the trip is over, right?"

"Of course," London assured him.

Oswinkle glanced around at the three women's faces, then he nodded.

"I'll go to my room and get it. I'll be right back."

He downed the rest of his drink and got up and left the lounge.

"So far, so good," Elsie said, starting to make another martini.

"This should get him to mix a little," London said. "He might actually enjoy himself."

"I just hope it doesn't backfire," Amy said.

Then Amy told Elsie all about Oswinkle's demand for a rock-steady room temperature.

"Wow, and I thought he was just an ordinary grouchy customer," Elsie said.

"But Archie Behnke took care of that," London said.

Amy looked surprised. "Archie told me it wasn't possible to get the thermometer set the way Oswinkle wanted it. What makes you think it's been settled?"

"Because Archie gave him a lecture on thermodynamics," London said.

"Thermodynamics?" Amy asked.

"You had to be there to appreciate it. But I don't think we'll have that problem with Mr. Oswinkle again."

Elsie held up the fresh martini. "Well, maybe this will help mellow him out."

"I hope so," London said.

Meanwhile, the passengers had moved back to their large dinner table and were chatting amiably. Elsie put the martini down at an empty place setting and London informed them that Mr. Oswinkle had gone to get his conductor figure and would join them.

"There he is now," Amy said with a smile.

But Oswinkle burst back into the lounge, waving his arms with agitation.

"There's a thief on board!" he cried.

CHAPTER EIGHT

London fought down a groan of discouragement.

What now? she wondered.

Kirby Oswinkle was storming through the lounge toward her, his arms still flailing wildly and his face red with anger.

She felt a nudge from an elbow and glanced over at Amy, who was standing next to her.

"Just remember—getting him involved was your idea, not mine," Amy hissed. "I didn't want any part of it."

The five passengers who had brought their musical figures to the lounge simply stared as Oswinkle arrived at the table where they were sitting.

"Why is everybody smiling?" he demanded, his voice hoarse with anger. "Is this somebody's idea of a joke?"

"I'm sorry," London told him. "But I don't know what you mean."

Amy spoke with exaggerated politeness.

"Why don't you just sit down with the others?" she said. "We can talk about this calmly, I'm sure."

Elsie chimed in, "Look here—we even brought you a martini."

"I'm not in a mood for a martini," Oswinkle said, pacing furiously. "What I want is an explanation."

"And we'd be glad to explain if we can," London said calmly. "Please tell us what you need explained."

"It was nowhere to be found," he sputtered. "I looked everywhere."

London's eyes widened.

"Do you mean … ?" she said.

"I mean it was stolen! When I went back to get my beautiful little music conductor, it was gone."

London and Amy exchanged confused glances.

"Are you quite sure?" Amy asked.

"Do you think I don't know the contents of my own suite?" Oswinkle said. "It was there in its proper place this morning, and now it's not."

"Well, it's just that you have so *many* things …" Amy began.

39

"And I know just where each and every one of them ought to be. The conductor has disappeared. It was stolen. There's no other explanation."

London doubted that very much.

"But who do you think stole it?" she asked.

"Maybe that's what *you* should tell *me*," he snapped. "I never let anyone into my suite who doesn't have some business there. Since we left Budapest, there have been two maids who've cleaned my room and changed my bed—"

Amy interrupted sharply.

"Now look here. I hope you're not accusing anyone on my staff."

Oswinkle let out a snort of disgust.

"Well, I'm certainly not accusing these passengers." He waved his hand to indicate those sitting at the dining table. "Not one of them has ever set foot in my suite." Then looking a little uncertain, he sputtered and added, "Not as far as I know. With all the chaos on board this ship, how am I supposed to know who to accuse?"

London could see that Amy was angry now. She fought down her own rising irritation and said, as pleasantly as she could manage, "Now, Mr. Oswinkle, please think about this. *Why* would anyone want to steal such a thing?"

"Why does anybody want to steal anything?"

"But surely you don't think that anybody on the staff—" Amy replied sharply.

"What am I supposed to think? Staff members have been milling around in my suite ever since we first set sail—including you, and also Ms. Rose, and that maintenance man, Mr. Behnke."

"We didn't just come 'milling around' for no reason," Amy said, her voice now shaking with barely suppressed anger. "We came to your room because of your complaints about your room temperature. And we did everything we could to help."

"Huh! You didn't do anything at all!"

Amy put her hands on her hips and leaned toward him.

"Maybe that's because there was nothing we *could* do. Your complaint was just …"

Amy stopped herself.

"Was what?" Oswinkle demanded.

"It was *unreasonable*," Amy blurted.

London felt a surge of alarm. She could see that Amy recognized her mistake. But the words were out, and there was no taking them back.

"Who are you calling unreasonable?" Oswinkle's voice was beginning to get shrill now.

"I'm not calling anybody anything," Amy said, trying to backtrack. "I'm just sure that nobody on our staff stole your little toy."

"My little toy!" Oswinkle yelped. "I'll have you know it's a work of art. A collectible example of local craftsmanship."

"Whatever you want to call it, then. If you just go back to your room and look more carefully—"

"I've searched my suite from top to bottom."

Amy couldn't seem to help but scoff.

"Now really, Mr. Oswinkle. You just left here a few minutes ago. You can't have looked very thoroughly. Maybe I should come back with you and help look around."

"Huh! Do you think I want my entire collection to disappear? No thanks!"

He stabbed the air with his finger, glaring at London and Amy.

"I'm going to get to the bottom of this, believe me! And there *will* be consequences!"

Before anyone could reply, Kirby Oswinkle whirled and stalked away.

The bar patrons, especially the ones who had brought the musician figures, all stared after him as he left the lounge.

Elsie muttered to London, "Even grouchier than I had thought," and hurried back to her usual place behind the bar.

London turned to the group seated at the table and saw that their expressions ranged from mild shock to amusement.

"I'm sorry for all this unpleasantness," she told them.

"I'm sure it'll all turn out all right," Carol Weaver said with a smile.

"I'm sure it will," London said—although she felt doubtful. "Anyway, I think putting your musicians on display was a marvelous idea. It makes for a charming arrangement."

The group thanked London for the compliment and began to chatter to each other. Since they all appeared content to go back to their drinks and conversations, London turned to Amy and led her aside.

"Amy, you called him 'unreasonable.'"

"Well, he *was* being unreasonable."

"That's not the point. You don't ever say something like that to a

41

passenger. You know better than that." London paused for a moment, then added, "The customer may not always be right, but the customer is always the customer."

"What's that supposed to mean?" Amy asked.

"It's London's motto," Elsie said.

"Huh," Amy grunted. "It's a very nice policy when it comes to dealing with sane people. It's not much good when dealing with a lunatic like Kirby Oswinkle."

He's not a lunatic, London almost said.

But right now, he certainly seemed like one.

"I give up," Amy said crossly. "It's been a long day, and I could use a good night's sleep."

Amy walked out of the lounge, leaving London standing near the bar.

"So what are you going to do now?" Elsie asked her.

London stepped closer and leaned on the polished surface of the long bar top, thinking about the question. Should she walk straight to Oswinkle's room and apologize? She doubted that it would help, at least not right now. It certainly wouldn't resolve the issue of the supposedly missing musician doll. And he would likely be offended that she might be checking up on him.

"I guess we should sleep on it—me and Mr. Oswinkle both," London replied. "Maybe he won't be this upset tomorrow. Maybe *I* won't be this upset."

"Do you really think somebody stole his little music conductor?"

"I find that very hard to imagine," London said. "You should see all the trinkets he's collected all over the world. It's probably still there somewhere, just misplaced. Maybe tomorrow he'll let me help him look for it."

But I doubt it, she thought.

"How about a drink to unwind?" Elsie asked, pointing. "There's an untouched martini over there on that table. Or I could make you your favorite drink—a Manhattan, if I remember right."

"Thanks, but I'll pass," London said. "It's getting late, and I've got a long day ahead tomorrow."

She left the lounge and headed for the elevator, which she took down to the Allegro deck.

She felt a new wave of worry as she walked down the passageway to her stateroom. When she opened the door and switched on a light,

42

she breathed a sigh of relief to see Sir Reggie sleeping soundly on the bed. She latched the doggie door for the night, checked his food, and refilled his water bowl. She was glad that the dog potty was self-cleaning. Sir Reggie truly was a self-sufficient, low-maintenance roommate.

She sat down beside him and gave him a gentle scratch of his head.

"What have you been up to tonight, pal?" she asked. "Did you stay inside, or make use of your new door to go out and party?"

Sir Reggie replied with a half-asleep sigh.

"Well, I hope your evening was better than mine turned out to be."

London took a nice hot shower, then put on her nightgown and got ready for bed. Before she lay down, she opened the curtains of her high window and looked outside. It was very dark out now, with little to see—only a few scattered lights here and there. The *Nachtmusik* was apparently sailing through forests and hills, not a city or a town.

But she knew that tomorrow she would wake up to a very different sight.

"Vienna," she murmured aloud.

As if in reply, she heard her cell phone buzzing on her bed stand.

London sighed as she wondered—was this another complaint?

Was Kirby Oswinkle calling her, angrier than before?

She saw that it was a long distance number, and one that she didn't recognize. She considered letting the call go to her voice mail.

Whatever it is, I'd better face it now, she decided.

She took the call and was surprised to hear a pleasant tenor voice singing softly ...

"Edelweiss, Edelweiss ..."

As the singing continued, it seemed uncanny to hear the same song she'd heard the choral group singing in the Habsburg Restaurant a little while ago.

But she knew that voice well.

CHAPTER NINE

London sat down on the edge of the bed, reeling from surprise.

"Hi, Dad," she said.

"Hi, sweetie," London's father said in reply.

She struggled to think how long it had been since she'd talked to her dad on the phone.

Months, maybe.

And it had been at least a year since they'd seen each other face to face. It wasn't due to a lack of interest in each other's lives—the two of them always felt emotionally connected, but their paths just didn't cross very often anymore.

"I—I didn't recognize the number when you called," she said.

"Oh, that. I lost my cell phone a couple of days ago—you know how I am about losing things. The one I'm calling on is brand new."

"Where *are* you?" London asked.

Because her father was an airline attendant, she knew he could be just about anywhere in the world right now.

"I'm on a layover in Tokyo," he said.

London looked at her clock and did some quick math in her head.

"It's eleven o'clock at night here," she said. "That means it's six in the morning there."

"Well, I always was an early riser. It comes with the job. You know that as well as anybody."

Yes, I do know that, London thought.

She and her older sister, Tia, had spent their childhoods dashing all over the world with Dad and Mom, who'd both been flight attendants.

But even so ...

"This is an odd hour for a phone call," London said.

"Aren't you glad to hear from me?"

"Oh, Dad, I'm *always* glad to hear from you. You know that. It's just that ..."

Her voice faded. She was having a hard time processing her thoughts. She realized she hadn't told him about her new job aboard the *Nachtmusik.* She'd been offered the job suddenly just a few days ago, and hadn't gotten around to letting him know. But he spoke up before she had a chance to explain.

"How's Austria?"

London felt another jolt of surprise.

"How did you know—?"

"Hey, I know everything. Isn't that what I always tell you?"

"Yes, but—"

"Did you like my rendition of 'Edelweiss'? Appropriate, now that you're in Austria, huh?"

"Yes, but—"

"Hey, did you know 'Edelweiss' is *not* Austria's national anthem?"

"You've told me a hundred times. But Dad—"

"And that the Trapp Family Singers never sang any of the songs in *The Sound of Music*?"

"Yes, you've told me that too, but …"

"Well?"

"How did you know where I was?"

"Oh, that. I called your sister yesterday. The last I'd heard, you were supposed to be staying with her right about now, between ocean cruises. I thought maybe I could talk to both of you—and to my grandkids as well. Tia told me you'd gotten a new gig with the same company you've been working for, this time aboard a river tour boat. I looked it up online and found out the boat is called the *Nachtmusik*. The name really caught my attention. I'm sure you remember …"

His voice faded, but London knew what he meant.

"Yes, Mom used to play it on the piano—Mozart's *Eine Kleine Nachtmusik*."

She could still remember the glowing expression on her mother's face whenever she'd played it. Learning the name of the boat had really hit an emotional button for London.

"From the pictures, it looks like a nice boat," Dad continued. "A nice design too—long and low like most river tour boats, but smaller and more … elegant I think is the right word … than any others I've seen. How many passengers does it board?"

"About a hundred," London said.

"Wow, that's really a change from those gigantic oceangoing cruise ships you worked on before."

"It sure is. I have more responsibilities, but I get to know the passengers better. I'm beginning to really like it."

He said, "I also looked up the itinerary—I'm nosy like that, you know—and found out you'd gotten into Vienna yesterday. And I just called to ..."

His voice trailed off, but London had some idea of what he was leaving unsaid.

He's worried about me.

And maybe, she thought, he was right to be worried.

"Actually, we aren't in Vienna quite yet," she said. "We'll be docked there by tomorrow morning."

"That's odd. This itinerary must be wrong."

"It's not the itinerary. We got held up for a whole day in Gyor, because ..."

London felt a sharp lump of emotion in her throat.

"Oh, Dad, so much has been going on. I wish we could sit down over a couple of drinks and talk about it."

"What's the matter?"

London swallowed hard.

"Someone died—I mean, someone got killed. A passenger. And elderly woman."

She heard Dad gasp.

"You mean she was murdered?"

"It was a homicide, anyway. It was really crazy. I—I just don't know where to start."

"Did you catch the killer?"

London was startled by the question.

"Um, yeah, I kind of did."

"Really? Good for you."

"But how did you know ...?"

"Oh, I didn't really," Dad said with a laugh. "It was just sort of a slip of the tongue. But whenever there's a crisis, you've always been the first to plunge in and try to fix it."

A silence fell between them. Finally Dad spoke again.

"I guess you might have realized ... I called because I was worried ..."

"About me being in Vienna," London said, finishing his thought.

"Well, it's the first time you've been there since you were little, and also since ..."

Again, London knew what he was leaving unsaid. The last time anybody had heard anything from Mom, she'd been in Vienna. Then she had completely disappeared. That had been twenty years ago, and London had never returned to any part of Europe as an adult.

"How does it feel to be on your way there?" Dad asked.

"It feels strange," London said. "I haven't processed it. I guess I probably won't until I get there."

"Well, try not to do *too much* 'processing.'"

"What do you mean?"

"Your mother's disappearance isn't another mystery for you to solve. You've always had some idea that something terrible happened to her. That's not true. I'm sure of it. Deep down, I'm sure of it. She just ... needed to get away."

London felt a familiar bitterness rising up inside her.

"From all of us, you mean," she said. "From Tia and me and ..."

"It was my fault, London," Dad said, gently interrupting. "Her leaving, I mean. I should have known she ..."

London heard Dad's voice choke up a bit.

"It wasn't your fault, Dad," London said in a comforting tone. "If you're right, and nothing terrible happened to her in Vienna, then she made her own decision to go away. You're no more responsible for her leaving than Tia or me."

Another silence fell.

"You do understand that, don't you, Dad?"

Dad forced a slight chuckle.

"I guess so," he said. "But maybe I need to hear someone say it now and then."

London smiled again.

"Well, whenever you need to hear it, I'm always available."

"I'll keep that in mind."

"I'll try to stay in better touch. You do that too."

"I will."

"I love you, Dad."

"I love you too, sweetie."

They ended the call, and London wiped a tear from her cheek. She noticed that Sir Reggie was awake now, and he was gazing at her with a seemingly sympathetic expression.

"It's nice to have you around, pal," she said, ruffling the fur on the top of his head.

He let out what sounded like a small grunt of agreement.

London got up from the bed and walked over to a mirror that was

47

hanging on a wall. Her uniform was rumpled and she realized she looked sad and tired.

She wondered …

Do I look like her?

She thought that her five and a half feet of height and her slender build were similar to Mom's image in family photos. But in her own vivid memories, Mom's face was stronger than her own and her hair was redder. How much had Mom changed over the years? Did she still have such beautiful red hair, or had it turned gray?

She climbed under the covers and thought about the conversation she'd just had with Dad.

It feels weird to him too—my going to Vienna.

She wished he wouldn't blame himself for Mom's disappearance. She didn't feel as though he had anything to blame himself for.

She closed her eyes and remembered those days when Mom and Dad had both been flight attendants, and she and Tia had followed them all over the world, hearing one language and then another, being privately tutored as frequently as being in school. Tia still resented that lack of stability, but London didn't feel that way at all. To her, her childhood had been one nonstop adventure, and she wouldn't have missed a moment of it for the world.

More than that, she'd always thought of Mom and Dad as perfect parents. Even when Dad had come out as gay when she and Tia and London were little girls, he and Mom negotiated the change with grace and humor and love. They'd kept right on being the best of friends and had continued to devote themselves to raising London and Tia as well as they possibly could.

But then …

Something happened.

When Tia was fourteen and London turned eleven, Mom and Dad had mutually agreed that it was time to give their children a more stable home. They rented a nice house in Gaitling, Connecticut, and Mom had quit working as a flight attendant to become a full-time parent. Dad was home as often as he could be, but it wasn't like the old days, when Tia and London had always been traveling with one parent or another.

Then, just three years later, Mom had announced that she was going to take a break and spend some time in Europe. The last any of them had heard from her was when she'd arrived in Vienna.

Poor Dad, London thought.

48

He still seemed to think that her disappearance had been his fault—that maybe if *he'd* stayed home with the kids and let Mom keep working, she wouldn't have succumbed to wanderlust and gone away like that.

But is that really why Mom went away? London wondered.

She'd just wanted to get away for a couple of weeks, she'd said.

But that couple of weeks had turned into forever.

London felt herself drifting off to sleep now. And in her mind, she could hear a lovely voice singing …

"Climb every mountain!"

The night before Mom had flown to Europe, she'd sung that song to Dad, Tia, and London, accompanying herself on the piano. That was why London had felt such a stab of emotion at hearing the choral group singing that song in the Habsburg Restaurant.

Fortunately, she was too sleepy to cry now.

Curled up nearby on top of the covers, Sir Reggie was snoring lightly. As London drifted off to sleep, she didn't know whether to welcome or dread the images that began to form in her dreams.

CHAPTER TEN

London flung open the curtains of her stateroom window and gazed out into the morning light. The view across the Danube wasn't what she had expected to see.

Last night she had dreamed of wandering beautiful streets in a venerable city that she'd visited as a child. Among the crowds, she'd caught repeated glimpses of a woman who looked like Mom ... a woman who always disappeared when London tried to approach her.

Of course, she knew very well what she was looking at now. During the night, the slight lurching and noisy activity of the *Nachtmusik* docking had told her they'd arrived at their destination. She shook her head to clear away the fragments of those dreams, then reached down and picked up her little dog.

"See that city, Sir Reggie? It's Vienna."

From here, it seemed very different from the cities where the *Nachtmusik* had docked back in Hungary—Budapest and Gyor. While those cities were proudly old and historic, this view featured a modern skyline. Across the sleek Reichsbrücke Bridge she saw tall buildings, including the two tallest structures in Austria—the spindly Danube Tower and the newly completed skyscraper, Donau City Tower 1.

But she knew that the view was deceptive. On the other side of the boat, on the left bank of the Danube, lay Vienna's Old Town with its wealth of history and culture.

And mystery, London couldn't help reminding herself.

The last postcard Mom had sent to the family was of the sights of old Vienna. After that, no one had ever heard from her.

She reminded herself of what Dad had told her last night.

"Your mother's disappearance isn't another mystery for you to solve."

He was perfectly right, of course. She wasn't going to be able to learn the truth about a twenty-year-old mystery during a single day in Vienna. The visit had been cut short because Mrs. Klimowski's death had disrupted their original schedule.

And besides, she had a job to do.

She put Sir Reggie down and sat at her table to eat the breakfast that had been delivered to her room just minutes ago. Next to a silver compote was a little folded card with a greeting written on it.

"Willkommen in Wien, London and Reggie!"

London recognized Bryce Yeaton's handwriting. She read it aloud, then looked down at Sir Reggie.

"Did you hear that? Bryce says welcome to Vienna!"

Sir Reggie yapped cheerfully.

She lifted the compote, and under it found a mouth-watering breakfast—Eggs Benedict, which Bryce knew she loved, and a side dish of his exquisite apple strudel. There was even a saucer with several of the dog treats he'd made especially for Reggie.

A perfect breakfast, she sighed. *From a very attractive chef.*

She coaxed Sir Reggie into sitting up for a treat, which he crunched and gulped down in a single swallow.

London smiled at his voraciousness.

"I'm going to take a bit more time with my food, if you don't mind," she told him.

She was supposed to begin her day by meeting Emil and a tourist group in the reception area very soon, but there was still time to savor every bite. Then she hurried to change out of her nightgown into her dark blue uniform and prepare herself for work.

As she left her stateroom, she unlatched the dog door and looked at Sir Reggie.

"So what are your plans for the morning, kid? Do you want to stick with me, or go roaming around on your own, or maybe just laze around the stateroom?"

Seeming to understand the question, Sir Reggie yapped and trotted along with her into the passageway and up the stairs. As they entered the reception area, they encountered Captain Hays on his way out.

"Willkommen in Wien, you two!" he said, tipping his hat.

"Danke," London replied with a smile. *"Willkommen* to you as well."

The captain glanced behind him, then at London again. He seemed to be on the verge of telling her something, but at the moment he was apparently in too much of a hurry to do so.

"I'll give you a call shortly," he said breathlessly. "Meanwhile, duty calls. I'm off to the bridge."

Without another word, the captain dashed on up the stairs toward

51

the Rondo deck.

"Such a busy man," London said to Sir Reggie.

In fact, it now occurred to her that she couldn't remember him ever leaving the ship since the beginning of their voyage. He hadn't had the time to get out and explore Budapest or Gyor.

"I hope he gets a chance to see a bit of Vienna while we're here," she said to Sir Reggie.

Since neither Emil nor any of the passengers had showed up for the tour yet, London picked up Reggie and stepped outside the reception room doors onto the gangway. She saw that the ship was pulled up very close to shore. Beyond the short gangway lay a wide, concrete promenade. Morning pedestrians were walking about casually, hardly impressed by as commonplace an event as the arrival of a tour boat.

Otherwise, she couldn't see much of the city from here—just rows of trees and hotels beyond a highway that ran parallel to the promenade. A chartered bus was parked in a nearby parking lot, ready and waiting for her tour group.

When she returned to the reception area, a short, stocky man was standing there, scratching his head. He was wearing sneakers and a plaid shirt and mirrored sunglasses. The man appeared to be in his sixties, and his wheeled suitcase looked brand new. She had never seen him before.

By now she knew the face of every passenger on board, including the hermit next door to her stateroom. And she wasn't expecting any new passengers to come aboard.

What was this addled-looking guy doing in the reception room this morning?

She stepped toward him and asked, "Can I help you, sir?"

He turned toward her and shrugged.

"Maybe you can, miss. Maybe you can. What's your name?"

"I'm London Rose, the ship's social director."

"London Rose. A pretty name. That's a cute little doggie. What's its name?"

"Sir Reggie," London replied, realizing she was still holding him. "But I do have to ask you …"

I'm Bob Turner. I'm looking for either room 113 or 114. I'm not sure which."

London squinted at him curiously.

"Are you here … to visit somebody?"

"Naw, I'm here on business," he said in a rumbling monotone. "The captain expected me. He greeted me just now and told me which room I'd be staying in. He said it's right down that passageway, and I went down there, but then I realized I didn't catch whether he'd said 113 or 114, and he had to take off in a hurry before I could ask him for sure."

London remembered how rushed the captain had seemed.

Bob Turner pointed down the passageway. "He said I'd find the room unlocked, and I should just go on in and make myself at home. I thought about trying the doors myself, but I didn't want to barge in on anybody if I got the wrong room. That could be really awkward, if you know what I mean."

London's brain clicked away, trying to make sense of what she was hearing.

Room 113 or 114 ...

She knew that stateroom 113 was occupied by Cyrus Bannister, an enigmatic man who could sometimes be unpleasant. Room 114, on the other hand, was the suite where Mrs. Klimowski had been staying until she'd died. Had the captain really meant to put this fellow there? It was one of the ship's grand suites, which seemed like an odd sort of lodging for a scruffy-looking character like this.

But the choice made sense in an odd way. Room 114 happened to be the *Nachtmusik*'s only unoccupied stateroom. There wasn't any other place available for a new passenger.

But what is he doing here, anyway? London wondered.

She thought maybe she should touch base with Captain Hays.

"Give me just a moment," she said politely.

She put Sir Reggie down, then took out her cell phone and sent the captain a text message.

Bob Turner is here. He says you know him. Please advise.

Although the message was immediately marked "delivered," London knew better than to expect an immediate reply if the captain had urgent business to attend to at the moment.

Meanwhile, what was she supposed to do? The newcomer was bending over patting Sir Reggie on the head, and the dog seemed to be approving of him.

The man straightened up and stifled an agonized yawn.

"Miss Rose, if you don't mind, I just flew in from Miami, and I'm awfully tired, and I'd really like to get off my feet."

London didn't suppose it would do any harm to show him to his

53

room. She led the way down the passageway and he followed, wheeling his suitcase along behind them. When London turned the knob, she found that Room 114 really was unlocked.

The man walked on inside, but Sir Reggie lagged behind in the hallway. London could guess why. This had been his room when Mrs. Klimowski had still been alive. Mrs. Klimowski hadn't really known how to handle a dog, so Sir Reggie's memories of this room probably weren't very pleasant. He wasn't taking any chances on being shut up in here again.

She left the door open, but the little dog trotted away.

When London turned back to Bob Turner, she still couldn't see his eyes behind his mirrored sunglasses, but his mouth was hanging open with amazement.

London understood how he felt. The suite was vast by riverboat standards, with a separate seating area and elaborate décor. Piano music played softly over the room speakers to welcome the new guest.

"Hey, wait a minute," Bob Turner said. "Are you sure this is the right place?"

"It is room 114."

"Man oh man," he said, looking all around. "This place is a palace. Are all the rooms like this?"

"No, this is one of the two really grand suites."

Bob Turner grunted with surprise.

"Huh. So what's a bum like me doing in a getup like this?"

London couldn't help but chuckle at his self-deprecation.

She decided it would be impolite to tell him that this was the only room available.

Turner cupped his ear and listened.

"What's this tinkling music?" he said with a hint of disapproval.

"Uh, it's Beethoven. *Für Elise.* It's playing to welcome you here."

"Beethoven, huh?"

"That's right. The suites aboard the *Nachtmusik* are composer-themed. This is the Beethoven suite."

"Is it, now?"

His eyes fell on the enormous picture hanging above the head of the bed. It was a portrait of Beethoven looking down with crossed arms and a severe scowl on his lips.

Turner let out a chuckle at the sight of the portrait.

"And here he is—the big guy himself! Hey, Mr. B, it looks like

54

we're going to be roommates. I hope that suits you."

Then he turned toward London with a wink and added, "Maybe I should speak louder. Folks say he's kind of hard of hearing."

Well, he's got a sense of humor, anyway, London thought.

Turner pointed to a speaker, which was still playing *Für Elise.*

He said to London, "Listen, I've got nothing against this old-style music. But I'm more of a classic rock kind of guy, if you know what I mean. So I wonder if maybe ..."

London immediately understood what he meant.

Indicating a list on the end table next to the bed, she said, "You choose just about any kind of music you like. Or none at all."

She switched off *Für Elise.*

"Oh, I like music all right," Turner said. Looking intently at the portrait, he added, "Mr. B and I will look at our options, won't we, Mr. B? Hey, Mr. B, did you know Chuck Berry wrote a song about you? You'd get a kick out of it, I think. Maybe you've heard it—'Roll Over Beethoven.'"

Turner sat down on the edge of the bed.

"Man oh man," he said with a groan. "I ache from head to toe, and I'm tired as all get out. Folks aren't kidding when say this jet-lag thing is murder."

"Did you say you flew in from Miami?" London asked.

Turner nodded.

"That must have been a long flight."

Turner nodded again.

How can I draw this guy out? London wondered.

"If you don't mind my asking," she said, "what brings you aboard the *Nachtmusik?*"

Turner didn't reply. She wondered if maybe he'd fallen asleep while sitting up. With those mirror sunglasses, London couldn't tell whether he was staring into space or had closed his eyes.

Finally he spoke in his seemingly perpetual monotone.

"I hear you had a murder aboard."

London felt a jolt at his mention of the murder.

"Yes, back in Gyor," she said. "It was a terrible thing. Fortunately we caught the killer."

"So I hear," Turner murmured sleepily. "So I hear. Well ..."

He yawned and added, "I'm just here to help out however I can."

He kicked off his sneakers and stretched out on the bed.

"You can't get too much help," he said in a near-whisper. "That's what I always say."

London squinted with confusion. The man wasn't being the least bit forthcoming. But she felt as though prodding him with further questions would be rude.

"Welcome aboard the *Nachtmusik*, Mr. Turner," she said. "Please give me a call if there's anything you want or need."

Turner's mouth dropped open and a long snore rumbled out. The man was already fast asleep, and he was still wearing his sunglasses.

London stepped quietly out of the room and closed the door. Sir Reggie was nowhere in sight, but after all, he had the run of the ship now.

She knew that the passengers who were going on the morning tour must be gathering in the reception area. She needed to join them, but she still wanted to find out more about the new passenger.

Just then her phone buzzed. She saw that the call was from Captain Hays himself.

Maybe he can tell me who this guy is, she thought.

And also what he's doing here.

CHAPTER ELEVEN

Captain Hays's voice on the phone was crisp and chipper.

"So you met our new arrival," he said to London. "What can you tell me about him?"

She was a bit startled.

"Um … sir, I was kind of hoping you could tell *me* about him."

"Oh, dear. Being mysterious, is he? What is his name again?"

"Bob Turner."

"Yes, that's it. Well. I got an email just this morning from Mr. Lapham. Let me see …"

London heard the clacking of computer keys before the captain spoke again.

"It reads thus: 'Expect the arrival of a certain Bob Turner very shortly. He will assist you on security matters during the rest of your voyage.'"

"Is that all he wrote?" London asked.

"Yes, it is. Then Mr. Turner showed up at the gangway just a few minutes after I got that email."

"Didn't he tell you anything about himself?"

"Well, to be fair, he didn't have much of an opportunity. I was called away on an urgent matter on the bridge and had to rush off. But I did tell him where to find the only accommodations we currently have available. I was just starting to call and tell you to stop by and make him feel at home, but when I got your message, I gathered you were already taking care of that."

"Yes, he had a little trouble finding his room, but I managed to get him there."

"Weren't you able to draw him out just a little?" Captain Hays said.

"I'm afraid not. He fell fast asleep right away."

"Well, I suppose we'll learn more about him in good time."

"I hope so," London said, feeling disconcerted that even the captain wasn't clear on what the odd Mr. Turner was doing here. But she had no time to worry about that now.

"How's your morning shaping up?" the captain asked.

"In just a few minutes, Emil and I are taking a tour group into Vienna."

"Capital. We need to do whatever we can to put the last couple of days behind us. Do your best to keep folks busy and happy."

"I'll do my best, sir."

They ended the call, and London hurried back to the reception area. The tour group was gathering, and Amy was on hand to take their names. Emil was circulating among the passengers chatting with them.

London saw some thirty passengers milling around, which was about the number she'd expected. There were some familiar faces, including the five people who had shared their musician dolls for display in the lounge last night. She was happy to see Gus Jarrett in his usual golfing outfit and his buxom, gum-chewing wife, Honey, with her heavily dyed red hair. Those two were far from polished or sophisticated, but London had come to like them during the last couple of days.

She wasn't as glad to see the moody, dark-clad Cyrus Bannister, the occupant of the Schoenberg grand suite across the hall from where Bob Turner was now lodged. But she knew it was up to her to make sure that everybody enjoyed the trip, so she said good morning to him with a smile.

As she surveyed the group, a nearby voice said, *"Guten Morgen, Fräulein."*

She turned to see Emil's suave smile.

"Guten Morgen, mein Herr," she replied. "How does it feel to be in a country where people speak your native language?"

"Refreshing. How is your German?"

London replied with a smile.

"Ich hoffe, es gut genug, um es zu schaffen," she replied. Good enough to get by, I hope.

"Ich bezweifle es nicht," he replied. I don't doubt it.

Actually, London felt reasonably confident about her German— much more so than she'd felt about Hungarian, anyway.

Just then, Amy pushed in between them, wielding her clipboard.

"Everybody's accounted for," she said.

Then she added in a slightly petulant tone, "I guess I'd better get back to my other duties. Lord knows you keep me busy."

As Amy stalked away, London knew why she was cross. The concierge would rather be out conducting tours of her own today

58

instead of staying aboard the boat. But there was a lot to take care of with the rest of the passengers right here on the *Nachtmusik*, and not much time to spend in Vienna.

And besides ...

The last time Amy had gone ashore, she'd developed a crush on the jewel thief who had killed Mrs. Klimowski. That poor judgment seemed reason enough to keep Amy on the boat for a while at least.

London and Emil led the group across the gangway, where they all boarded the chartered bus that awaited them. A moment later, the bus was headed toward the heart of Vienna.

Standing in the aisle, London picked up a microphone and spoke to the passengers.

"Willkommen in Wien, fellow Epoch voyagers!" she said.

"Danke," many of them said cheerfully in near-unison.

London was pleased that most of them had picked up at least a few German words in preparation for their visit.

She continued, "As you know, our tour is behind schedule due to the unfortunate events of the last few days."

The group murmured in sad agreement.

"Our stay in Vienna will be shorter than we'd originally planned. This morning's tour will give you a brief introduction to the city. If you would like to see more, you can spend the rest of the day exploring as you like. There are plenty of modes of transportation available, including cabs, buses, trains, and subways. Emil and I can help out with schedules and routes. I hope you enjoy your time here."

She sat down beside Emil and looked out the window. So far, the city didn't look at all as she'd remembered. The buildings appeared distinctly sleek and modern as the bus headed along the bustling, four-lane *Lassallestrasse.*

Then the first significant landmark came into view on their left. It was truly an impressive sight, and London swallowed hard as memories of being here before swept over her. The passengers on the right got up to get a better look, and London handed the microphone to Emil.

"Ladies and gentlemen," he announced, "here you see the famous *Wiener Riesenrad*—the Vienna Giant Ferris Wheel. It was built in 1897, which I believe makes it the world's oldest operating Ferris wheel. And with its height of 212 feet, it was for many years the tallest Ferris wheel in the world, until the Technostar was built in Japan in 1985."

The group let out exclamations of awe.

"The *Riesenrad* is, as you might say, a true survivor," Emil continued. "All the other early great Ferris wheels—in Chicago, Paris, London, and St. Louis—were destroyed within a few decades after their construction."

"Why did this one survive?" one of the passengers asked.

Emil chuckled.

"I was hoping somebody would ask me that," he said. "It was scheduled for demolition in 1916. But due to a lack of funds, nobody got around to tearing it down! So here it stands, well over a hundred years later."

The passengers laughed, echoing his amusement.

Emil continued, "But do not let its age worry you, in case you want to take a ride on it later today. It is far from decrepit. Oh, like many structures here it was almost destroyed during World War Two, but it was rebuilt and has been excellently maintained ever since. You might remember Orson Welles taking a ride in it in the movie *The Third Man.* And I can tell you from personal experience that the view from the top is stunning."

Stunning is right, London remembered. Many years ago, when she was just a little girl, she had ridden in one of those large gondolas. They were built like passenger train cars, and Dad had lifted her so she could see through a window. From the very top of the wheel she could see all of Vienna, and even beyond into the surrounding forests and hills.

London felt her throat tighten at the memory. Even so high above the ground, she hadn't been afraid. She couldn't remember ever being afraid when she was with Mom and Dad.

It seems like so long ago, she thought.

As the bus continued on its way, Vienna seemed to undergo a magical transformation from a modern city into a picturesque center of history and culture. Emil took the microphone as the bus crossed the bridge over a narrow waterway flanked by stone embankments.

"We are now crossing the *Donaukanal*—the Danube Canal—which borders the city center. Once a natural branch of the Danube River itself, it has been managed as an artificial channel since 1598."

Finally the bus pulled to a stop in front of what looked like a magnificent palace with rows of massive arches and columns. London knew that it was not a palace, but something even more wonderful in its

60

way.

Taking her turn with the microphone, she announced, "This is our first destination—the *Wiener Staatsoper,* the Vienna State Opera. It was completed in 1869, and the opening performance was attended by Emperor Franz Joseph and Empress Elisabeth."

The enigmatic Cyrus Bannister raised his hand and asked a question.

"What was the first opera performed here?"

London felt a twinge of irritation at Bannister's quiz-like tone. She was sure that he already knew the answer to his own question, but hoped to trip her up.

No such luck today, Mr. Bannister, she thought.

She said, "The first opera performed here was *Don Giovanni,* Mozart's version of the story of Don Juan, the legendary womanizing rogue."

The stout, formally dressed Letitia Hartzer spoke up.

"Isn't *Don Giovanni* playing here right now?"

"That's right," London said. "I believe tickets are available for tonight's performance, if any of you are interested in attending."

A few people voiced their interest, including Ms. Hartzer.

Everybody climbed out of the bus and walked toward the great building.

London pointed upward and said, "Those two equestrian statues on the roof were created by the sculptor Ernst Julius Hähnel in 1876. The riders of the horses are the Muses of Harmony and Poetry."

Emil added, "Hähnel also created the five statues in the upper row of arches. They represent heroism, tragedy, fantasy, comedy, and love—all the necessary ingredients of great opera!"

We really are a good team, London thought as she and Emil shared information with the group. She felt a momentary temptation to reach over and hold his hand as they continued along. But how would he react? And what might that lead to? She was sure it was best to keep some distance between them—at least for now.

She realized that the towering opera house was stirring up some vague, long-forgotten memories, but she couldn't bring them into focus.

Emil gave her a friendly nudge as they passed through the arched entryway.

"I have a little surprise waiting in there," he said.

CHAPTER TWELVE

A "little" surprise?

London couldn't imagine that anything about the *Wiener Staatsoper* could possibly be "little." As for the surprise that Emil had mentioned …

What has he got up his sleeve?

She could tell from the astonished gasps that the vast foyer itself was surprise enough for the passengers in the tour group. The gold-leafed interior glittered brightly under the glow of wall and ceiling lamps, even though the gigantic chandelier wasn't lit. But she was sure that even this wasn't what Emil was referring to.

A uniformed gentleman greeted them with a smile.

"Guten Morgen, Fruende. Good morning, friends."

With a nod of his head he added, "And you must be Herr Waldmüller. I've been expecting all of you. Would you like a tour of this great palace of music and drama?"

Emil looked at him with a slightly haughty expression.

"We will not need your services," he said in German. "I know the building extremely well."

The man's smile disappeared and he nodded curtly.

"The 'effect' you requested is quite ready," he replied sullenly in German.

Effect? London wondered.

Just then Gus Jarrett's voice echoed through the vaulted lobby.

"Did you ever see so much gold in your life? This joint is a regular Fort Knox!"

Honey answered sharply, "Show some class, Gus. This is a place of great art and culture and stuff like that. Don't be an uncouth jerk."

Some members of the group laughed, and Gus blushed with embarrassment.

Even so, London understood why he was impressed. The spectacle took London's breath away. But her memories of it were still vague and indistinct.

Emil lectured on in a hushed, reverent purr.

"This interior was created by the great Austrian architect Eduard van der Nüll. Now believe it or not, the design of the *Staatsoper* was not well regarded when it was completed. Even the Emperor didn't like it much. Alas, van der Nüll took such criticisms quite personally. He committed suicide by hanging."

After letting his words sink in, Emil said in a significant tone, "Genius often goes unrecognized in its own time. And sometimes there is a steep price to pay for having it."

London was slightly jarred by this comment. True though it might be, she thought that Emil was sounding rather pompous.

She followed as he led them up a flight of stairs and out onto a balcony into the theater itself. Nothing could prepare them for the sight that met their eyes. The horseshoe-shaped auditorium surrounded by four tiered balconies seemed almost too gigantic for the building's palatial exterior.

"The auditorium's current capacity is two thousand two hundred eighty-four," Emil said. "It used to hold more people, but it has undergone many changes over the years. Like much of the rest of Vienna, the *Staatsoper* building was badly damaged by Allied bombing during World War Two and had to be rebuilt."

Gus Jarrett looked positively pale with amazement.

"How many, er, shows get put on in this place?"

"'Shows'?" echoed Emil with a condescending laugh. "Well, let me see. I believe there are some three hundred fifty performances every year, including many ballets and some fifty or sixty operas. It is one of the busiest opera houses in the world."

"Wow," Gus murmured.

Suddenly, Emil clapped his hands. As the noise echoed through the auditorium, the lights dimmed, as if a performance was about to begin. Because of the sheer size and emptiness of the place, it felt as though dusk was suddenly falling.

So this is Emil's "little" surprise, she realized.

Although it was really quite simple, it hardly seemed "little." She actually felt a bit woozy as the fading light cast an unexpected spell over her.

Suddenly, her vague childhood memories became much sharper and more distinct. As she looked down at the stage, she could imagine it filled with color and movement, while her mind filled up with beautiful music.

Emil touched her on the shoulder.

"You seem to be rather entranced, my dear," he said.

London nodded silently.

"A memory of something you saw here as a child?" he asked.

London glanced at him in surprise. She had told Emil that she had visited Vienna with her parents, but she hadn't expected him to pick up her emotional reactions to being here again.

"It's so vivid," she said. "As if it were happening right now."

"What do you see?"

"I see … a serpent chasing a handsome prince through a deep forest … a bird-catcher all dressed in feathers, his lips padlocked as he rings magical bells … a great ceremony in a mystic temple … and a beautiful but terrifying goddess all dressed in stars …"

Her voice faded as the images kept crowding through her mind.

Emil spoke in a soothing murmur.

"Ah. The opera must have been *Die Zauberflöte.*"

London looked at him.

"Yes, that's it. Mozart's last opera—*The Magic Flute.*"

Suddenly, a woman's voice echoed elegantly through the auditorium, singing a familiar aria beautifully at a high pitch.

"Ah-ah-ah-ah-ah …"

This was no memory!

London turned and saw that the singer was the stout, dignified Letitia Hartzer. Then the woman's voice fumbled and she coughed with embarrassment.

"Oh, dear," she said. "I guess my voice isn't what it used to be."

"Were you an opera singer?" asked one of the tourists.

"I wanted to be," Ms. Hartzer said, blushing a little. "I studied voice in college and performed in some college opera productions. I played the Queen of the Night in *The Magic Flute*—the goddess dressed up in stars.*"

"A very difficult role," Emil remarked.

"Indeed. I can't say I ever came close to mastering it, but I did sing it much better way back then. Oh, I simply adore Mozart!"

She added wistfully, "I just couldn't resist trying out my voice in this wonderful place. I hope the ghosts of great singers past weren't offended. If so, I offer them my sincerest apologies."

Emil clapped his hands again, and the lights rose back to their earlier brightness.

He turned to the group and smiled.

"I suggest we presently pay a little visit to the man who wrote that great opera," he said.

London knew exactly where Emil intended to go next.

As the rest of the group left the auditorium, London paused to take one last look into the cavernous space. She remembered something else now—how good it had felt to sit in that audience as a little girl, with Mom and Dad on either side of her.

Her throat caught a little as she followed after the group.

*

After exploring the opera house for a little while longer, London and Emil led the group outside for a short, brisk walk to the Mozart Monument in the Burggarten, the beautiful park at the city's center. A few people were lounging about on the grass or sitting on park benches.

And there was the twenty-five-foot-tall marble statue of Wolfgang Amadeus Mozart himself, mounted on a handsome pedestal. In the grass in front of the sculpture, a huge treble clef was shaped in a garden of brightly colored flowers.

"This statue was unveiled in 1896," London told the group. "Like so much else in Vienna, it was damaged during World War Two, but it was moved here and restored in 1953."

She pointed to sculpted figures flanking the pedestal. "These cherubic-looking winged fellows represent the power of Mozart's music. The two bas-reliefs at the base show scenes from *Don Giovanni*—the first opera ever staged at *Wiener Staatsoper*, and the one that's playing there right now. Now let's look at the back of the pedestal."

She led them behind the monument, where there was another bas-relief.

"This shows Mozart as a child playing the keyboard, accompanying his father on the violin and his older sister as she sings. As you probably know, Mozart was a great child prodigy who spent much of his childhood performing for aristocratic audiences."

Emil spoke up, pointing to the child on the bas-relief and then the adult statue.

"Let's pause for a moment to compare these two likenesses," he said. "Both of them, I think, hint at Mozart's inborn genius, one an

65

image from his childhood, the other of him in his full maturity—older and wiser, but still young. I believe they both suggest a certain perpetual youthfulness, appropriate for a master whose artistry was apparent from the start—an artistry that never grows old, no matter how many years may pass."

Well said, London thought.

And again, she imagined she heard strains of music from *The Magic Flute.*

She remembered vividly being here with Mom and Dad many years ago on a sunny afternoon, sitting right here on the monument's semicircular railing for a pleasant picnic. She thought she could almost taste the Austrian pastry she'd eaten back then.

What was it?

Apple strudel?

No, she was sure it hadn't been that.

What was it, then?

One of the tourists interrupted her thoughts.

"Is it true Mozart was murdered by a rival composer?"

London heard Letitia Hartzer let out a scoff. Cyrus Bannister looked more than a little offended.

"You should know better than to believe everything you see in movies," Cyrus growled at the passenger. "*Amadeus,* for example."

London and Emil exchanged glances of concern. They knew that Cyrus could be brusque about his authority on music.

"Then he wasn't killed by Antonio Salieri?" another passenger asked.

"No, and I can hardly believe any of you are entertaining such a foolish notion," Cyrus snapped. "There was probably some rivalry between the two of them. But as far as anyone knows, Salieri and Mozart seem to have been mutually supportive and even friendly. They even collaborated on at least one piece of music."

Letitia Hartzer chimed in, sounding markedly more pleasant than Cyrus.

"Of course there *were rumors* about such a murder, untrue though those rumors certainly were. But even while suffering dementia on his deathbed, Salieri very clearly denied the rumors to a friend, saying, 'Tell the world that old Salieri, who will soon die, told you so.'"

The group let out a murmur of appreciation.

"How sad that Mozart died so young, though," Ms. Hartzer added, "at only thirty-five years of age."

There was a collective sigh of agreement. But London noticed that Emil had crossed his arms and was scowling. She realized that he didn't like to be upstaged in his role as the ship's historical authority.

It was time to move on. Fortunately she had made plans in advance.

"Let's go get some coffee and something scrumptious to eat," she said.

*

London had made reservations for the whole group at the famous Café Landtmann. As they headed there along the broad, tree-lined boulevard called the *Museumstrasse*, the group passed the grand edifices of the Museum of Art History, the Natural History Museum, and the Austrian Parliament Building, which was fronted by a huge fountain with a statue of Athena standing on a pillar at its center.

As they approached the broad awning of the Café Landtmann, Emil smiled with approval.

"You made an excellent choice, my dear," he said.

London couldn't help but agree. In a city that was famous for its cafés, the Landtmann looked especially attractive.

Like all Viennese cafés, it was more than a mere eating place—it was a cultural institution, a place where ordinary people could rub shoulders with some of the most remarkable people of their times. Since 1873, the Café Landtmann had been a regular haunt of the likes of composer Gustav Mahler, psychologist Sigmund Freud, novelist James Michener, and even Paul McCartney.

The tourists dispersed to their tables, and London and Emil sat down together on the outdoor terrace under the awning. They had a nice view of the bustling boulevard called the *Ringstrasse*.

They both ordered espresso, then mulled over the pastry menu.

"I believe I will have the Sachertorte," Emil said. "Perhaps you would enjoy it as well."

London was familiar with the layered chocolate sponge cake coated on top with apricot jam and chocolate icing. She knew that it was perfectly delicious.

But even so ...

She was trying to remember a pastry she had eaten with her parents all those years ago.

67

"I've got something else in mind," she said tentatively. "Something I ate when I was just a little girl. I really liked it, but I can't remember what it's called ..."

"Can you describe it for me?" Emil asked.

London thought for a moment.

"I think it was like a thin piece of pie with a crisscross crust on top."

Emil pointed to the menu and said, "You might be talking about Linzertorte. It is thought to be the oldest cake in the world, first made in 1696 named after the city of Linz where it was invented."

The name sounded familiar, so when the waiter returned, London ordered the Linzertorte, and Emil ordered the Sachertorte. When thin pie-like dessert arrived, London took a small taste of it. The crust was buttery and delicate, with hints of lemon, cinnamon, and hazelnuts. The filling was an uncommon blend of tartness and sweetness—redcurrant jam, London suspected.

Yes, that's it, she thought.

And it was every bit as delicious as she remembered.

She closed her eyes and took another bite, savoring the cluster of wonderful flavors. The taste was almost intoxicating, and London felt dizzy at the rush of memories it stirred up. A little alarmed, she opened her eyes.

For a moment, she thought she was dreaming last night's dream all over again.

There, in the midst of the crowd on the busy *Ringstrasse*, was a woman with reddish hair and a face shaped much like London's own.

London gasped and dropped her fork.

"Mom?" she whispered.

CHAPTER THIRTEEN

Overwhelmed by anticipation, London barely noticed Emil's voice calling after her as she dashed away from their table. She rushed out of the café terrace into the crowd of people on the wide sidewalk.

Mom, she repeated breathlessly.

But now the woman she'd seen had disappeared in the sheer density of pedestrians. It was like being back in last night's dream, with her repeated glimpses of a woman who vanished whenever London tried to approach her.

I've lost her, she thought in despair.

But then she caught a glimpse again—the same color and arrangement of hair that had gotten her attention before. The woman was now farther away, but she was definitely there, and definitely real. Then dozens of other pedestrians clustered and intermingled in the space between them.

London pushed her way into the crowd, bouncing chaotically against other moving bodies.

"Entschuldigen Sie," she said, begging pardon as she bumped into a tall man.

"Entschuldigen Sie, bitte," she repeated as she pushed against a woman harder than she meant to. She heard murmurs of surprise, and wished she could stop and explain and apologize, but since that could be Mom out there, she needed to keep moving.

The woman came into view again—very nearby. Now it was more than her hair that held London's attention. It was her posture, her distinctive stride, her manner of movement.

It's Mom. It's got to be.

She reached out and touched the woman's shoulder.

"Mom!" she exclaimed.

The woman stopped in her tracks, and so did London. Then the woman turned and looked at her.

London's heart sank.

It wasn't Mom at all.

She knew it immediately because of the brown eyes. Mom's eyes

69

were a vibrant bright blue, like London's own. And up close like this, there really wasn't as much resemblance as she'd thought.

London gasped aloud at her mistake.

Fortunately, the woman didn't seem angry. She spoke to London with polite surprise.

"Darf ich Ihnen helfen?" she asked. May I help you?

London swallowed hard and struggled to catch her breath.

"I'm sorry," she said in German. "I thought you were someone else."

"That's all right," the woman replied in German with a short laugh. "Are you an American?"

"Yes," London said.

"You speak German well."

"Thank you."

"Are you here as a tourist?" the woman asked.

"Yes," London said. She didn't want to explain anything more.

The woman seemed on the verge of introducing herself, perhaps of even making conversation. Under different circumstances, London would have welcomed the chance to chat with a Viennese local. But she didn't want to explain the circumstances ... and besides, Emil must be wondering where she'd rushed off to.

The woman seemed to detect London's reticence.

"Enjoy your stay," the woman said.

"I will," London said, still in German. "Pardon me for disturbing you."

"It was nothing."

London felt her whole body slacken with exhaustion and disappointment. The distance back to the café now seemed considerably greater than she thought she'd run. She made her way back through the crowd to the terrace and sat down again with Emil.

"Are you all right, London?" he asked a bit anxiously. "What just happened?"

"Nothing," London said. "I thought I recognized someone I knew."

"Ah," Emil replied.

London knew he must be waiting for more of an explanation, but she'd never told him much of anything about her past, let alone her mother's disappearance.

Anyway, this is not the time to share, she decided.

London picked up her fork and took another bite of the Linzertorte.

70

Just as before, the pastry crust melted on her tongue and the filling was absolutely luscious. All the same, it no longer stirred up those uncanny memories of her childhood.

*

The next stop on the tour was just a very short walk from the Café Landtmann.

"Ladies and gentlemen," Emil announced as the building came into view, "welcome to Vienna's celebrated Burgtheater, the National Theater of Austria—perhaps the most important German language theater in the world."

The majestic building with its swirling Baroque architecture and rounded facade wasn't as overwhelming as the titanic *Wiener Staatsoper,* but it was still stunning.

As they approached the entrance, Emil continued his lecture.

"This building is from 1888, but the theater was founded almost a century and a half earlier. In 1776, Emperor Joseph II declared that all performances would be in German. Now, that may sound unremarkable to you, but at the time it was quite revolutionary."

"How so?" one of the tourists asked.

London noted the pride in Emil's voice as he replied, "Throughout Europe at the time, and even here in Austria, the German language was looked down upon in elite circles. French and Italian were considered the languages of high culture, but only the wealthy and privileged understood them. The German language gained respect from the emperor's decree—and the plays became accessible even to ordinary people. In a sense, it was the true beginning of German drama."

She gazed upward at the sculptures placed high above the doorways. They were busts of great German playwrights, and she recognized some of the names.

There was Goethe, Kliest, Schiller, and ...

Shakespeare?

London blinked and looked harder.

Sure enough, there was the familiar face with the name "Shakespeare" on a plaque beneath it.

Emil patted her on the back and said, "You look a bit surprised to see your friend Will Shakespeare here."

"A little," she admitted.

Emil chuckled, but said nothing more as they continued on their way.

When they entered the theater's great foyer, with its chandeliers and parquet floors and marble columns and walls, they were again greeted by a uniformed man who seemed prepared to serve as a guide. And again, Emil waved him aside.

London brought the group to a stop as they reached a magnificent stairway.

"Have a look," she said, pointing straight above them.

The group gasped at the sight that met their eyes. A series of enormous and beautiful paintings stretched across the high vaulted ceiling.

She said, "Those paintings were created in 1888 by the great Viennese painter Gustav Klimt."

Certain that Emil knew much more about the paintings than she did, she prompted him with a nod.

He pointed to them individually. "That one is of the altar of Dionysus, the Greek god of wine and drama. That one pictures the great ancient amphitheater at Taormina in Sicily. And that one shows Thespis, whom legend holds to be the world's first actor, performing aboard his traveling stage. And the last picture ..."

He paused and grinned.

"Well, perhaps some of you recognize the scene."

London almost laughed as she peered at the painting carefully. Judging from the collective murmur, others in their group recognized the scene, too.

On a jutting theater stage, a young woman lay on her bier, with a young man sprawled dead beside her, while rapt spectators watched the performance. The painting was of the last moments of a performance of *Romeo and Juliet* at the original Globe Theater in London.

Emil said, "Perhaps you also recognize at least one member of the audience."

"Why, that's Queen Elizabeth herself!" one tourist said.

"That's right," Emil said. "And although you probably don't recognize their faces, Gustav Klimt and his brother are also in the audience watching the performance. This is the only self-portrait Klimt ever painted."

Without further explanation, Emil led the group to a great theater with a massive chandelier and four tiers of horseshoe-shaped balconies.

He cautioned them, "I believe a rehearsal is in progress."

The hushed tourists filed into the auditorium, where three actors on the stage below—two men and one woman—were speaking in German

The first few words London heard sounded oddly familiar.

The two men stepped out of sight, leaving the woman alone onstage.

Then another young man entered and remained silent for a few moments.

"I believe you are familiar with this play," Emil whispered in London's ear. "Just listen!"

Facing the empty auditorium, the actor spoke solemnly and dramatically.

"Sein oder Nichtsein, das is hier die Frage ..."

London's eyes widened as she understood the words.

"'To be, or not to be'!" she whispered to Emil. "Why, they're rehearsing a production of *Hamlet*!"

Emil smiled and nodded.

As they all listened, the words wove a startling spell indeed. When the soliloquy ended, she and Emil quietly led the group out of the auditorium.

"So," Emil asked her as they left the building, "was that your first taste of Shakespeare in the original German?"

Now London laughed aloud. She'd heard that Germans sometimes joked about how much better Shakespeare was "in the original German."

But Emil wasn't laughing. He shrugged in an ambiguous manner.

"We Germans like to think of Shakespeare as one of our own," he said. "His plays are actually performed in Germany more often than they are in England. Did you know that?"

"No," London admitted.

"His language translates into German with uncanny grace and beauty—or is it the other way around? We speakers of German sometimes wonder. Even during his lifetime, his plays were performed by *Deutsche Wanderbühne*—German traveling players. There is actually an early version of *Hamlet* that exists only in a German version. So which came first—Shakespeare in English, or Shakespeare in German?"

London didn't know what to say.

There wasn't a doubt in her mind that Shakespeare was English, and he wrote his plays in English. But what did Emil really think? Was that a note of wryness in his voice, as if he wasn't being quite serious? His manner was so dry, she couldn't be sure. Did he really think that Shakespeare wrote his plays originally in German?

He's a hard man to read, she thought.

But as they left the theater, London heard that famous line echoing through her head.

"Sein oder Nichtsein, das is hier die Frage."

She couldn't deny that it sounded beautiful in German.

*

The visit to the Burgtheater brought the morning tour to an end. The group assembled in front of the building to discuss their activities for the rest of the day, now that they were free to go out on their own. Many wanted to spend the afternoon exploring the rest of Vienna, including the museums of art and natural history. Several asked Emil to lead them on a tour of the Austrian Parliament Building, which he gladly agreed to do.

Several others wanted to return to the *Nachtmusik* to relax, or to rest up in preparation for a long performance of Mozart's *Don Giovanni* that night at the *Wiener Staatsoper*. Since London had plenty of tasks awaiting her on the boat, she boarded the chartered bus along with them and returned to the riverboat.

When they arrived and she went up the gangway and into the reception area, a charming sight awaited her. Sir Reggie was entertaining several passengers with his antics.

London was especially pleased to see that Sir Reggie was sitting up and begging for a dog treat that Walter Shick held in his hand. She was the only one aboard who knew that Walter and Agnes Shick had been in a witness protection program for thirty years. The presence of police aboard the boat back in Gyor had been especially traumatic for them. She'd been afraid that the elderly couple might stay sequestered in their stateroom during the rest of the voyage. But here they were, enjoying themselves just like other people.

Walter toss tossed the treat up in the air, and Sir Reggie jumped up and caught it.

Seeing London, Walter said, "Bryce the chef gave us some of these a while ago. Sir Reggie will do anything for them."

Several other people showed London the treats that Bryce had given them as well. London couldn't guess how many passengers aboard the *Nachtmusik* might be carrying dog treats by now.

London wagged her finger at Sir Reggie.

"You've got to be careful, or you'll get fat," she said.

Sir Reggie let out a whine of protest, which made everybody laugh. Then, as the group broke up, London picked up the dog and looked him in the eye.

"I mean it, Sir Reggie," she said. "You'll get sick if you eat too much. And don't let all this attention go to your head. I don't know what I'll do with you if you get all conceited."

At that moment, London heard the elevator door open behind her, then the sound of a man's voice.

"Don't you worry about it, sir. I'm on the case now. I'll get to the bottom of this nasty little crime before you know it."

CHAPTER FOURTEEN

"Nasty little crime?" London wondered, as she turned and saw two men stepping out of the elevator. One of them was Kirby Oswinkle, wearing his nautical cap and looking as disgruntled as always.

From the slicked-back hair and mirrored sunglasses, she recognized the second man as Bob Turner. The last she'd seen that new arrival, he'd been lying fast asleep in the Beethoven suite earlier this morning. When he caught sight of London, he stepped toward her.

"London Rose—I'm glad we ran into you. Did you know that this gentleman has been the victim of a robbery?"

Before London could reply, Oswinkle spoke sharply.

"Oh, she knows, all right—don't you, Miss London Rose?"

He's talking about the musician doll, London realized.

She'd almost forgotten about that. And she'd hoped she'd heard the last about it.

Oswinkle continued, "You were right there last night when I discovered the theft. But you didn't do a single thing about it, did you? Well, that's about to change."

London was still holding Sir Reggie, who was starting to tilt his head again in apparent sympathy with Oswinkle. The last thing London needed was for Oswinkle to get irate at the dog again, so she set Sir Reggie down.

Bob Turner gave Oswinkle a reassuring pat on the back.

"You needn't worry, sir. I'll get to the bottom of this. I'll get your precious keepsake back."

"And bring the culprit to justice?" Oswinkle said through clenched teeth.

"You can count on it."

Oswinkle turned to London again.

"It's about time you brought some big guns aboard to deal with the shenanigans that have been going on."

Then he headed off down the passageway toward his suite.

Bob Turner shook his head at London.

"Poor guy," he said to her. "He's really bent out of shape about

76

this."

"Yes, well—I'm not sure how seriously we should take it."

"Oh, we should take it *very* seriously," Turner said, leaning toward her. "It's our job. No problem is too small for us to tackle. It's the little things that wind up turning into the big things."

London felt a flash of resentment. She didn't like being lectured by this man about her duties aboard the *Nachtmusik*—especially since she really knew so little about him or what he was doing here.

"Bob—may I call you Bob?" she said.

"If I can call you London."

"Please do. The thing is, I'm not sure this is even a real problem. I wouldn't be surprised if Mr. Oswinkle just misplaced the doll. If you could only see all the stuff he's got in his stateroom—"

"Oh, I saw it, all right," Bob said. "He showed it to me. It's really an impressive collection. And he and I combed through every bit of it, item by item, to make absolutely sure the little conductor doll wasn't hiding there somewhere. But it's gone for sure. Somebody definitely stole it. And now it's up to me to find the thief."

He shook his head and shuffled his feet.

"And just a couple of days ago there was a murder. What next? We've got some real problems on this boat. I'm glad I got here when I did. Just in the nick of time. You leave all that to me."

He stood looking at her for a moment—or at least she *thought* he looked at her. With those mirror sunglasses, it was hard to tell.

"Well, London, I'll get right to work," he said. "I'll be seeing you tonight at dinner."

London stood staring at him as he headed away down the passageway. She found the security man more than a bit mystifying.

And what was he saying about dinner? she wondered.

She wasn't aware of any dinner plans involving him.

Who is this guy, anyway? she asked herself.

She remembered what Jeremy Lapham had written in his email to Captain Hays.

"He will assist you on security matters during the rest of your voyage."

So whoever Bob Turner was, he seemed to have been brought aboard the *Nachtmusik* as some sort of security expert. And although

77

London thought the man was rather odd, she figured he couldn't do any harm in that capacity. Actually, maybe he could be of help.

Maybe he could even find Kirby Oswinkle's missing musician doll. Apparently he'd already taken an interest in it, and that might keep Oswinkle happy—which would be an achievement in itself.

Looking down at Sir Reggie, London said, "I guess I won't have to worry about the doll anymore."

Sir Reggie let out a little yap of agreement.

"But what did he mean about dinner?"

Sir Reggie made no reply, and it was only when London went back to her stateroom to prepare herself for the afternoon's activities that she found the answer.

Perched on her table was a tent-folded card. She picked it up and read its attractive calligraphy.

Captain Spencer Hays
"respectfully commands" you
to join him and a select group of colleagues
for dinner at the Palmenhaus
courtesy of Epoch World Cruise Lines.

The invitation—or the "command," as it styled itself—went on to state the time when the group would gather in the reception area.

The Palmenhaus, London mused.

She knew the restaurant by reputation, but she hadn't expected to get a chance to eat there.

I'm about to be pampered, she thought with a smile.

Apparently Bob Turner had been invited as well. But who else would be coming along?

Meanwhile, she had lots of work to do. She sat down at her table and began to make a list of what she needed to take care of and to check on.

*

London's frantic afternoon flew by very quickly. Yesterday, she'd set up a suggestions box for activities that passengers might like to request. Now she found lots of interesting proposals, including a book club, a drawing class, and a meditation group. She introduced the

78

prospective book club members to Emil in his library, and found locations for the other two pursuits.

Next, she helped set up a particularly interesting little musical game called "Drop the Needle." A passenger had even brought along a phonograph player and a large collection of classical music vinyl records. The game involved someone dropping the needle randomly on a randomly chosen record. Players scored points by being the first to recognize what piece was being played.

London herself wasn't much good at guessing whether the passages were by Bach or Vivaldi, Mozart or Haydn, Rachmaninoff or Tchaikovsky, Bartok or Stravinsky, much less at identifying the piece itself. Nevertheless, those passengers were having a good time with it.

Her afternoon's duties came to an end just in time for her to feed Sir Reggie and get ready for tonight's dinner at the Palmenhaus. She surveyed her closet for something to wear. She had a traveler's standard variety of black mix and match items, so she could put together a dinner outfit from those.

But she thought something more colorful might help reenergize her after a long day.

She took a brightly patterned tunic out of the closet and showed it to the dog.

"What do you think of this, Sir Reggie?"

The dog lowered his head and gazed up at her skeptically.

"You're right," London said. "I wore this to dinner back in Budapest. Mustn't repeat myself."

She put the tunic back and took out a long straight maxi dress with spaghetti straps. She knew that the dark moss green color emphasized her auburn hair.

"What about this?" she asked the dog.

Sir Reggie let out a disapproving whine.

"What's wrong with it?"

Sir Reggie made no further comment. Although talking aloud to him seemed to help her decision-making process, London knew she had to rely on her own critical eye. She concluded that although the neckline was high, the two leg-baring side slits made it too sexy for a dinner with the captain.

But maybe not for ...

She wondered if others, maybe Emil or Bryce for example, might react favorably to the slinky outfit. But she didn't even know if either

79

one of them would be at dinner tonight. And she certainly wasn't interested in looking enticing to either Bob Turner or Captain Hays.

She put it back in the closet and took out a navy-blue dress with white polka dots. With this one, she would be fully covered, and the soft fabric belted with a sash was definitely figure-flattering. She showed to Sir Reggie, who at least didn't seem to disapprove.

"OK, I'll go with this," she said.

After a refreshing shower, she dressed and hurried to the reception area, where the captain was waiting already. The other dinner guests arrived quickly—Elsie, Amy, and yes, both Emil and Bryce.

The captain said, "After the events of the last few days, I think you people in particular deserve a night on the town."

Everybody smiled.

Yes, I suppose we do deserve a treat, London thought. The captain seemed to have chosen the people most responsible for solving the mystery of Mrs. Klimowski's death.

But she'd almost forgotten about Bob Turner, who arrived last. She wasn't sure why he'd been included in Captain Hays's invitation. She guessed the captain might be trying to please Jeremy Lapham, since bringing the "security expert" aboard had been the CEO's own idea.

Now that everybody had arrived, the captain led them all down the gangway toward a waiting van.

A night on the town, London thought as she got into the chauffeured vehicle.

She felt more than ready to enjoy herself.

*

After a twenty-minute drive through Vienna, the van pulled up to the *Palmenhaus.* Even though she knew that the name "palm house" meant a type of greenhouse, London gasped with amazement. The structure with arching roofs and walls of glass was simply gigantic—nothing less than a palace made mostly of glass.

As they got out of the van and climbed an elegant stone stairway to the entrance, Emil was his usual informative self.

"The *Palmenhaus* was opened in 1882 by Emperor Franz Joseph the First as a greenhouse for Austrian royalty. It covers about twenty-two thousand square feet and includes exotic flora from all over the world. It is one of the world's largest botanical exhibits, featuring some forty-five hundred plant species in all."

The captain added with a smile, "And it also happens to have an excellent restaurant."

The group was shown into a vast dining area beneath a vaulted glass-and-steel ceiling, where tables were interspersed among towering plants. When they reached their table, Bryce pulled out a chair for London, then sat down in the one next to her.

He leaned toward her, apparently about ready to say something, when Amy plopped down in the chair on the other side of him.

"What a beautiful place!" Amy commented, tugging on his jacket sleeve. "Was eating here your idea, Bryce?"

Bryce looked a bit surprised at Amy's undisguised flirtation.

"No, it was the captain's choice," he replied. "But I certainly approve."

"Well, your approval counts a lot as far as I'm concerned," Amy said sweetly.

London was rather bemused. This was the first time she'd noticed Amy's interest in Bryce. Then she saw that Emil was still standing on the other side of the table, and he seemed to be frowning at Bryce.

As Emil finally took a seat opposite her, London realized that the evening might not be as relaxing as she had hoped.

Oh dear, she thought. *This is liable to get complicated.*

CHAPTER FIFTEEN

London noticed Elsie grinning at her across the table. When their eyes met, Elsie gave a sly wink.

She sees what's going on, London thought. *Maybe she understands it better than I do.*

London's face suddenly felt warm. Emil apparently saw Bryce as a rival for her attention. And Amy definitely saw London as a rival for Bryce's attentions.

And as for Bryce—well, London couldn't tell how he felt. For a moment, London wondered if she should have worn the slinky dress after all.

She was relieved by the distraction when a waiter came and took their drink orders. London chose her favorite, a Manhattan, and turned her attention to her dinner menu.

Then she heard Amy's voice. "Oh, Bryce, I simply can't make up my mind," she chirped. "You're the culinary expert. Could you please order for me?"

London's eyes widened with disbelief. Now Amy was acting like Bryce was her date

She glanced over to see Elsie's reaction, but her friend's attention had shifted to the bar. And London could see why. The Palmenhaus bartender was an especially handsome young man with an excellent physique, a strong jaw, and wavy, blond hair.

So London wasn't the only one whose attention was divided this evening.

She felt relieved that Bryce seemed reluctant to fulfill Amy's request.

"Well, I can make a suggestion, anyway," Bryce said.

He seemed to be speaking to both Amy and London when he offered his advice.

"I hear the Palmenhaus is especially renowned for its Austrian beef steak fillet," he said. "I think that's what *I'll* order."

"Then that's what I'll order as well," Amy said.

London was about to say the same thing when Emil spoke up.

"Austrian beef is all very well and good for tourists, but it is hardly the best choice at the Palmenhaus. I have dined here before, and can vouch for their kitchen's *gedämpftes Lachsforellenfillet.*"

Then with a patronizing smile, he said to Bryce, "That means steamed salmon trout fillet."

"I know," Bryce said, apparently impervious to Emil's condescension. "But I think I'll stick with the fillet of steak."

Both Captain Hays and Bob Turner made their choices. Now London had to make up her mind. Whose advice was she going to follow, Emil's or Bryce's?

She was starting to feel annoyed with herself.

Act your age, she told herself. *You're not a teenager.*

She decided to order the Wiener schnitzel.

The waiter brought their drinks, and everybody ordered their meals. Then London took a sip of what struck her as the best Manhattan she'd ever tasted. The rye whiskey cocktail had an underlying sweetness that mingled splendidly with the dash of orange bitters.

She was a bit surprised to hear Elsie complain about her bright pink cocktail.

"Oh dear. I'm afraid the bartender doesn't have the first idea how to make a cosmopolitan."

Sitting at the head of the table right next to her, the captain said, "May I try it?"

Elsie offered the captain a sip.

"It tastes perfectly good to me," he said.

"Can't you tell what's wrong with it?" Elsie said.

"I'm afraid not."

"It doesn't have nearly enough triple sec."

The captain shrugged and said, "Well, if it's not to your liking, my dear, let me wave for the waiter and—"

"Oh, that won't be necessary, Captain Hays," Elsie said hastily. "This is a professional matter as far as I'm concerned. I'll go talk to the bartender myself. I'm sure I can teach him a thing or two."

I'll bet you can, Elsie, London thought with a smile as her friend headed away to meet with the handsome bartender. In a few moments, just in time for before-dinner soups and salads, Elsie returned to the table, looking quite pleased with herself. London doubted very much that there was anything wrong with Elsie's drink at all.

She choked back a giggle and focused on her own mixed salad

flavored with pumpkin oil.

When the main meals arrived, the Wiener schnitzel was served with creamed cucumbers and warm parsley-flavored potato salad. As soon as she tasted it, she realized this was the first time she'd ever eaten authentic Wiener schnitzel. The delicately breaded, deep-fried veal escalope was less than an inch thick, and as tender and luscious as any pastry.

Before he started eating his own salmon trout fillet, Emil peered at London's dish with a scholar's eye.

"Many people don't understand the difference between 'schnitzel' and 'Wiener schnitzel,'" he said in his most pedantic manner. "Schnitzel is typically made from tenderized pork or some other meat. True Wiener schnitzel simply *must* be made with veal. That's actually an Austrian law!"

Tasting his own beef filet, Bryce said, "Of course, it's also true that Wiener schnitzel may not be native to Vienna at all. It's very similar to *costoletta alla Milanese*. Legend has it that the Austrian Field Marshal Joseph Radetzky brought it to Austria from Milan, which was then ruled by the Habsburgs, in 1857."

Bryce managed to share this information casually, without the slightest hint of pretension. Looking peeved, Emil ate in silence for a while.

Sitting on the other side of the Elsie, Bob Turner had kept rather quiet so far, but now he spoke to London over the restaurant clatter.

"I hear you discovered the old lady's body."

His voice was loud enough that people at the next table turned and glared at him.

"Um, yes," London replied, almost gagging on a bite of veal.

"And you found her corpse in a church, eh?"

London nodded. Bob chuckled as he continued eating his Paris-style beef dish.

"I'd sure like to hear how you and the dog cracked the case," he said. "I hear the dog did his share of the detective work. That must be some story."

London was dumbfounded. Was Bob going to demand the whole story right here and now?

Fortunately, the captain spoke in a tone of mild protest.

"Surely we can talk about this unpleasantness some other time."

Bob nodded and kept eating.

Recorded music began playing from somewhere nearby, and the captain explained that there was dancing in the lounge if any of them would like to go there later. To London's relief, the conversation settled down to occasional comments on the delicious meal.

Desserts were finally served, and London basked in a serving of flawlessly caramelized *crème brûlée,* warm on its lightly scorched surface while the custard interior remained deliciously cold.

Just as everybody finished their dessert, the music burst out with a fanfare-like opening that led into a waltz melody.

Emil's face lit up.

"Ah, a truly authentic Viennese waltz tune!" he said. "'Tales from the Vienna Woods,' by the Waltz King himself—Johann Strauss the Second."

He rose from his chair and said to London, "May I have this dance, *fraulein?*"

London gulped nervously.

She loved to dance, but …

"I'm not sure about my waltzing skills," she said.

Emil chuckled knowingly.

"I believe you may be surprised, *fraulein.*"

The two of them left the table and ventured through a wide doorway into the Palmenhaus lounge, where only a handful of couples shared a spacious dance floor. They were already whirling about to the tune.

London felt terribly nervous. She remembered Dad teaching her the basic waltz steps when she was still a little girl, but she'd never seriously tried waltzing before.

Emil took her right hand in his left and bowed slightly. Then he placed his right hand on her waist and she put her free hand on his shoulder. He began moving, and to London's surprise, she found herself in effortless motion as Emil led her gliding across the dance floor.

She realized that Emil's assuredness and skill were somehow contagious, and all she had to do was follow him instinctively. At times, it seemed as though her feet never touched the floor, as if she and Emil both were utterly weightless. She felt breathless and increasingly dizzy as they spun round and round—and even a little alarmed. She wasn't used to surrendering so much control to another human being, and as thrilled as she was, she wasn't quite sure she liked it.

She felt somehow both relieved and disappointed when the piece came to an end. Then a new melody started—something slow, sentimental, and vaguely familiar. After the whirling waltz, London wasn't sure she was ready to join Emil in a slow dance.

She was a bit grateful to see Bryce stepping toward them.

"May I cut in?" he asked, reaching for London's hand.

Emil crossed his arms and frowned, but he politely stepped aside.

A moment later, London found herself moving and swaying slowly in Bryce's arms. As they turned near the doorway, she glimpsed the bar in the dining room. Elsie had returned there and was flirting contentedly with the handsome bartender. There seemed to be a touch of romance in the air tonight.

"I can't place this tune," London said to her new dance partner.

"It's an old Lombardo and Loeb song," Bryce said. "'Seems Like Old Times.'"

"Oh, yes, that's right."

London was pleasantly startled as she felt a wave of comfort come over her. She fairly melted into Bryce's embrace. She couldn't help being amused at herself. The rather mawkish melody wasn't the sort of thing she normally liked. Even so, she found herself slipping under its sentimental spell.

She remembered a quote she'd heard somewhere.

"Extraordinary how potent cheap music is."

Bryce chuckled, and London blushed to realize she'd said the words aloud.

"Noel Coward said that, didn't he?" Bryce observed.

"I believe so," London said at the mention of the witty English playwright's name.

She found herself murmuring the song's title lyric—"Seems Like Old Times." The words struck an emotional chord with her. She'd been obsessing about "old times" ever since she'd come to Europe, and especially since she'd been in Austria.

Her throat tightened with emotion, but she found Bryce's presence soothing. Part of her realized how emotionally vulnerable she was to him at this moment. Another part of her simply didn't care. She put her head on his shoulder and let it rest there during the rest of the song.

*

86

During the ride back to the *Nachtmusik*, London found herself awkwardly seated between Bryce and Emil. None of the three of them seemed to know what to say, and London could almost feel Amy's piercing glare from the seat behind her.

The other people in the van seemed perfectly relaxed. Elsie and Bob shared cocktail recipes, and Captain Hays and the chauffer chatted about sports.

When everybody got out of the van at the end of their ride, Amy hurried over to Bryce and brazenly took his arm. Bryce looked rather puzzled but politely walked up the gangway with her. Telling herself she didn't care, London followed along with Emil.

As soon as the dinner companions stepped into the reception area, Letitia Hartzer came rushing toward London, looking alarmed.

"I'm so relieved to see you!" she exclaimed.

"Is something the matter?" London asked.

"Yes! There's been another theft!"

CHAPTER SIXTEEN

Without another word, Letitia whirled away and headed toward the lounge.

Another theft? London thought.

As she started after the distraught woman, other crew members who had just returned from dinner continued on their various ways.

But London felt a hand on her shoulder. She turned and found herself staring into a pair of mirrored sunglasses.

"You needn't trouble yourself," Bob Turner told her. "I'll get to the bottom of this."

Then the diligent security man strode off to the lounge.

For a fleeting moment, London felt tempted to leave the entire matter to him. After all, dealing with this sort of thing seemed to be Bob's job aboard the *Nachtmusik*. And earlier today he'd promised Kirby Oswinkle, *"I'll get your precious keepsake back."*

But she really couldn't just ignore the problem. She had to check out whatever was missing this time, and whatever Bob was doing about it.

She followed after him.

It was late, and the Amadeus Lounge was fairly quiet except for a buzz of activity around the little table where the musician dolls were displayed. A familiar group of people was gathered there with Letitia— Rudy and Tina Fiore, Steve and Carol Weaver, and Kirby Oswinkle. Elsie had joined the group, and Sir Reggie was trotting around looking up at all the people.

London stepped close enough to get a look at the table. Sure enough, there were only four figures there now, not five. The bass player, clarinetist, violinist, and drummer were still on display. But Letitia's trumpet player was gone.

Oswinkle, whose conductor figure had gone missing yesterday, appeared to be as angry as if another of *his* keepsakes had been stolen. He glanced at London, then ignored her.

"Am I glad to see you!" he said to Bob Turner. Then turning to others, he announced, "This is Bob Turner, our new security man. If anybody can get to the bottom of this outrage, he can."

Bob turned his mirrored sunglasses toward Elsie.

"Were you working at the bar when this happened?"

"As you know, I just now got back from the captain's dinner," she said. "But I've asked my bartenders and none of them saw anything unusual. Of course, they've been pretty much busy with customers."

Bob nodded sagely.

"This is a tricky case," he said. "Finding your lost treasures is going to take some special skills ..."

He was interrupted by a yap from Sir Reggie.

The little dog was crouched beside the table, peering under the dark tablecloth that hung almost to the floor.

"Did you find something, boy?" Bob asked.

The sleuth leaned down and lifted the tablecloth, then reached under the table.

"Aha!" he cried.

Bob straightened up, holding the little trumpeter figure in his hand.

"I believe *this* is what you're looking for," he said to Letitia with a note of triumph, as if he'd achieved some remarkable investigative feat.

"Oh, goodness, yes!" she said as he handed her the doll.

Most of those watching let out a sigh of relief in unison.

"Obviously nothing to worry about," Rudy Fiore said.

"Yes, it must have just fallen off the table and gotten knocked underneath," his wife added.

The others murmured in agreement as Letitia put the musician doll back in its place among the others.

"Thank you so much!" Letitia squealed. "It's so nice to have an actual investigator on board."

Bob chuckled and stooped down to pat Sir Reggie on the head.

"Well, I couldn't have done it without the help of Sir Reggie the Wonder Dog," he said.

"So this was just a false alarm," Kirby Oswinkle growled. "But don't forget, there has been a *real* theft that remains unsolved! I won't be satisfied until my little music conductor is safely returned to my collection!"

Kirby stormed out of the lounge.

"I suppose he's got a right to be upset," Carol Weaver said.

"Oh, bother," her husband, Steve, protested. "I'll bet that man's doll isn't missing at all. He probably just misplaced it. Let's try not to get upset over every little thing that happens—or doesn't happen."

There was another murmur of agreement, and then the group headed to the bar for one last drink before closing.

Bob drew London aside and spoke to her confidentially.

"I don't want to cause a panic," he said. "But this was no false alarm."

London's eyes widened.

"Do you mean—?"

"I mean there's more to what just happened here than meets the eye," Bob said, scratching his chin.

"Please explain," London said.

"Not yet, not yet," Bob said with a shake of his head. "Not without further evidence. Suffice it to say, there's somebody aboard this boat who is up to no good. And I've got a pretty good idea of who it is."

"Then I wish you'd tell me—"

"All in good time, London. All in good time."

Bob shoved his hands into his pockets and wandered out of the lounge, looking deep in thought.

London looked down at Sir Reggie.

"All I know is, it's been a busy day and I'm tired," she said to him. "And we've got another busy day ahead tomorrow. Let's turn in for the night."

As she and Sir Reggie left the lounge, the songs London had danced to back at the Palmenhaus played in her head. She found herself moving and swaying to "Seems Like Old Times" as she walked toward her stateroom.

*

The next morning, London had just gotten up and dressed when her cell phone buzzed. She saw a command-like text message from Emil.

Come quick to the Rondo deck!

She had a pretty good idea of what Emil's message was about, so she took a few bites of the breakfast she'd ordered, then left her stateroom and hurried up the stairway.

When London stepped out into the warm morning sunlight, she felt a fresh breeze. The *Nachtmusik* was in motion, having departed from

Vienna during the wee hours of the morning. For part of this day, the ship would be traveling the Danube through Austria's beautiful Wachau Valley. Now they were passing a sight she hadn't wanted to miss.

Perched on the rocky hillside above a quaint medieval Austrian village were the ruins of a once-magnificent castle with sheer, high stone walls. Emil was at the starboard rail, pointing and lecturing a group of passengers.

"... and there it is, Durnstein Castle, built by Hadmar the First of Kuenring during the early twelfth century. It was plundered when Hussite forces raided this area in the 1400s, and further damaged by the Swedes during the Thirty Years' War. It hasn't been habitable since 1679, when it was abandoned."

One of the passengers raised his hand and spoke.

"I read that Durnstein Castle once hosted an interesting house guest."

Emil smiled.

"I was just getting ready to tell that story," he replied. "Although he was rather a reluctant 'guest,' to put it mildly. England's Richard the Lionheart passed through this region on his way home from the Third Crusade. He was captured by Duke Leopold and imprisoned in this castle. He was eventually ransomed back to England for some one hundred fifty thousand marks—an enormous amount of money that staggered even the prosperous English economy. But the historical facts make for a rather dry version of the story. The *legend* is much more interesting."

As the boat glided past the village of Durnstein, another remarkable sight came into view. Built into the hillside were the large statues of two figures—a chainmail-wearing nobleman on horseback and a more humbly dressed man playing a stringed musical instrument, walking alongside of him.

Emil continued, "That is a statue of King Richard the First, with his loyal minstrel, Blondel, at his side. After Richard was captured, it is said that Blondel traveled all over Europe looking for him, singing the first verse of one of the king's favorite songs. Finally Blondel came this way, and when he sang that verse, he heard Richard sing the second verse from his castle cell. He had found his king at last."

The passengers let out exclamations.

"Do you think the story is true?" one of them asked.

91

Emil's smile turned just a bit mischievous.

"As a historian ... well, I am not sure it is my place to say."

Another passenger spoke up.

"As they say, 'When the legend becomes fact, print the legend.'"

Emil tilted his head with interest.

"An interesting quote," he said. "Who said it?"

"It's from an American Western movie starring John Wayne and Jimmy Stewart," the passenger replied. *The Man Who Shot Liberty Valance.*"

Emil looked a little taken aback—and also a little embarrassed. London realized he surely considered that movie to be a lowbrow piece of entertainment. She looked around for a way to change the subject and saw that the ship was now gliding past the terraced hills of a vineyard. She knew they would see many such hillsides today, with vines planted in rows almost down to the water on both sides of the Danube.

She moved over to the railing and began telling the passengers about those vineyards.

"The story of how Wachau became a fine winemaking region goes back literally millions of years, to long-ago ages before human beings even lived here. First the Danube carved its twisting way through the rocky land, and then rock dust settled on crystalline slopes, making the soil perfect for raising grapes.

"Back around 500 B.C.," she continued, "the Celts were the earliest grape-growers in Austria. They were followed by the Romans, and then by Catholic monks who became the region's first true master vintners ..."

She finished her little lecture by announcing the Wachau Valley wines that were available from the bar in the lounge or with meals in the ship's restaurant. Afterward, some passengers broke up into social groups and some plopped down into deck chairs to relax and continue enjoying the view.

When Emil walked over to join London at the railing, she was glad to see that he seemed to be in better spirits now. But she felt a tingle of alarm at his next remark.

"I have a marvelous tour planned for Salzburg tomorrow," Emil said. "I'm exceptionally prepared."

"Uh, Emil ..."

"Yes?"

"I thought you knew. You won't be conducting tomorrow's tour. Epoch World accepted the offer of a local tour guide to show us around Salzburg."

Emil let out a snort of anger.

"What? Whose decision was this?"

"I don't know," London said. "Someone high up on the company ladder—maybe Jeremy Lapham himself."

"This is outrageous!" Emil almost shouted, then stormed away toward the elevators.

Uh-oh, London thought. *I hope we're not in for trouble about this tomorrow.*

CHAPTER SEVENTEEN

The next morning, Emil was nowhere to be seen when the group began to gather in the reception area for their tour of Salzburg. As London got things organized and checked off the passengers' names, she heard someone calling from outside the ship.

"Willkommen!"

She looked out the glass doors and saw a well-dressed young man with ruddy cheeks and sandy hair waving from the bottom of the gangway. She opened a reception room doors and waved back to him.

"Willkommen in Salzburg, birthplace of Wolfgang Amadeus Mozart!" he called with a broad smile. She heard the passengers clustered behind her calling back *"Danke"* and "Thank you." Someone even replied with a cheerful, even if out of place, *"Gracias."*

It wasn't an especially large group, just twenty of them, but they all seemed excited and ready to go. She knew that, as usual, some passengers had opted to do their touring on their own and others were just more interested in activities aboard the *Nachtmusik* than in visiting an ancient city.

And one is writing a murder mystery, she thought, noting without surprise that Stanley Tedrow wasn't with the group.

London saw some familiar faces in the group, including Cyrus Bannister, Letitia Hartzer, and the honeymooning young couple, Rudy and Tina Fiore.

But where was Emil? Surely he wouldn't be skipping this trip out of vexation at not leading the tour himself.

Meanwhile, Sir Reggie was trotting around London's feet, looking eager to join her.

"I'm sorry, old sport," she said, "but it's better for you not to come with us this time. We just got here, and we don't know just how welcome you'll be. Stay aboard and do your job—keep everybody safe."

Sir Reggie whined a little, then dashed away.

As London headed down the gangway herself, she glanced back and forth along the narrow, swiftly moving Salzach River. She

94

marveled at the versatility of the *Nachtmusik* to navigate just about any kind of waterway. During the early hours of the morning, the pilot had steered them off the Danube onto the smaller Inn River, then onto this still smaller tributary called the Salzach. It seemed that the *Nachtmusik* could travel almost anywhere.

The guide continued his garrulous greetings as the passengers gathered on the barge that was moored at the bottom of the gangway so that they could cross the shallower water between the boat and the shore. He introduced himself to each one individually, and London sensed that he was quickly learning all their names by heart.

"Willkommen, willkommen! My name is Olaf Moritz—please just call me Olaf—and I will be your guide today!"

To London's relief, Emil Waldmüller finally came walking down the gangway to join the tour. He nodded curtly to London and coldly shook Olaf's offered hand. London was disappointed in Emil's silent pettiness, but she was glad that he hadn't snubbed the tour completely. There was still a lot she didn't understand about the intelligent, handsome, but sometimes stiff and standoffish historian.

On the other side of the barge, a flight of stairs led up a steep grassy embankment to the streets of Salzburg. Olaf guided them all into a town that looked like something out of a fairytale, with its Baroque buildings and the enormous medieval Hohensalzburg Fortress towering protectively on a hilltop above them.

"We'll reach our first destination before you know it!" Olaf said, leading them through stone-paved pedestrian streets flanked by quaint buildings, some of which had tunnel-like arches leading into the next courtyard or walkway.

Sure enough, they soon arrived in front of a six-story building marked with the words *Mozarts Geburtshaus*—Mozart's Birthplace— in graceful cursive letters across an orange-painted edifice. As Olaf continued explaining things to them, London was impressed by his fluent German-accented English.

"This house was old and venerable even before Salzburg's most famous son was born here. It was built in the twelfth century on what was once a garden owned by Benedictine monks. A whole book could be written about the people who lived and worked here over the years."

He pointed to an engraved image showing a serpent entwining a staff.

"Perhaps some of you recognize this image."

One of the passengers chuckled with surprise.

"I sure do," he said. "I'm a physician, and that's the Rod of Asclepius, a symbol of medicine."

"That's right," Olaf said. "This is guild sign of Chunrad Fröschmoser, the apothecary to the Austrian court who set up business here in 1585."

The tour began on the third floor, the apartment where the Mozart family had lived. There they visited Mozart's study, the bedroom where he was probably born, and an authentic eighteenth-century middle-class kitchen with low-hanging ceiling beams and the place where food was cooked over an open fire.

"Not much of a kitchen," one visitor complained. "And someone had to haul firewood all the way up here."

But the others found it quaint and attractive.

In the apartment, they saw countless paintings of Mozart's family and friends and acquaintances, and also handwritten letters, original scores, and personal items displayed in museum cases. There was even a violin Mozart had played as a child.

Then Olaf led the group down to the second floor, which was themed "Mozart at the Theater" and was devoted to his operas. The displays included models of set and costume designs and paintings and photographs of productions.

But perhaps the most remarkable item on exhibit didn't look all that impressive at first glance. It was a small keyboard that looked almost like an antique toy. What would have been the white keys on a piano were black, and what would have been the black keys were white.

Letitia Hartzer gasped at the sight of the instrument.

"Oh, my goodness!" she said. "Is this ...?"

"Yes, this is Mozart's original clavichord," Olaf said, "which I happen to have permission to play."

When he played a few notes, the instrument produced a soft and delicate sound, and London recognized a Mozart piano sonata. An enchanted hush fell over the group, and London fell under the same spell. For a moment, more than two centuries seemed to disappear, and they were transported to the days when Mozart had lived and worked here.

"The clavichord wasn't used as a concert instrument anymore in Mozart's time," Olaf explained as he played. "It was used for practice, and for composing. In fact, this was the very instrument on which

Mozart composed ..."

Instead of finishing his sentence, he played a series of chords.

Letitia could barely contain her excitement.

"He composed *The Magic Flute* on this very instrument!" she cried.

"So you're familiar with that opera?" Olaf asked.

"Familiar with it? Why, I played the Queen of the Night in a college production!"

"Then perhaps you'd like to sing a bit of it for us," Olaf said.

Letitia blushed shyly as Olaf began to play a few introductory chords.

"Oh, I couldn't," she said. "Those days are long gone."

"Try it. You might be surprised."

As Olaf accompanied her, Letitia began to sing the aria she'd attempted yesterday. Her voice sounded strong and full at first. But just like yesterday, she fumbled when she tried to hit some especially high notes.

Letitia looked understandably crushed that her voice had failed her while she was being accompanied on this legendary instrument. But from the woman's dark glances at Olaf, London sensed that Letitia was more than just embarrassed. She seemed furious at their tour guide for coaxing her into attempting the aria.

As Letitia slunk away into the group, Emil spoke the first words he had said during the tour.

"I'm sure we would all like to hear you play *'Land der Berge, Land am Strome.'*"

"Austria's national anthem?" Olaf asked with surprise. "I mean no disrespect, but—why on this instrument?"

"Well, as I explained to some of these people yesterday, Mozart *did* write the melody. Perhaps on this very keyboard."

Olaf chuckled as he played a few notes of the anthem.

"That's a common longstanding misconception, my dear sir. It's been known for quite some time that Mozart almost certainly did *not* compose the melody for *'Land der Berge, Land am Strome.'* It was probably written by either Paul Wranitzky or Johann Holzer—with at most a very little help from Mozart himself."

As Olaf resumed playing the Mozart sonata, he seemed not to notice that Emil was glaring at him with his arms crossed. Emil was obviously mortified—and incensed—at having his expertise contradicted.

London wondered how it was possible that the friendly and cheerful Olaf had, perfectly innocently, managed to enrage two of her companions on this tour.

When the tour of the *Mozarts Geburtshaus* came to an end, Olaf led the group on foot to their next destination. The short walk took them among shops selling food, crafts, flowers, clothes, and of course cheap souvenir trinkets. They soon arrived at the House for Mozart, a theater devoted primarily to music and opera.

As they walked across a terrace toward the broad, modern facade with its row of glass entryways, Olaf told the group, "This building has gone through many transformations since it was first built on the site of some stables and a riding school in 1925. It was then called the *Kleines Festspielhaus,* the 'Small Festival Hall.' Above the entrances you can see three bronze reliefs showing scenes from Mozart operas—*The Marriage of Figaro, Don Giovanni,* and *The Magic Flute.*"

The group continued on into the expansive, gleaming foyer.

"The former festival hall is no longer so 'small,' as you can see," Olaf said. "Its latest remodeling was completed in time for Mozarts two hundred fiftieth birthday in 2006, when it was renamed *das Haus für Mozart*—the House for Mozart."

The group murmured with awe at their surroundings, which included towering windows, bronze busts on marble pedestals, and enormous murals. Most impressive was a curving, gilded wall with horizontal openings through which could be seen a gigantic human profile.

"Why, that's Mozart himself!" one of the tourists said.

"That's right," Olaf said. "His face is made out of Swarovski crystal. And take note of the construction materials in this lobby—a startling mix of glass, marble, concrete, and gold leaf."

"A most impressive piece of architecture," Emil said as he took in the view.

London happened to notice something much more prosaic farther along the marble floor—a yellow plastic sign that read *"NASSER BODEN."* She was about to warn her charges that the words meant "wet floor." But the warning seemed unnecessary as Olaf led them up a flight of stairs to a gallery that overlooked the lobby.

The music aficionado Cyrus Bannister gasped aloud at the sound of piano music from inside the theater.

"Someone's playing Beethoven's *Hammerklavier* sonata in there!"

he commented.

"Yes, one of the most difficult sonatas in the classical repertoire," Olaf agreed. "It's no mean feat. That's a talented young pianist named Wolfram Poehler, practicing for a recital here tonight."

"He's playing extremely well," Cyrus said. "But I don't believe I've heard of Herr Poehler."

"I'm not surprised," Olaf told him. "He's just now making his reputation."

"May we ... go in and ...?" Cyrus said, indicating an entrance to the auditorium.

Olaf tilted his head thoughtfully.

"I'd hate to disrupt Herr Poehler's rehearsal," he said. "But of course you will want to see the auditorium. That's the main attraction here."

The group murmured in agreement.

"Perhaps we can be very quiet," he added, as he opened a door slowly.

They all filed into the spacious auditorium, with its rows of red-cushioned seats and two balconies that wrapped around all the way around the auditorium to the stage itself.

A young blond man wearing a T-shirt was on the stage playing on a grand piano. London was familiar with the indescribably complex *Hammerklavier* sonata, and she was impressed by the power and quality of his playing—and also by the hall's perfect acoustics.

Wolfram Poehler was in the middle of the thunderous fugue of the last movement when he noticed the arrival of visitors. He suddenly stopped, smiled at the intruders, and shut the lid over the piano keys.

"Sorry," he said quite pleasantly in German. "Rehearsal is over."

Then he left through a stage door.

"Well, you can hardly blame him," Olaf said, laughing. "If we want to hear his *Hammerklavier*, we'll just have to buy tickets for tonight's performance. Come on, let me show you the rest of the building."

*

The visit to the House of Mozart brought the morning's tour to a pleasant end. Only Emil and Letitia refrained from warmly thanking the tour guide for his services. With a final bow and a wave, Olaf turned back into auditorium while the visitors made their way outside.

99

At that point, London's passengers were free to spend the afternoon as they pleased, and most wandered off in various directions. She heard some mention that they planned to visit sights such as the Mirabelle Palace and Gardens and the city's various museums. She saw that others apparently just wanted to go shopping, and they began checking out the nearby shops and stalls. London wasn't sure where Letitia or Emil had gone, but they were nowhere to be seen.

Just two passengers, Rudy and Tina Fiore, were still standing there in front of the House of Mozart.

"I'm hungry," Rudy announced.

"London, we'd love for you to join us for lunch," Tina added.

London realized she was both tired and hungry, and also grateful for the company. They chose a nearby sidewalk café and sat down at a table with an umbrella. A waitress promptly gave them menus, but before they could even think about what to order, Tina let out an exclamation of alarm.

"Oh dear," she said, reaching around in her purse. "I seem to have lost my cell phone."

"Where do you think it happened?" her husband asked.

Tina thought for a moment.

"When we went into the auditorium I took out my cell phone to snap a picture. I must have dropped it then. I believe we were in the aisle right by the fourth row of seats."

"Don't worry about it," London said. "I'll go back and find it. Just order me anything that looks good, and a cold drink."

London hurried back to the theater and was relieved to find the door still unlocked. She thought that Olaf might still be inside. As she crossed the lobby, she again noticed the plastic *"NASSER BODEN"* sign, now placed in a different area. She climbed the staircase and continued on inside the auditorium.

She was startled to find the place was now quite dim inside. London turned on her cell phone flashlight, but before she could look for the missing phone, her beam fell on a large, dark object heaped over some chairs in a nearby row.

London couldn't tell what that object was, and couldn't imagine why anything would have been left draped across those chairs.

"Ist hier jemand?" she called out. "Is anyone here?"

She heard no answer, not even the slightest sound in the cavernous space.

She shined her flashlight around the auditorium and didn't see anybody.

Finally London walked up the aisle to the row of seats where the object lay, then made her way over to it. She shined her flashlight directly on the object, then leaped back with a cry of alarm.

Her flashlight had revealed a pair of unmoving staring eyes.

Olaf Moritz was dead.

CHAPTER EIGHTEEN

London stood frozen with horror and disbelief. Those eyes staring at her here in this vast darkness seemed like some horrible dream.

This can't be happening, she tried to tell herself.

But it was happening.

A man she'd seen so lively and smiling just a little while ago lay dead and broken right here over the backs of the theater seats.

She heard herself shout "Help!" at the top of her lungs.

Then, remembering she was in Austria, she shouted, *"Hilfe!"*

Her shouts echoed through the auditorium. She felt as though all of Vienna must have heard her. And yet, how could anybody have really heard her in this cavernous empty space? Was there even anyone else in the whole building?

I've got to find somebody, she thought.

Using her flashlight to guide her, she staggered along the row of seats back into the aisle.

"Hilfe!" she kept yelling. *"Ein Mann ist tot!"* A man is dead!

Moving toward the entrance, she kept her beam focused on the floor in order not to stumble. Along the way, the light caught the reflection of an object on the floor.

Sure enough, it was Tina Fiore's cell phone—the very thing London had come back here to find. But finding it in these circumstances, at this particular moment, felt beyond bizarre. Nevertheless, she mechanically picked it up and dropped into her bag and continued on her way.

"Hilfe!" she cried out again.

When she pushed her way out the door into the lobby, she was momentarily blinded by the bright lighting. She yelled again and this time a voice answered.

"Was ist da los?" What is the matter?

A figure was running toward her

"We've got to call the police!" London cried out in German. As her eyes adjusted, she saw that it was a pretty, young blond woman, wearing a gray maintenance worker's uniform. Remembering the

"NASSER BODEN" sign, London guessed she must have been mopping a restroom.

"Why?" the young woman asked.

"An accident," London replied breathlessly. "Inside."

Near the entrance to the dark auditorium, the woman stepped over to a little metal door on a wall and flipped an electrical switch.

Lights came up in the auditorium, and the body heaped over the chairs was clearly visible.

The young woman let out a bloodcurdling shriek.

She ran toward the body.

"Olaf! Olaf! Olaf!"

When the young woman got near enough to see those open staring eyes, she burst into tears and collapsed into a seat.

London struggled to overcome her own state of shock. No one here was going to be of any help.

She fumbled for her cell phone. As she gripped it in a shaking hand, she briefly had to remind herself *not* to dial 911.

I'm in Vienna.

Austria.

As always when she led tours, she had entered the local emergency numbers in her phone—133 for the police and 144 for an ambulance. She wavered for just a moment as to which to call. But there wasn't a doubt that the man was dead. It was too late for an ambulance. She dialed 133.

A calm, professional-sounding woman's voice asked in German, "What is the nature of your emergency?"

"A man ... a man is dead," she stammered in German.

"Where are you?"

"In the auditorium at the House for Mozart."

"And your name?"

"London Rose. I'm here with the tour boat *Nachtmusik.*"

"I'll send the police right over," the woman on the phone said. "Stay where you are."

"I will," London said.

The call ended, and London became aware of the young woman sobbing as she sat near the body.

She knew him, London thought.

For her, this tragedy was clearly painfully personal.

Meanwhile, London's mind reeled as she wondered what she

should do next. Did she need to call Captain Hays right away?

And tell him what? she asked herself.

She still didn't understand what had happened.

Instead, she dialed Emil's number.

"Emil, where are you right now?" she said when he answered.

"Out walking," Emil replied, sounding a bit startled by the question.

"Are you still near the House for Mozart?"

"Quite close, actually. Why?"

"Emil … that's where I am, and …"

Words failed her for a moment.

"Please come here right away," she finally said.

"I will," Emil replied.

They ended the call, and London made her way back along the row of seats where the body lay crumpled. She sat down next to the young woman.

"Can I … help?" London asked.

The woman just kept repeating the same name again and again.

"Olaf … Olaf … Olaf …"

Whatever its cause, the poor woman's anguish was palpable. London knew that her own shock couldn't begin to compare with it, although she was deeply shaken.

But what happened to Olaf? she wondered.

It looked as though Olaf had fallen from one of the balconies. From the way his head was twisted, he appeared to have broken his neck.

But how?

Had he fallen by accident?

It just can't be another murder, she thought miserably.

Surely it's not that.

Soon the sound of police sirens pierced through the auditorium walls, and then a group of uniformed police officers swarmed into the building.

Two officers briskly escorted London and the young woman back into the lobby and had them sit down on facing marble benches. London spotted a name tag on the young woman's blouse—Greta Mayr.

She said, "Greta … my name is London."

The woman didn't reply, but her sobbing had subsided.

"I take it you knew … the victim," London said.

The woman nodded.

"Do you have … any idea …?" London began.

"No, I don't know anything," Greta said. "I don't know anything at all."

She said so with a strange tremor, as if she knew more than she could bring herself to say.

A female police officer approached them from the auditorium.

"I'm afraid I must ask you both to stay and answer a few questions," she said.

"What can you tell us right now?" London asked.

"Just that you will need to answer some questions."

London didn't like the evasiveness of the policewoman's words.

"Couldn't you just tell us—?" she began.

"The *Landespolizeidirektor* will be here momentarily," the policewoman interrupted. "He will want to talk to you."

Landespolizeidirektor—the police director, London realized.

Surely the police director wouldn't be on his way here if the officers already on the scene didn't suspect something sinister.

The officer took a few steps away and stood nearby, alert and vigilant, as if keeping watch.

Suddenly one of the glass front doors flew open, and Emil came rushing in.

"London!" he exclaimed as he caught sight of her. "What has happened?"

London got up from the bench and hurried toward him.

"Something terrible … our tour guide …"

"Yes? What happened to him?"

"He's dead."

Emil's eyes widened.

"What do you mean? How do you know?"

London opened her mouth to speak, but her voice failed her.

At that moment, the front door opened again. A tall man wearing a dark blue uniform with insignias on his shoulders came striding into the lobby.

"Is that the *Landespolizeidirektor*?" Emil asked London, looking alarmed.

"I think so. I was told he was on his way here."

The policewoman who had just spoken to London and Greta hurried over to him. She spoke to him, pointing at London. The man glanced at London, but went on into the auditorium.

"Please just tell me it is not another murder," Emil said to London.

London was startled by his query, which seemed weirdly inappropriate.

Wasn't he worried about the trauma she was going through?

Why doesn't he ask me how I am? she wondered.

He didn't seem concerned about her at all.

"I don't know … what happened," she replied.

"But you must know something," Emil insisted.

London felt a flash of anger. She had called on Emil for help, but now she wished she hadn't phoned him.

"I said I don't know, Emil! All I know is … something terrible has happened."

Emil just frowned, almost as if he thought all this was her fault.

"At least tell me how you happened to find—" he began.

London interrupted sharply.

"I don't want to talk about it. I don't think I *should* talk about it—at least not with you, not before I talk to the police."

London and Emil stood in tense silence for a few long moments. Then the *Landespolizeidirektor* came back out of the theater.

"Come with me, please," he said to London.

He escorted her to a different section of the lobby and told her to sit down. Emil followed, but after a sharp stare from the police director, he kept his distance.

The police director appeared to be about fifty years old. He had a white mustache, round-rimmed glasses, and an alert twinkle in his eye.

"I am *Landespolizeidirektor* Fritz Tanneberger," he said to her in German. "And you are …?"

"My name is London Rose," she said.

"An American?" he asked, apparently noticing her accent.

"Yes. I'm the social director aboard a tour boat …"

"Ah, the *Nachtmusik*," Tanneberger said. "Yes, I heard. You docked here this morning, didn't you?"

"That's right," London said.

"A rather large craft, I hear. How many passengers?"

London wondered why that could possibly matter.

"About a hundred," she said.

"Then it was an impressive feat, navigating our narrow little Salzach River. The *Nachtmusik* must be very maneuverable."

106

"It is," London agreed.

He seemed to be genuinely curious about the *Nachtmusik*. If not, he was taking an indirect approach toward asking her questions.

Emil suddenly stepped toward them and spoke up.

"London and I brought a tour group into Salzburg shortly after the *Nachtmusik* landed."

Tanneberger squinted through his thick lenses at Emil.

"And you are …?"

"My name is Emil Waldmüller. I am the ship's historian."

"And you are German."

"I am."

"Were you here when the body was found?"

"No, but—"

Tanneberger interrupted gently but sternly.

"Then kindly let Fraulein Rose answer my questions, if you don't mind."

Emil's face reddened—London wasn't sure whether from embarrassment or irritation. But he kept silent.

"How many passengers did you bring ashore?" Tanneberger asked London.

"About twenty."

Tanneberger tilted his head with interest.

"A rather large group. And was Herr Moritz your tour guide?"

London noticed that he seemed familiar with the name.

"He was."

"And did he bring your whole group here to this theater?"

"He did."

"And you all went inside the auditorium—you and all twenty of the tourists?"

"That's right."

Tanneberger scratched his chin.

"And yet … you were alone when you found the body. How could that be?"

London winced at the note of suspicion in his voice.

"The tour ended here, and everybody went their separate ways," she said. "Olaf—the victim—stayed behind in the theater. I went to a café with a couple of passengers, right outside. When one of them told me she thought she'd dropped her cell phone in the auditorium, I came back to look for it."

"Did you find it?"

London was a bit startled by what seemed like an irrelevant question.

"Why, yes—but only after I found ... the body."

Tanneberger held her gaze for a long moment.

London stammered, "Do you think it was ...?"

"Murder?" Tanneberger said, finishing her thought. "I prefer not to jump to conclusions. Suffice it to say, it appears that the body fell from the uppermost balcony. However, the position is odd. The trajectory does not suggest that the victim simply tripped and fell."

London felt as though the world was swirling around her. It was starting to sink in that this impossible situation was very real.

"Meanwhile, I need to come aboard the *Nachtmusik* and speak to your captain. I shall accompany you and Herr Waldmüller back to the boat. But first, give me just a moment, please."

He turned away and walked toward the policewoman.

Emil was seething as he murmured under his breath to London.

"So this policeman is going to come aboard the *Nachtmusik* and wreak havoc with our tour. And over nothing at all."

"It's hardly over nothing," London murmured back.

"Well, it is nothing that concerns any of us. It is not another one of our passengers who is dead this time. And none of us could have had anything to do with what happened—even if it *was* murder, which I doubt. Suicide seems much more likely."

Suicide? London thought.

The idea hadn't occurred to her for a second.

And now, as she remembered the cheerful, smiling tour guide, she couldn't bring herself to believe it. Besides, it seemed like a peculiar way to commit suicide. A fall from that height into the rows of seats below might not have proven fatal, but would definitely have proven painful and probably paralyzing.

Tanneberger finished giving his instructions to the policewoman, who walked over to where Greta was still sitting, apparently to question her. Then Tanneberger and another police officer led London and Emil through the lobby toward the front entrance.

As the group stepped out into the open air, London saw Rudy and Tina Fiore approaching them from among the parked police vehicles.

"London!" Tina exclaimed.

"We heard sirens!" Rudy said. "What's going on?"

London's spirits sank even lower as she remembered having to share the terrible news of Mrs. Klimowski's death.

It's starting all over again, she thought.

She numbly heard herself say, "Our tour guide is dead."

"What?" Tina said.

"How did it happen?" Rudy said.

"No questions right now," Emil said, his tone suddenly protective. "Surely you can see that London is very upset. We're heading back to the *Nachtmusik.*"

"Someone needs to call Captain Hays so he'll be prepared," London said.

"I'll take care of it," Emil said, taking out his cell phone.

After his curtness just a few minutes ago, London felt grateful for his show of consideration. But she knew it was only a short reprieve. Soon she'd have to deal with an entire ship full of confused and upset people—again.

Emil spoke on his phone to the captain, walking a little too far away for London to hear what he was saying. As Tina and Rudy trotted along with London, Emil, Tanneberger, and the policeman, a weirdly incongruous thought crossed London's mind.

Tina's cell phone.

The reason I went back to the theater in the first place.

She reached into her bag and took out the cell phone and handed it to Tina, who simply looked puzzled.

As London and her companions walked back toward the *Nachtmusik,* she flashed back to *Landespolizeidirektor's* skeptical attitude as he'd questioned her.

He considers me a suspect, she realized with a deep chill.

CHAPTER NINETEEN

When the group arrived at the Salzach River and the *Nachtmusik* came into sight, London saw that Captain Hays was standing at the top of the gangway. Sunlight reflecting off a pair of mirrored sunglasses revealed that Bob Turner was standing there too.

They crossed the barge where the ship was docked, and the police director strode ahead of the others up the gangway. Now London could see that the captain looked very distressed.

Tanneberger tipped his cap and asked in English, "You are the captain, I presume?"

"Yes, I am Captain Hays," the captain replied in German. "We need not speak in English. My German is fairly good."

The police director nodded and continued in German, "And I am *Landespolizeidirektor* Fritz Tanneberger. My English is also fairly good, and we may speak however necessary for clarity. I am sorry we have to meet under such unfortunate circumstances."

"Indeed," Captain Hays said. "I can't say I know much about the circumstances, except what little Herr Waldmüller was able to tell me over the phone. Perhaps we should adjourn to my quarters and discuss this matter."

"Yes, I believe we should—you, Fraulein Rose, and myself," Tanneberger said.

"I think our security specialist Bob Turner should join us as well," Captain Hays said, gesturing to the man standing beside him.

"Very well," Tanneberger replied.

Apparently unable to understand a word of German, Bob Turner was looking thoroughly perplexed. Captain Hays quickly explained to him in English what Tanneberger had just said.

Emil was still just standing there with a frown on his face, along with Tina and Rudy Fiore, who appeared to be thoroughly confused. London realized that Emil had expected to be included in any discussion that ensued, and that the young couple must still be trying to deal with the news that their tour guide was dead.

Tanneberger spoke firmly in English to Emil and the Fiores, "I think it would be best for all of you to go to your staterooms for the time being. I would prefer that you not discuss this matter with anyone else at this time."

Emil seemed on the verge of protesting, but London silenced him with a shake of her head. She understood that she herself was the focus of Waldmüller's interest for the time being, and there was no reason to get Emil involved. She hoped they would all go along with Tanneberger's request not to talk about the death, at least for now.

Soon enough everybody will have to be told, she thought with dread.

Tanneberger instructed the policeman who had accompanied them to stay right where he was at the top of the gangway and take note of passengers as they returned to the ship. When London followed Tanneberger and the captain and Bob Turner into the reception area, Sir Reggie came trotting up and jumped into London's arms.

Tanneberger looked understandably surprised.

London was about to put Sir Reggie down and tell him to go somewhere on his own when Bob Turner spoke in English to the police director.

"No, no, the dog should join us, sir. Sir Reggie is no ordinary animal, I can assure you. He has a proven record for crime solving."

Bob didn't sound like he was kidding in the least. He said the words in all seriousness, as if he truly considered Sir Reggie to be some sort of investigative peer. Tanneberger shrugged in noncommittal agreement, and they all took the elevator down to the Allegro deck.

Captain Hays escorted the group into his spacious but modestly decorated suite, where they all took their places in a sitting area that was also outfitted as an office. London was the only one to sit down, feeling shaky from the morning's events, and now somewhat daunted at being the focus of attention. She chose a nice armchair, and Sir Reggie jumped up with her. Seeming to sense her mood, he crouched tensely on her lap and glared up at the three men who remained hovering there before them.

"Before we begin," Captain Hays said, "in this case, I do suggest we speak in English, for the sake of our security man."

"Very well," the *Polizeidirektor* said. "Fraulein Rose, perhaps you could offer your own account of what happened."

London swallowed hard. She'd expected this, of course. But she felt unsettled at the task of repeating to Captain Hays and Bob Turner

111

exactly what she'd told Tanneberger a short while ago—this time in English.

She thought carefully over the events as she related them—a brief account of the group's tour that morning, their visit to the Theater for Mozart, how she'd joined Rudy and Tina Fiore for lunch only to rush right back to the theater in search of Tina's cell phone, and finally her grim discovery in the darkened auditorium.

While she was talking, she found herself weighing her words against what she'd said earlier.

Am I contradicting myself? she wondered, aware that while certain elements of her story were sharp and clear in her mind, others might well be becoming blurred by her panic and confusion.

Surely that would be understandable, she told herself. After all, she was telling the truth and had nothing to hide. But she worried about misremembering details.

I can't make any mistakes.

Tanneberger was listening attentively, as if he'd never heard her story before. Naturally this made perfect sense. She knew that the police director was listening carefully for contradictions, and she was especially aware of his sharp gaze. She thought the captain just looked astonished, and she couldn't tell what Bob might be feeling behind his mirrors.

By the time she finished her account, the captain's mouth was hanging open with shock. He drew himself up and growled at Tanneberger, "But surely you don't imagine that any of our passengers had anything to do with this unfortunate event. I mean, what motive could any of them have? None of them even knew the man before today."

"Can we be sure of that?" Bob asked. "There's a lot we don't know at this point. Seems to me there are many questions still to be asked here."

Certain that he was looking at her, London sensed a suspicious glare. She felt a flash of annoyance at Bob.

So far, she had no reason not to respect *Polizeidirektor* Tanneberger. He was doing his job in much the same way London herself thought she would in his place. He also seemed to be quite sharp and competent, quite unlike the blundering police chief they'd had to deal with back in Gyor.

But she wasn't so sure about Bob Turner. Was he going to make the coming ordeal even worse than it had to be?

"I'm not ready to draw any conclusions," Tanneberger said. "But until I've investigated the case further ..."

He hesitated, but Captain Hays clearly caught his meaning.

"You don't need to tell me," the captain said miserably. "The *Nachtmusik* must remain in Salzburg until you say otherwise."

Tanneberger nodded sympathetically.

"I'm afraid so, Captain Hays."

Bob nodded in stern agreement.

"And everybody has to stay on the boat," Bob added.

Tanneberger looked a bit surprised.

"Oh, I hardly think that's necessary, Herr Turner. I think it's sufficient that no one aboard your craft leave the jurisdiction of Salzburg."

Bob crossed his arms and spoke in his perpetual monotone.

"I'm sorry, sir, but that just won't do—not as long as there's any possibility that any of our people committed a murder."

The captain looked shocked at Bob's protest. London felt the same way.

Bob continued, "London, how many people were with you on the tour?"

"About twenty," London said, worried about what he was about to say next.

"I'll need to talk personally to each and every one of them."

London's worry grew sharper.

"But—Bob," she stammered, "most of them haven't even come back aboard. They're still out seeing Salzburg."

"They need to come back right now," Bob said to London. "Give me a list of their names, including phone numbers and emails. I'll contact all of them and make arrangements to meet with them personally, in small groups."

London was dumbfounded.

Are we really going to do this?

Not for the first time, she wondered whether Bob Turner was really the sharp security guy that CEO Lapham thought he had hired. Or was the supposed sleuth just given to random suspicions? She remembered his comment yesterday that somebody aboard the boat was up to no good. But he wouldn't tell her who he suspected of stealing Oswinkle's music figure, and she wasn't sure that it had been anything more than a

113

bluff.

She glanced at Captain Hays, who also didn't look happy about Bob's demand. Nevertheless, he gave London a reluctant nod.

"As you saw, the ship's historian was with us," London told Bob. "And also the Fiore couple. I'll have to email you the rest of the list."

Bob gave her an approving smile and hurried out the door.

It occurred to London that if this meeting was over, she should warn Emil that he was about to be questioned by the security man.

But the police director took a couple of steps toward the door, then turned back toward London and Captain Hays.

Landespolizeidirektor Tanneberger stared at London with his sharp gray eyes.

"Oh—there's one more issue we need to discuss," he said. "And it especially concerns you, Fraulein Rose."

His tone and expression had grown just a bit more ominous.

London felt a sudden chill.

What now? she wondered.

CHAPTER TWENTY

The *Polizeidirektor* held London's gaze for just a moment.

"You had rather an adventure back in Hungary, in Gyor to be specific—very recently, I believe."

"Yes, sir," London said.

"The news circulated rapidly," Tanneberger continued. "Glint had been on the watch list of every law enforcement bureau for years. Your name was rather prominent in the account of his capture."

London gasped. Glint was the popular name of the expert jewel thief and master of disguise Swain Warrington.

Tanneberger was watching her closely as he added, "And that situation involved another suspicious death."

"That's right, sir."

"And you found the body on that occasion as well."

"Yes," London said, wondering what he could be implying.

"Now, see here, sir," protested Captain Hays. "If you're insinuating that London is in any way responsible for either of these tragedies, I can assure you that you are very much mistaken. The fact is, London actually solved the case and found the victim's killer."

"I'm making no insinuations," Tanneberger said with a trace of a smile. "But you must admit—the coincidence is striking."

London's heart sank.

Yes, the coincidence really is striking, she thought.

But how was she going to convince him it was only that—a mere coincidence? A part of her resented Tanneberger for bringing it up. But she knew it wasn't rational for her to feel that way. After all, he wouldn't be doing his job if he ignored such a coincidence.

But she was also anxious that he not waste his time. If there was still a killer out there, any suspicion of her might be worse than just a problem for London herself. It might be a dangerous distraction.

I need to give him some sort of assurance, she thought.

"*Polizeidirektor* Tanneberger," she said, "you can count on my cooperation in every possible way."

"Very good," Tanneberger said. "Meanwhile, my team and I will begin our investigation ashore. I will leave you all to your own tasks. This is truly an unfortunate set of circumstances, and I hope we can resolve things to all of our satisfaction soon."

"Yes, the sooner the better for all of our sakes, I'm sure," Captain Hays said.

The *Polizeidirektor* gave cards with his contact information to London and the captain. Then he tipped his hat and turned toward the door. As Hays saw him out with a few more encouraging comments, London pulled out her cell phone. She sent Bob her complete list of those who had been on the tour and their contact information.

The captain returned and sat down, drumming his fingers nervously on his desk.

He said, "London, I can't tell you how deeply sorry I am about what you're going through. Of course I know that *Polizeidirektor's* suspicion of you is completely unfounded. Even so, it must upset you terribly. I know it's quite terrible for you."

London felt a surge of gratitude. It occurred to her that these were the first words of sympathy she'd heard from anybody since this terrible event had occurred.

"Thank you, sir," she said.

"I suppose you may go for now, London," he said. "You've got your own daily duties to attend to. Just be ready for—well, any eventuality."

"I will, sir," London said, getting up from her chair.

"Meanwhile, I'll make an announcement to everybody aboard," the captain said. "I also have to call Jeremy Lapham at corporate headquarters. He's not going to be happy to hear all this. Another delay is going to be very hard on the company. I suppose I'd better take care of that right now."

London felt a pang of sympathy for the captain—and, for some reason she couldn't quite put her finger on, a sense of personal responsibility.

"I'll do it," she said.

"Are you sure?" the captain replied.

London nodded.

"I appreciate it," Captain Hays said.

Sir Reggie trotted alongside London as she went out into the passageway and walked the short distance to her own stateroom. Sir Reggie popped through the doggie door before London could even let herself in.

She sat down and took a few long, slow breaths to gather up her courage.

This isn't going to be easy, she thought.

Then she called Mr. Lapham's personal extension. His secretary put the call directly through to him.

"Good morning, London Rose," he said. "Although of course it's afternoon where you are." Then with a sigh, he added, "But I suppose you're calling with bad news. It seems as though that's always the case."

"I'm afraid so, sir," London said.

"I'd better hear it, then."

"Yes, sir. I'm sorry to say … there's been another death."

A short silence fell.

"Oh, no," Lapham said. "Please tell me it's not another case of foul play."

"It's too soon to say for sure but … the police think probably so."

"Was the deceased one of our passengers?"

"No."

"And did the incident occur aboard the *Nachtmusik?*"

"No."

"Where did it occur?"

"In the auditorium of the House of Mozart."

"How dreadful! And are any of our passengers under suspicion?"

London swallowed hard.

"For the time being, the police can't eliminate the members of a tour group I was conducting through Salzburg at the time."

"So I feared. Do you think any of them are guilty?"

"I … I can't imagine why, sir," London said. "None of them knew the victim, at least not as far as I know. I'm sure the Salzburg police will soon eliminate our clients as suspects soon."

"The Salzburg police, yes …"

London detected a note of distaste in his voice. She knew from the awful events back in Gyor that Mr. Lapham had scant respect for local law enforcement anywhere in the world.

"They never get to the bottom of anything," he'd told her. *"They always look for the laziest explanation."*

"The police director seems like a very capable man, sir," she said.

"I do hope so. Meanwhile, I suppose the *Nachtmusik* won't be able

117

to leave Salzburg on schedule."

"I'm afraid not."

"And there will be a delay in reaching Regensburg."

"I believe so."

Mr. Lapham heaved a long, weary sigh.

"Very well then," he said. "Keep me apprised of any new developments."

London was taken aback by the note of resignation in his voice. He'd reacted very differently when she'd told him about Mrs. Klimowski's death. Then he'd been angry with her and had even held her responsible.

I ought to be grateful he's not mad at me, she thought.

But in a way, this was worse. She'd come to like the eccentric Mr. Lapham, and she hated the thought of him being disappointed.

I've really got to fix this, she thought.

"Mr. Lapham, I just want to assure you, I'll do everything I possibly can—"

"Don't say it, London," Mr. Lapham interrupted. "Don't say you're going to solve the crime. I talked you into playing Nancy Drew back in Gyor. And I very nearly got you killed in the process."

"Sir, it wasn't your fault that—"

"It certainly was my fault. I put you up to it. You were following my orders. And I want no more of your amateur sleuthing, do you hear? That's what Bob Turner is there for."

London remembered the email Mr. Lapham had sent to the captain.

"He will assist you on security matters during the rest of your voyage."

"Um, sir," London said cautiously, "who *is* Bob Turner exactly?"

"He's a former New York City police detective. He's also a cousin of mine, although we've never been close—in fact, I'm not sure we've ever met. He retired to Miami a few years ago, and I heard he was restless, and I figured he was exactly the kind of man you need aboard the *Nachtmusik*. After all, the *Nachtmusik* seems to be a bit trouble-prone as tour boats go."

"I see," London said doubtfully.

"So leave the investigating to him. That's what I hired him for, to keep you safe and out of trouble. Mind your own business. Stick to your job. Keep the passengers happy. That's all you really have to do— and I know you're good at it."

118

"I'll do my best, sir."

"Glad to hear it. Now let's both get back to work."

They ended the call, and Sir Reggie jumped up into London's lap.

"I don't know about all this, buddy," she said, petting him. "What do you think of Bob Turner?"

Sir Reggie let out an uncertain growl.

"I'm not sure what to think of him either," London said. "But I guess I'd better follow orders and mind my own business."

Or try to, anyway, she thought.

Then she heard the captain speaking over the PA system.

"Hello, Epoch World Voyagers. This is your captain speaking. I am sorry to report that we will be experiencing another delay on our cruise. Due to our proximity to a suspicious death in Salzburg, the authorities have ordered us not to depart for Regensburg on schedule. Also, passengers must stay within the city's jurisdiction. Hopefully we won't be detained for long. Meanwhile, enjoy your stay in Mozart's beautiful hometown."

London's heart sank at the captain's words.

He did that well, she thought. *As well as anyone could have, anyway.*

Even so, his message would come as scant comfort to the crew and passengers, who now had more questions than answers—and plenty of well-founded anxieties. London's mind boggled at the thought of trying to keep everybody's morale and spirits up until the ship could set sail again.

London was just starting to think through the rest of her day when her cell phone rang. It was a text message from Bob Turner.

Meet me at once in the ship library.

London sighed and said to Sir Reggie, "This can't be good."

CHAPTER TWENTY ONE

Sir Reggie trotted alongside London as she left her room.

"You don't have to come if you don't want to," she said to Sir Reggie. "I sure would skip this if I didn't think it would cause a scene."

The dog let out a little yap of interest and continued along at her side.

"OK, then," she said. "I guess I might need your support."

They took the elevator back up to the Menuetto deck, then went straight to the ship's library, a room at one end of the lounge. The walls were completely covered with books, and the space was equipped with a large-screen computer and folding chairs for lectures to small groups of passengers.

Six people were already there—Emil, Letitia Hartzer, Rudy and Tina Fiore, Cyrus Bannister, and of course Bob Turner. Emil was leaning against a bookshelf, looking annoyed at this invasion of his space, and Bob was pacing energetically. The others were seated and waiting for whatever was about to take place.

"I'm glad you could join us for the beginning of my investigation, London," Bob said. "Have a seat, make yourself comfortable."

The beginning of his investigation! London thought as she unfolded another chair. She had no idea what Bob might be up to, and the possibilities boggled her mind.

Feeling anything but "comfortable," she sat down, and Sir Reggie jumped up into her lap. Bob nodded at the dog with approval, as if pleased to have a professional colleague on hand.

"I don't want the five of you to feel singled out for suspicion," Bob said, peering at everybody through his mirrored sunglasses. "I'm going to meet with everybody who went on your morning tour, in small groups at a time." Then with a chuckle he added, "That is, until I find out the truth. Who knows? That might happen during the next few minutes."

Emil rolled his eyes.

"Kindly get on with it, Mr. Turner," he snapped.

Bob's eyebrows popped up above the frames of his sunglasses. "I'll do just that, Mr. Waldmüller," he replied, taking out a notepad and a pencil. "But I don't see any reason why this needs to be unpleasant. Let's all try to be polite and civil."

London bristled a little herself.

Now he's sounding like a grade school teacher, she thought.

Still pacing, Bob said, "All of you were ashore at the time of Moritz's murder."

Turning to London with a frown he said, "Or should I say, at the time when Moritz's body was discovered by this young lady here."

London couldn't help but cringe at the remark—but not just for her own sake. Bob seemed determined to subject about twenty passengers to exactly this sort of pushy questioning. It would definitely hurt morale aboard the *Nachtmusik.*

Am I really going to let this happen? she thought.

On one hand, as the boat's social director, she felt like she ought to put a stop to it.

But on the other hand ...

She didn't see that she had any choice about it. She wasn't in a position to order Bob to stop disturbing the passengers, especially since Mr. Lapham had put him in charge of such matters.

Meanwhile, Letitia Hartzer drew herself up haughtily.

"Sir, you can strike me off your list right now," she said. "I went nowhere near the House for Mozart after our group visit there."

"Is that so, Mrs. Hartzer?" Bob said, sounding as if he knew that already.

"That's *Ms.* Hartzer," Letitia said sharply.

"I beg your pardon, Ms. Hartzer," he said, starting to take notes. "Where did you happen to be at the time?"

"Well, if you must know, I was in the *Museum der Moderne Salzburg* looking at a rather obnoxious contemporary painting. I can't say I much liked their collection as a whole."

"Can anybody confirm your whereabouts?" Bob asked.

Letitia's mouth dropped open with incredulous annoyance.

"There were other people about, if that's what you mean. But you'd be very hard-pressed to track them down, much less get them to remember seeing me. I certainly don't remember anything about any of them."

Bob peered at her skeptically.

"That's kind of ... inconvenient," he said.

"For you, I suppose it is, since you seem to suspect me of doing God knows what, which you can't possibly prove," Letitia said huffily. "If you're going to accuse me of something, why don't you just come right out with it?"

Bob smirked without replying, then turned his attention to Rudy and Tina Fiore.

"And what about you two?" he said. "You happened to come back to the *Nachtmusik* accompanied by the local cops, along with London, Herr Waldmüller, and Mrs.—*Ms.*—Hartzer."

Rudy shrugged, looking perplexed.

"We hurried over to the theater as soon as we heard sirens and saw the police arrive," he said. "But they wouldn't let us anywhere near the building."

Tina added, "The truth is, we *still* don't know exactly what this is all about—except that someone got killed there."

"And where were you when you heard the sirens?" Bob asked.

"We were at a café—the *Altstadtcafé,* I believe it's called," Rudy said.

"We'd just sat down for snacks there with London when I noticed that my cell phone was missing," Tina said.

"And London went to the theater to look for it?"

"That's right," Tina said.

"Can anybody confirm that you were at the café?" Bob said.

"Well, there's London herself, I suppose," Rudy said.

Bob shook his head.

"I mean someone who can confirm you stayed there until you heard the sirens."

"The waiter, I guess," Rudy said with a shrug.

"I think his name was Max," Tina added.

"That's very helpful," Bob said, jotting down the name. "And London returned your missing cell phone?"

"Yes, she did—when we were walking back to the *Nachtmusik*."

"Very interesting," Bob said, jotting something down.

London couldn't imagine what could possibly be interesting about Tina's cell phone. She also still didn't see how this questioning was leading in any productive direction.

Then Bob turned his attention to Cyrus Bannister.

"And may I ask where you happened to be during the events in question?" he asked.

Cyrus crossed his arms and scowled.

"I was having a look around *Stift Sankt Peter*—St. Peter's Abbey," he said. "I suppose you could ask some of the monks if they remember someone answering to my description. But I'm afraid that's rather a long shot."

Bob let out a discontented grunt, then turned again to Emil, who had finally taken a seat.

"And you, sir—why did you happen to show up at the scene when you did?"

"London called me from the theater," he said. "She told me to come there right away. She did not say why. I did not find out about the tour guide's death until I got there."

"And where were you when you got the call?"

"I was taking a pleasant stroll along Hoffstallgasse, viewing the architecture. And no, I have no way to confirm my whereabouts. And if I did, I am not sure I would bother to tell you. The local police are already investigating this matter. By whose authority are you pestering us about it?"

London almost spoke up to warn Emil against making matters worse with his sour attitude. But she was afraid a full-scale quarrel might ensue. The last thing she wanted was for all hell to break loose right here and now.

Bob looked unperturbed as he answered Emil's question.

"By the authority of Jeremy Lapham, CEO of Epoch World Cruise Lines. He hired me, and he flew me out here from Florida. It's my job to deal with these sorts of shenanigans whenever they come up."

Looking as if he were trying to keep his temper, Emil turned his face away.

"Well, now," Bob murmured as he moved among the group. "None of this is especially informative. But maybe I'm asking the wrong questions. Did any of you happen to know Olaf Moritz prior to today?"

Everybody murmured that they hadn't.

"Let's get right down to the nitty-gritty," Bob said. "Did any of you have a motive for killing Olaf Moritz?"

What a silly thing to ask, London thought as the rest of the group grumbled in protest. Bob looked around the group skeptically for a moment. Then he turned toward Rudy and Tina Fiore.

"What about you two?" he said to them. "Did either of you know Olaf Moritz?"

"No," Rudy said.

"Certainly not," Tina added. "How could we have known him? We haven't even been in this country before."

Bob kept steamrolling right along. "And did either of you have any reason to mean him harm?"

"How could we if we didn't know him?" Rudy said.

"He seemed like a nice guy," Tina said. "I liked him."

"I did too," Rudy said.

Bob peered at them through his mirror glasses for a moment, then turned to Letitia.

"And as for you, ma'am—what was your relationship with the deceased?"

Letitia laughed aloud. London couldn't help smiling herself at what seemed to be a cliché and ridiculous question.

"I knew nothing about him, of course," Letitia said. "I never saw him until this morning. I thought he was quite likeable."

Cyrus let out another snort of derision.

"You did at first," he said. "But you didn't like him so much after he talked you into singing the Queen of the Night's aria from *The Magic Flute*, and then you fumbled it so badly."

Letitia's eyes widened with embarrassment and anger.

"My voice wasn't properly warmed up," she said. "Surely he knew that. He shouldn't have tried to talk me into it, and I shouldn't have let him."

"So you admit being angry with him, then," Cyrus said.

"Certainly not enough to *kill* him," Letitia said. "And now that he's dead, I'm quite distraught about it. Just how vain do you think I am, anyway?"

Cyrus let out a yelp of cynical laughter.

"I'll do you a favor and not answer that question," he said.

"Well I never …!" Letitia gasped.

Bob turned next to Emil.

"What about you, Herr Waldmüller? Did you know Olaf Moritz prior to today?"

"Of course not," Emil said. "And as for my having anything against him, the very idea is ridiculous."

Cyrus Bannister let out a noisy scoff.

"Nothing against him, eh?" he said. "Olaf made a fool of you right in front of the rest of us."

"I am sure I don't know what you mean," Emil said stiffly.

"No? What about your little musical request?" Cyrus said. "You asked him to play Austria's national anthem, *'Land der Berge, Land am Strome'*—because Mozart wrote the melody, you said. And you were mistaken. As he told you, Mozart didn't write it."

Emil's face reddened.

"So the man claimed," he said. "I have yet to check out the truth of his assertion."

Cyrus scoffed again.

"Go ahead and look it up," he said. "I can tell you right now, Mozart *didn't* write it, as anyone with any real knowledge of classical music knows."

"Now look here ..." Emil said, almost rising out of his chair.

"Ah, ah, ah," Bob said, tapping Emil on the shoulder so that he stayed seated. "Let's keep our cool, OK? You're not going to make your case look any better by losing your temper."

"My 'case'?" Emil snarled. "You have got no case against me, you meddling fool."

For a moment, London worried that Emil might be on the verge of starting a fistfight with Bob. But Bob was nothing if not composed, and he seemed almost amused by the insult.

"Don't worry, Herr Waldmüller," Bob said. "You've got nothing to worry about—as long as you're innocent. The truth will out, as they say."

Still seated, Emil sputtered with wordless exasperation.

London felt a flash of worry as she remembered how angry Emil had been yesterday when he'd been told someone else would be conducting the tour through Salzburg. She also recalled the anger in his expression when he saw Olaf Moritz for the first time.

Is it possible ...?

She quickly decided that the idea was absurd. And she didn't intend to make this scene any more confusing and chaotic by mentioning Emil's palpable resentment of the tour guide.

Finally Bob turned to London, and she saw her own face reflected in those twin mirrors of his glasses.

"I'd be pretty derelict at my job if I didn't ask you the same question," he said to her. "Did you know him? Did you have anything against him?"

London felt too unsettled by everything else that was going on to take offense at the question. She figured it best to keep her answer simple and matter-of-fact.

"I also never saw him until today," she said. "And he didn't do anything that bothered me."

Bob glanced over at Cyrus, as if expecting him to contradict London as he had with Emil and Letitia. This time Cyrus only shrugged. Then Bob turned back toward London.

"But you *did* discover the body, though," he said to her.

"Yes, I did," London said, trying to stay calm in the face of his insinuation. "It was horrible and shocking and completely unexpected."

Bob stared at London for a moment. Then he sauntered about scratching his chin as if deep in thought. Finally he looked down at Sir Reggie, who was still sitting in London's lap.

"Well, partner," he said to the dog, "it looks like we've got some work to do."

Sir Reggie didn't make a sound in reply. Instead he tilted his head curiously, almost as if he were asking, *"What do you mean 'we'?"*

At that moment came a sharp knock at the door.

Bob opened it, and Kirby Oswinkle came inside, looking angry as usual.

"What's going on in here, anyway?" Oswinkle asked, glaring at everybody in the group.

"A murder investigation," Bob said dryly, putting his hands in his pockets.

Oswinkle looked unsurprised and unimpressed.

"You'd better come with me," he growled at the group. "Something really serious has happened."

Nothing worse than a murder, I hope, London thought. She noted that Emil just looked relieved and stayed in his library, shutting the door after she and the others followed Oswinkle out into the Amadeus Lounge.

CHAPTER TWENTY TWO

As the group hurried across the large, open lounge, London could see no sign that "something really serious" had happened. Only a few passengers were scattered about chatting, snacking, and drinking quietly. Off to one side, a Scrabble game was underway.

Then she spotted Elsie standing near the table where the musician dolls were on display. And as they grew near, she could see that Elsie looked dismayed.

When they all reached the table, Tina Fiore let out a gasp of alarm.

"My drummer!" she exclaimed. "It's gone!"

"We shouldn't have left it here after all," her husband, Rudy, commented.

Sure enough, there was a gap among the four remaining dolls. The double-bass player, the clarinetist, the violinist, and the trumpeter were all still there—but not the drummer.

"See!" Oswinkle said angrily. "I thought you deserved to know— another figure is gone. I noticed it right away when I came in here for a beer just now."

Steve and Carol Weaver entered the lounge and joined them.

"We got your text message," Steve said to Oswinkle.

"What's going on?" Carol wanted to know.

Oswinkle just pointed at the figures on the table.

"What happened to the drummer?" Carol asked.

"That's a very good question," Oswinkle said. "First someone stole my conductor, and now this! Whatever is going on here, it has gotten way out of hand."

London felt a twinge of mental whiplash. Just a moment ago, she, Letitia, the Fiores, and Cyrus had been discussing the mystery of Olaf Moritz's murder with Bob. And now here they were, agitated about the disappearance of a little souvenir trinket. It seemed unreal somehow.

"Let's not jump to conclusions," Elsie said.

"That's right," Carol Weaver agreed. "Remember, just yesterday Letitia was sure her little trumpeter had been stolen. But she was mistaken. Sir Reggie found it right under the table."

As if on cue, Sir Reggie tucked his head under the floor-length tablecloth, wagging his tail as he looked around.

"What do you see, partner?" Bob said.

Sir Reggie backed out from under the tablecloth and turned around and looked up at Bob with a tilt of his head. Bob himself stooped down and lifted up the tablecloth.

"You're right, partner," he said. "There's nothing under here."

"But who would do such a thing?" Tina asked.

Bob turned slowly, looking over all the faces in the group.

"Who, indeed?" he said. "It's just possible that somebody right here knows the answer to that very question."

"You mean you think that one of *us* stole both of the dolls?" Carol asked.

"It's a possibility," Bob said.

"If so, I'd sure like to know who it was," Oswinkle said.

Everyone else just looked puzzled.

"And why would anybody do such a thing?" Steve asked.

Bob jabbed the air with his finger.

"When we know *that*, we'll have solved this mystery," he said. "And we will solve this mystery. I'm sure of it."

London and Elsie exchanged startled glances. Elsie shrugged as if she had no idea what to make of Bob.

He sure enjoys playing the sleuth, London thought.

She remembered what he'd told her yesterday, when Letitia Hartzer's trumpeter had momentarily gone missing.

"There's more to what just happened here than meets the eye."

He'd also said that he had "a pretty good idea" about the identity of the thief.

She wondered—what had he been thinking then?

And what was he thinking now?

"Bob, let's not get carried away," London said, worrying again about the effect Bob's nosiness was having on her passengers. But Bob didn't act as though he'd even heard her.

"Let's review," Bob declared. "Mr. Oswinkle's conductor was the first doll to go missing, the day before I got here."

"But not from right here," Oswinkle said. "It was stolen straight out of my room. Someone came right in and took it."

"Right," Bob said. "And then yesterday, Ms. Hartzer here *thought* her trumpet player was gone."

128

Stooping down to pat Sir Reggie on the head, he said, "But my furry colleague here found it right here under this table."

"Yes, to my considerable relief," Letitia said.

Bob stepped toward Letitia and peered at her suspiciously.

"So you say, ma'am," he muttered. "So you say."

Letitia drew herself up haughtily.

"Just what are you accusing me of, Mr. Turner?"

Bob looked at her silently for a moment.

Then he said, "Tell me about that song you had trouble with over in town—the one that got you so mad at Olaf Moritz because he tried to get you to sing it."

"I was hardly *mad* at him," Letitia snapped. "And you weren't even there."

Cyrus Bannister chuckled and said, "You looked pretty mad to me."

Letitia's eyes widened with anger and frustration.

"Why does it matter whether I was angry or not?" she sputtered. "What on earth has it got to do with these missing dolls, anyway?"

"That's what I'd like to know, Ms. Hartzer," Bob said, sounding almost as if he thought Letitia could explain it to him if she wanted to. "And it's my job to keep close track of everything going on around here," he added.

Cyrus Bannister smirked at the others.

"You people are making such a big deal out of this," he told them.

"That's easy for you to say," Oswinkle replied. "Nothing of yours was stolen."

Cyrus shrugged and added, "If you're so anxious about your precious little dolls, maybe you should just take turns sitting here watching over them. That way nobody will try to steal them. Or if anybody does, you'd be sure to catch them."

"And spend the rest of the trip fretting about them night and day?" Letitia said, picking up her little trumpet player. "I hardly think so. I'm taking mine back to my room to keep it safe."

The two couples murmured in agreement and picked up their dolls as well. As they headed out of the lounge, Oswinkle stood by the table and called after them.

"So you think they'll be safe in your rooms? Good luck with that! Nothing is safe on this boat! Not one single thing!"

Letitia and both couples ignored him and continued on their way. Oswinkle stomped his foot with frustration and strode out of the lounge himself.

Bob stood stroking his chin as if deep in thought.

Then he wagged his finger at London and said, "So far, two dolls are missing—a conductor and a drummer. Does that suggest anything to you?"

London squinted at him curiously.

"I'm not sure it suggests anything," she said.

"Oh, but it does, London, it does. I'm not quite sure what it is yet, but ..."

He thought for a moment.

"Without a conductor, a band can't stay together. Without a drummer, a band can't keep time."

He nodded slowly.

"Someone's trying to send us a message, London Rose."

Bob looked down at Sir Reggie, who was standing beside London.

"Come on, pal," he said. "We've got some investigating to do. Let's start on the top deck and work our way down through the boat."

So much for interviewing everybody who was on the tour, London thought wryly.

He hadn't gotten very far with that. And London figured it was just as well.

Bob sauntered out of the lounge, apparently not noticing that Sir Reggie wasn't following him. Instead, the dog stayed right where he was, looking up at London as if he, too, couldn't make any sense of what was going on.

Meanwhile, Elsie looked thoroughly baffled.

She said, "London, please tell me what's going on. It's not just stolen dolls, that's for sure. Everybody's acting so weird. And what did Captain Hays mean when he said there had been a 'suspicious death'? Please don't tell me there's been another murder."

London heaved an overdue sigh.

"Let's sit down," she said to Elsie. "I'll tell you what I can."

They chose a table apart from other customers, and London began to describe the day's strange events. She felt numb as she talked, as if she were listening to someone else, or even as if she was hearing her own words in a recording.

None of it seems real, she kept thinking.

When London finished her account, she remarked, "I'm afraid Bob is doing more harm than good."

"What a peculiar guy," Elsie said. "What's he doing aboard the *Nachtmusik* anyway?"

London let out a wry, sarcastic chuckle.

"He's here to keep me out of trouble," she said.

"Huh?"

"That's what Mr. Lapham told me over the phone a little while ago. He doesn't want me to risk my neck playing detective anymore. So he hired his own personal security man—an ex–New York cop who also happens to be a relative of his. I'm supposed to leave everything to him. I'm not supposed to go playing 'Nancy Drew' anymore."

Elsie shook her head slowly.

"London, don't get me wrong," she said. "I agree with Mr. Lapham about one thing. I don't want you to go around almost getting yourself or Sir Reggie drowned or otherwise nearly killed like last time. But if Bob Turner really is seriously working on this case, and if he's going to be reporting to the *Polizeidirektor* about it, I think you might have a real problem on your hands. I mean, for example, do you really think someone's stealing these dolls to send some kind of 'message'?"

"Well, I don't know …"

"It sure doesn't make sense to me. I'm not sure he's thinking straight. I think maybe he's some kind of a loose cannon. You'd better pay close attention to what he's up to."

London remembered Bob's departure from the lounge right now—how he'd said he was going to start investigating on the top deck and work his way down through the boat. She could probably reach him on her cell phone, but …

I'd rather talk to him face to face.

"You're right," London said to Elsie. "I'll go see him right now."

Sir Reggie trotted alongside her while she walked up the spiral stairs to the Rondo deck. She was relieved to see that everything looked pretty normal on the outdoor deck. Some people were playing a game of shuffleboard, others were playing in the pool, and others were taking in a fine view of Salzburg from the railings on either side. A few were lounging around on deck chairs, and a few of those had fallen fast asleep.

For a moment, London didn't see Bob Turner anywhere.

Maybe I should phone him after all, she thought.

But then her eyes fell on a figure lounging apart from the others. From behind, she could see that the person was twisted rather grotesquely as it lay stretched out on a lounge chair.

She walked around in front of the person sprawled on the chair and saw that it was Bob Turner. One of his feet was touching the deck, and the other dangled off the other side of the chair. His arms were twisted as if he'd just been flailing about in violent struggle. Although the mirror sunglasses were slightly askew, London still couldn't see his eyes. But his mouth hung open and she didn't see any sign that he was breathing.

Is Bob dead? London wondered.

CHAPTER TWENTY THREE

"Bob?" London leaned over and whispered to the unmoving figure in the lounge chair.

There was no reply.

"Bob?" she said again, louder this time.

Again there was no response.

London glanced around nervously at the other passengers on the deck. To her relief, no one seemed to notice the problem or her anxiety.

Before she could decide what to do next, Sir Reggie moved up and nudged his cold nose into Bob's dangling hand. Then the dog licked the hand with his wet tongue.

To London's relief, Bob let out a thunderous snore, writhed around a bit, grumbled inaudibly, and finally wound up in an even more grotesque position than he'd been in before.

He was obviously perfectly fine—and fast asleep.

Meanwhile, it seemed that Bob's top-to-bottom investigation of the boat hadn't gotten very far, just like his plan to interview everybody who had been on the tour. The ship's designated sleuth was all worn out and taking a nap.

So should I wake him up? she wondered.

Now she thought better of it. She shared Elsie's concern that Bob was something of a "loose cannon" who could make a lot of trouble to no good purpose.

But he's not causing any trouble right now, she thought.

It seemed best to let him sleep.

She walked over to the railing and looked out over Salzburg's Old Town. She was enchanted anew by the view of the Baroque spires of the Salzburg Cathedral, the clock tower of the Nonnberg Abbey, and most of all, the majestic white walls of Hohensalzburg Fortress gleaming down upon city. It was hard to believe that something as ugly as a murder could ever take place in such an exquisitely lovely setting.

She thought over all that had happened since this morning.

"Who killed Olaf Moritz?" she said, stooping down to pet Sir Reggie.

Of course, Sir Reggie didn't offer any theories.

London stood back up and gazed out at the city again, trying to organize her own thoughts. The more she thought about it, she just couldn't believe the killer was anybody aboard the *Nachtmusik*. And the truth was, she doubted that *Polizeidirektor* Tanneberger really believed that either. But he was still in the process of eliminating suspects, and he had to consider the people in the tour group—including London herself.

In the meantime, the real killer was still on the loose. And the *Nachtmusik* was going to be stuck in another city, causing Epoch World Cruise Lines another costly delay and possibly damaging the tour's reputation.

And what am I going to do about it? London thought.

She remembered Mr. Lapham's stern but well-intention command.

"Mind your own business. Stick to your job. Keep the passengers happy."

She tried to convince herself to do exactly what Mr. Lapham had said.

But how could she do that? And after all, nobody had been forbidden to leave the *Nachtmusik*. She just wanted to go ashore and do some investigating on her own.

"Sorry, Mr. Lapham," she murmured aloud. "I guess I'm not through playing Nancy Drew."

She still had a busy day ahead and knew she couldn't take much time away from her duties. But maybe it wouldn't take long to do what she had to do.

She wondered briefly whether she should somehow let Bob know what she was up to—maybe leave a note where he was sleeping, or send him a text message. But no, that didn't seem like a good idea. Bob might well know of Mr. Lapham's insistence that London not do any investigating. She didn't want word to get back to Mr. Lapham that she wasn't doing as she was told.

Instead, she took out her cell phone and called Amy Blassingame.

"Hi, Amy," she said. "I wonder if you could fill in for me for just a little while."

"How do you mean?" Amy said, already sounding a little annoyed.

"Well, I'd like you to just check in on a few activities. Make sure things are going smoothly with our new casino set-up."

Glancing at her watch, she added, "Also, there's a trivia game

134

scheduled to start in the restaurant in twenty minutes. Check and make sure it starts on time and everything is going OK."

Amy didn't reply.

"Uh, Amy," London said, "are you still there?"

"Yeah," Amy said, then fell silent again.

London fought down a sigh as she recognized one of Amy's pouting spells.

"You're doing it again, aren't you?" Amy finally asked.

"What do you mean?"

"I heard what the captain said over the PA. There's been another 'suspicious death.' So you're going ashore to play Miss Marple again."

London winced at the mention of Agatha Christie's fictional spinster detective. The last person who had made that comparison was the bumbling police chief back in Gyor, and he hadn't meant it as a compliment.

Ignore it, she told herself.

"I just need to go into town and check out a few things," London said.

"Hah. You're going to have some big adventure while I stay here and do all the boring work."

That's not true, London almost blurted.

"Amy, please just let me explain—" she began.

"Oh, don't worry, I'll do what I'm told," Amy interrupted. "I swear, I think that dog of yours gets to have more fun than I do around here."

Amy abruptly ended the call.

London looked down at Sir Reggie, who was standing beside her looking as if he'd been listening in on the conversation.

"I'm going into town," London said to him. "You can stay aboard if you like."

Sir Reggie let out a yap of protest.

"OK, you can come along," London said. "You might even be helpful. But behave yourself. And I hope you don't mind being on a leash."

London reached into her bag and took out Sir Reggie's leash and attached it to his collar. They went down the stairs and headed out to the gangway.

As she reached the top of the gangway, London pictured the eager guide standing down on the barge at the bottom of the gangway calling out to the tour group.

135

"Willkommen in Salzburg, birthplace of Wolfgang Amadeus Mozart!"

London felt a pang of sadness that the tour had ended so horribly for him. It occurred to her that she still knew almost nothing about him, including what friends or loved ones might be mourning his death.

But as she continued ashore, she felt sure of one thing.

Olaf deserves justice.

CHAPTER TWENTY FOUR

London and Sir Reggie began to retrace the tour's morning route through Salzburg. As they passed the *Mozarts Geburtshaus*, London could almost hear the hushed, delicate sound of Mozart's own clavichord as Olaf used it to play part of a sonata by the composer who had lived there.

She and Sir Reggie continued on directly to the House for Mozart. There were still a handful of police officers posted in front, but London was glad to see that the building seemed to be open. An officer at door the politely took her name and allowed her to walk on inside.

Again she found herself in the sparkling lobby with its blend of glass, marble, and gold, and its huge crystal profile of Mozart on its curving wall. London noticed that there was no longer a sign that read *"NASSER BODEN"*—"wet floor"—anywhere in sight.

As London and Sir Reggie passed by the marble bench where she'd sat while waiting to talk to the police, she remembered the attractive young maintenance woman who had sat on the opposite bench weeping inconsolably over Olaf's death.

What was her name?

Oh, yes. Greta Mayr.

She also remembered her almost desperately emphatic claim when London asked her if she had any idea what had happened to Olaf.

"No, I don't know anything. I don't know anything at all."

Hearing that voice again in her mind, London wondered—had she been lying? Did she really know the truth, or at least part of the truth? If so, what had she told the police?

There's a lot I don't know, London realized.

London walked back to the entrance of the auditorium. The door was wide open, but the way was barred by a thick rope. Sir Reggie started to go under the rope, but she pulled him back.

She peered into the auditorium, which was dark except for the light spilling in from the lobby. She could barely make out something white on a row of chairs, and realized that it must be a taped outline showing where Olaf's crumpled body had lain.

137

London peered upward toward the two balconies.

What must have happened here?

All she really knew was that Olaf Moritz had fallen from the upper balcony, and now she could see for herself why the police were suspicious about the trajectory of the fall. He certainly hadn't fallen straight downward.

But had he really been pushed?

Might there be some other explanation for why the body had fallen some distance away from the balcony's edge?

As her eyes adjusted a bit more, London could see that the balcony's center aisle was steep. She wondered—might he have entered at the top when the auditorium was dark like this, only to trip and fall and tumble all the way over the rail and ...?

Her thoughts were interrupted by a kindly voice speaking in German.

"May I help you, *fraulein*?"

London turned and saw an attractive, well-dressed, middle-aged woman smiling at her.

"I'm not sure," London said.

The woman extended her hand and said, "I'm Selma Hahn, the theater's managing director. I'd be glad to be of assistance in any way I can."

London stammered, "I—I just wondered if maybe I could go into the auditorium and have a look around. With the house lights on."

Selma Hahn tilted her head sadly.

"Under normal circumstances, I'd be happy to say yes. But not today. The police have declared this to be an active crime scene. Perhaps you've heard about the unfortunate events of earlier today."

"Yes, I—I know something about it."

"Then you understand the situation. Sadly, tonight's piano recital has also been canceled. Too bad, because everyone was so eager to hear Wolfram Poehler's performance of Beethoven's *Hammerklavier* sonata. He's an amazing new talent. Even I hadn't heard of him until recently. He seems to have appeared out of nowhere."

Selma Hahn looked as though she was about to escort London out of the building, but then she glanced down at Sir Reggie, who was sitting there quietly on his leash.

"Is that a Yorkshire Terrier?" she asked. "My aunt has one, she takes it with her everywhere."

"Yes, he's a Yorkie. I haven't had him very long, but he's a great little companion."

The woman's expression softened a bit. She peered at London's name tag.

"Your name is London Rose, I see," she said.

"That's right," London said.

Selma Hahn's expression had turned oddly curious.

She said, "And judging from your uniform, you must work aboard the boat that arrived today—the *Nachtmusik*, I believe it's called."

"That's right. I'm the boat's social director."

The woman gasped a little.

"Oh, then *you* must have been the one who discovered poor Olaf's body," she said. "Or so the police told me."

London nodded.

"How awful that must have been for you," Selma Hahn said. "I'm so sorry your visit to Salzburg was marred by such a terrible experience. But—why would you want to go back into the auditorium? I would think you'd want to avoid it like the plague."

London stifled a sigh.

"I guess I'm—trying to make sense of what happened."

"I can understand why you feel that way, of course. But I really must obey police orders."

"I understand," London said.

They stood silently for a moment. London could feel the inquisitiveness of Selma's gaze. She wondered—had the police told her that London might be a suspect? Possibly, but Selma Hahn seemed to be perfectly sympathetic.

Maybe she'd be willing to answer some questions, London thought.

"Did you know Olaf personally?" London asked.

"Some. He was well known in Salzburg. He was always around town, showing our lovely town to tourists. He was very knowledgeable, especially about Mozart."

London recalled Emil's theory that Olaf's death was a suicide.

"Were you aware of Olaf being ... at all unhappy recently?" London asked.

Selma let out a musical chuckle.

"Oh, no, anything but! He was always happy. He had an outgoing personality, was extremely friendly. And funny, too. Everybody liked him. I can't begin to imagine why anyone would ..."

Her voice faded and she shook her head.

"Where were you when it happened?" London asked cautiously.

"I was at home. I came right away when the police called me. I understand that there were only two people in the building when the police came—you and our maintenance woman."

"Yes—her name is Greta, I believe."

"That's right. Greta Mayr."

London hesitated for a moment.

"Greta seemed personally upset about Olaf's death. Did she have some kind of a relationship—?"

The woman gently interrupted.

"I really don't know much about our employees' personal lives, and … well, I'm afraid I'm not comfortable talking about them in any case. I believe in respecting people's privacy."

"Oh, of course," London said hastily. "I shouldn't have asked."

"It's quite all right. I wish I could be more helpful."

"It was very nice to meet you, Fraulein …"

"*Frau* Hahn. But everyone calls me Selma. It was nice to meet you too. I just wish the circumstances weren't so unfortunate."

London was about to say goodbye when Selma spoke again.

"Your last name is Rose?"

"That's right," London said.

"And you're American, judging from your accent."

"Yes."

Selma looked intently at London's face.

London wondered what she was thinking.

Selma said, "'Rose' is a rather common name in Europe, especially in England, I believe. How common is it in America?"

"I guess I never thought about it," London said. "Not very common, I guess."

"There's something about your face …"

Selma's voice faded for a moment.

Then she asked, "Are you by any chance related to a woman named Barbara Rose?"

London felt as though her heart jumped up in her throat.

Mom! she thought.

Selma knows Mom!

140

CHAPTER TWENTY FIVE

For a moment, London couldn't breathe.

She more than half-expected to wake up at any moment.

Finally, she took a gulp of air and managed to blurt out a reply.

"My ... my mother's name was ... is Barbara Rose."

Selma nodded.

"There's a very strong resemblance," she said. "The shape of her face. The sound of your voice. Even the way you stand and move."

"How ... do you know her?"

"I met her some months back. I ... well, I liked her."

"Is she here in Salzburg?" London gasped, barely able to get the words out.

"No, not anymore," Selma replied, looking puzzled.

London was starting to feel dizzy now.

Seeming to notice her discomfort, Selma gently took her by the arm.

"Let's go talk about it in my office," the older woman said.

Sir Reggie followed along quietly as London unsteadily but gratefully followed her up the stairs to her office in the gallery. It was a large, pleasantly decorated office, much simpler and less showy than the lobby, with minimalist artworks on the walls.

London and Selma sat down in deep upholstered facing chairs and Sir Reggie lay down on the carpeted floor.

"You seem surprised that I mentioned her," Selma said with a smile. "And I hate to pry but it seems clear ... you don't know where Barbara is. I mean, you had to ask ..."

London's mind was reeling.

"Selma, I hardly know where to begin. She and my dad both used to be flight attendants. She retired in order to raise my sister and me in Connecticut, while Dad kept on traveling. One day, when I was fourteen, she said she wanted to go on a little European tour all on her own, just to get away for a bit. The last we heard from her, she was in Vienna. Then she just disappeared without a trace. None of us saw her or even heard from her ever again."

Selma's expression was deeply sympathetic.

"Oh, how terrible for all of you," she said.

London swallowed hard.

"Over the years, I guess I ... tried to convince myself that something awful had happened to her, that she was no longer alive. I know that sounds awful, but in a way it seemed better than thinking she'd just ... gone away."

"I can understand that," Selma said with a nod.

And from the look in her eyes, London could tell she really meant it.

"Then you've just seen her ... after all these years ... so she's still alive?" London asked.

"As far as I know."

"What can you tell me about her? How did you know her?"

Selma sighed and leaned back in her chair.

"Late last year, she arrived in Salzburg looking for work as a tutor."

"Was that what she did for a living?"

"Yes, she was sort of an itinerant language tutor. I think mostly she just loved to travel, and tutoring wherever she went was how she kept herself going financially. As it happened, my teenaged daughter was studying English, and a tutor was exactly what my husband and I were looking for. And she was a marvelous teacher! Mia learned so much from her, and they both had so much fun. In fact, Barbara was fluent in all sorts of languages, so Mia picked up bits of lots of them. It was a wonderful experience for the girl."

Selma paused again. London noticed a deepening sadness in her expression.

"I got to know her as well. We often met for coffee, and we talked about one thing or another. She was very interested in my work here at the House for Mozart, and in all the wonderful talents we've got coming and going. She knew *so* much about music, and the other arts as well. She was a wonderful conversationalist. And she told me great stories about all the places she'd been—all over the world, it seemed."

London felt a lump of emotion rising in her throat. It seemed strange to hear Selma talking about Mom in the past tense.

London asked, "Did she ... ever talk about *us*? Her family, I mean?"

Selma seemed a bit reluctant to reply.

"She did, at least a little," she said. "But she never mentioned any

142

of you by name."

London felt a stab of sadness.

She realized that Sir Reggie must have been disturbed by the tone of her voice, because he whined and looked as though he wanted to jump up into the chair with her. She shook her head no, and the little dog lay down again.

"Why do you think that was?" she asked.

"Whenever she tried to talk about you, she'd look like she was about to cry. I was curious about her family, but I never pressed her about it. I thought that perhaps she had somehow lost all of you. I didn't want to add to her sadness. But now that you're here, I wonder … if maybe I was wrong. Maybe I should have asked more questions."

London wished she had. But she could certainly understand why she hadn't.

Selma continued, "She seemed very happy here in Salzburg. Although she didn't exactly say so, I got the feeling she was really thinking about settling down here at last. I would have liked that, and so would my daughter. Barbara got to be like an aunt to her. But one day Barbara said she was going away, and she did the very next day. I've not heard from her since."

So it's like she left another family, London thought with a trace of bitterness.

But why?

"Did she say where she was going?" London asked.

"Yes, she said she was on her way to Germany. I don't remember her saying exactly where, and of course, that was many months ago. I don't know where she is now."

London felt wave after wave of emotions rising up inside her.

"What else can you tell me about her?" she asked Selma.

"Only that she seemed … well, a little mysterious somehow. As though she just didn't want to talk about herself in any detail."

London suddenly couldn't contain herself.

She let out a sob, and tears started to flow.

"Oh, I'm sorry," Selma said, handing her a tissue. "Maybe I shouldn't have told you …"

London wiped her eyes and hastily pulled herself together.

"No, no, I'm glad you did. You helped. You really helped."

"I hope so," Selma said. "I wish I could tell you more, but that is all I know."

143

London nodded and said, "I'd better go now."

"Of course," Selma replied. "But about that other matter ... I suppose it would be all right for me to give you this ..."

Looking at her computer screen, she scribbled something down on a piece of paper. As she handed it to London she said, "The maintenance woman you asked about—perhaps this will help."

Glancing at the paper ,London saw the name "Greta Mayr" and a phone number. Unable to think about the maintenance woman now, she thanked Selma as she put the paper in her vest pocket and stood up to leave. Sir Reggie jumped up, ready to go along with her.

"*Auf Wiedersehen,* then," Selma told her. "Come back if you like."

"Thanks."

Trembling as she walked, London made her way down from the gallery and outside. She sat down on a bench in front of the building. She fought back her tears, determined not to let her emotions get the best of her. She had too much to deal with right now to let herself fall apart.

With a soft whine, Sir Reggie jumped into her lap.

London hugged the little dog, appreciating the sympathy. But her mind was reeling. What was she supposed to make of what Selma had just told her? And exactly what did she know that she hadn't known before?

That Mom's alive, at least, she thought.

Or at least she was several months ago.

Also ...

She went to Germany.

Of course, there was no possibility of finding Mom there without more information. She could be in another country by now. London simply didn't know. And now London almost wondered whether she'd have been better off not knowing that Mom had even gone there.

She remembered something her father had said on the phone yesterday.

"Your mother's disappearance isn't another mystery for you to solve."

But how could she help wanting to try?

London looked at her watch. More time had passed than she'd realized, and she still hadn't learned anything about Olaf Moritz's murder.

Maybe it's time to get back to the Nachtmusik *before ...*

Her cell phone suddenly buzzed with a text message from Bob.

"I know what's going on. Get back to the boat."

London groaned with despair. Bob obviously knew what she was up to, and he wasn't happy about it.

As if things couldn't get any worse, she thought, getting up from the bench and heading back toward the boat, carrying her canine companion in her arms.

CHAPTER TWENTY SIX

As London crossed the barge toward the *Nachtmusik*, she saw Bob Turner's sunglasses peering out of the big glass door at the top of the gangway. When he caught sight of her and stood waiting with his hands on his hips, the security man looked like he meant business.

I'm really in for it now, she thought anxiously.

She wondered if she should just admit to her little shore adventure, then try to talk him out of telling Mr. Lapham that she'd gone playing Nancy Drew again.

London set Sir Reggie down, and the little dog dashed on up the gangway. Although Bob grinned and bent over as if to greet him, Sir Reggie darted right by as if he figured it was best to avoid him right now.

Bob didn't look pleased that the dog had brushed him off. As London came up the gangway he scowled at her.

"Come on into the lounge," he said brusquely. "We've got to talk."

London followed him into the Amadeus Lounge, where they sat down at a small table apart from other customers.

She could only see her own reflection in his sunglasses as he leaned across the table toward her. She certainly looked as though she'd just been crying. She wondered whether Bob noticed that.

"Just so you know," he said, "I've got a brain like a steel trap. Nobody gets the best of me. And nobody can pull the wool over my eyes—not for long, anyway. It's best to keep that in mind."

London stifled a groan of dismay.

"Bob, I can explain—" she began.

Bob grunted with disbelief.

"Explain! I doubt that, missy! No sir, I really do doubt that very much! Not unless you've got a brain like mine!"

Now London was starting to feel more puzzled than alarmed.

Bob tapped a finger on his forehead.

"It's all in the synapses, you see. Mine are fast and quick, real live superconductors, and they're solid-state wired up to my whole entire sensory apparatus into whatchacallit, some kind of topnotch ultra-fast feedback loop. My nose, my eyes, my fingers—they don't miss a detail, they observe everything, bring in scads of data, and my brain puts all that data together like nobody's business."

Pointing to his chest, he added, "So be advised. Don't ever try to fool this guy. Nosirree, that's never a good idea."

"Bob, I really wasn't trying to fool—"

"Don't interrupt when I'm on a roll here," he went on with a note of triumph. "In case you're slow on the uptake, I've solved the case."

London felt a jolt of surprise. This certainly wasn't what she'd expected to hear.

"What?" she asked, trying not to sound dubious.

"You heard me. I solved the case. What did you think I was going to say?"

London decided not to tell him. Apparently Bob wasn't the least bit interested in her shore excursion.

She squinted at him uncertainly.

"Uh—which case?" she asked.

"What do you mean, which case?" Bob said with a shrug.

"Well, we've sort of got two mysteries," London said. "There's the theft of the musician dolls, and there's the murder that happened at the House for Mozart."

Bob chuckled heartily.

"Missy, you really don't get it, do you? It's all connected. Everything's always connected. That's a lesson I learned long ago. The trick is sorting through the whole tangle of connections. Don't you understand?"

No, I guess I don't, London thought.

He took out his cell phone and started showing her a series of photos.

"I've been busy since we last talked," he said.

Indeed, London could definitely see that he had been. Apparently Bob hadn't stayed sleeping on the Rondo deck for long after London had left the boat. He'd been up and busy since then. If nothing else, he'd been taking lots of pictures—although London couldn't make rhyme or reason of them.

There was one photo of a water glass with some ice cubes in it, another of a set of keys, another of a paperback book lying open on a table, another of a travel brochure in somebody's hand, and a bunch of others that seemed equally unrelated to each other—or to anything she could think of.

She briefly wondered if Bob really did have some kind of extraordinarily insightful mind. Was there something she'd been missing altogether?

Sounding more pleased with himself every moment, Bob kept talking.

"In just an hour or so, I've done what it would take a whole crack investigative team an entire week to do. I've been on the prowl after certain select passengers who went on your tour, catching them doing anything that might be the least little bit suspicious."

He's been taking pictures of the passengers, London realized with alarm.

Surely at least some of them wouldn't be happy to know they were being photographed without their knowledge. Besides, she couldn't see anything suspicious in any of the pictures she'd seen. They looked pretty much random and meaningless to her.

She was about to suggest that he really shouldn't do that, but he was plowing ahead.

"And my work isn't random. Not at all. It's methodical. I've been keeping an eye on one specific passenger. And I'll bet you can't guess who it is."

London flashed back to his behavior while questioning the group in the library, and how he'd focused on one of those people in particular.

"Is it Letitia Hartzer?" she asked.

Bob's mouth opened with surprise.

"Very good! It is indeed! And let me tell you why ..."

He leaned toward her with his elbows on the table.

"The day I came on board, I already had my eyes sharp for trouble—any kind of trouble at all. I happened to run into Mrs. Hartzer in the reception area. I saw how she was looking at a glass paperweight on the front desk. She picked it up gingerly-like and looked at it real close. She even opened up her purse and was about to drop it inside when she noticed me looking at her. Then she put it back down on the desk, trying to look nonchalant-ish about it."

London tilted her head with surprise.

"You mean ... she was thinking about stealing it?"

"You bet she was," Bob said. "And just twenty minutes ago or so, I saw her having a snack in the Habsburg Restaurant. And quick and quiet and catlike, I sneaked up on her and snapped this picture."

148

London looked closely at the picture and gasped slightly.

No doubt about it, Bob had caught her in the act of dropping a silver saltshaker into her purse.

"So now we know for sure who stole the music dolls," Bob said.

London was reluctant to agree. She hoped there was some other explanation.

"I don't know, Bob. Maybe you were wrong about her wanting to steal the paperweight. Maybe she just wanted some salt for her room and was borrowing it or—"

"Huh. You're drawing erroneous conclusions from whatchamacallit, the available data. You're not thinking like a crack detective, missy. That's what I'm here for. Salt and pepper are always delivered to rooms with food orders. There's no reason for anyone to snatch a shaker out of a restaurant."

London sputtered, "Still, maybe she's not really stealing it. Maybe she's only ..."

London's voice faded as she noticed something else in the picture—a feathered fountain pen in a small decorative stand on the table in front of Letitia. There were also several postcards on the table. Letitia seemed to have been using the pen to write postcards.

"Oh, no," London murmured.

"What is it?"

London pointed to the pen.

"I saw that pen earlier today. In fact, I used it myself to write down my name in the visitor book at the Mozart birthplace. So did everybody on the tour. That pen is museum property. Look, you can even see the little beaded chain that attached the pen to the desk. It looks like she cut it with a pair of scissors or something."

"Well, well, well," Bob murmured softly. "This is even bigger than I thought."

London stifled a scoff.

"So it looks like Letitia's a bit of a kleptomaniac," London said. "From what I've seen so far, that's hardly any big deal."

"You don't call murder a 'big deal'?"

London stared at Bob for a baffled moment.

"What's any of this got to do with the murder?" she asked.

Bob chuckled and pointed to his head again.

"It's like I said, missy. It's all connected. Everything's always connected. You've just got to have the right kind of brain to see that."

149

That's ridiculous, London almost blurted aloud.

And she was getting really tired of being called "missy."

But then a dim possibility began to play itself out in her mind.

What if Olaf Moritz had witnessed Letitia stealing the pen, or somehow found out about it, and maybe confronted her in the House for Mozart when nobody else was there, and things got out of hand and …

London's mind stalled.

That sounded pretty silly. She couldn't string the events together in a plausible way.

For one thing, no one in the group, including Letitia, had gone up onto the balcony during their visit there.

And yet …

Might she have gone back?

London only felt sure of one thing. She didn't want to share this germ of a theory with Bob. She remembered what Elsie had said about him earlier.

"I'm not sure he's thinking straight. I think maybe he's some kind of a loose cannon."

She didn't want to give Bob any ideas. He already had enough of them.

"And now," Bob added eagerly, "it's time for me to really connect the dots once and for all, put the final touch on things, so to speak. It's time for the *coup de grâce.*"

"What do you mean?" London asked apprehensively.

"Wouldn't you like to know?" Bob chuckled. "You just sit right here and wait a few minutes. I'll be back with the goods."

"What 'goods'?" London asked.

"Don't you want to be surprised?" Bob said.

"No," London said.

Bob frowned at her.

"You young people," he grumbled. "So impatient, always wanting answers right off the bat. I guess you never heard of delayed gratification. Well, this time you're just going to have to wait."

He got up to leave.

"Wait a minute," London said sharply.

As he stopped and turned toward her, London wasn't sure what to say next. Mr. Lapham hadn't told her whether she had any authority over Bob. She still wasn't completely sure just what his job was supposed to be. But she figured she'd better exert some authority, whether she really had it or not.

She crossed her arms and spoke to him sternly.

"I think you'd better tell me what you're up to."

Bob drew back a little, obviously surprised.

"Well, if you're going to be like that about it," he said, glancing around furtively as if to be sure he wasn't overheard, "I guess I can tell you. I'm going to sneak inside Letitia Hartzer's stateroom."

"You're what?" London said with a gasp.

"You heard me. I'll definitely find those stolen dolls. And about the murder, you can bet I'll find some kind of a 'smoking gun' in there— metaphorically speaking, of course, since she didn't kill the guy with a gun. But then, maybe she's got a real gun tucked away there. If so, we'd better find it before she kills someone else."

"You're doing nothing of the kind," London said.

"Why not?" Bob said.

"You don't have a key, for one thing."

"I sure do."

London's eyes widened as he produced a keycard just like hers.

"This will open every door on the boat," he said.

"Where did you get that?"

"From the captain. By order of Jeremy Lapham, who told him I might be needing it. I've got free rein all through this ship. I can come and go as I like."

London felt queasy at the thought of Bob doing exactly that.

It's bad enough that he's snapping pictures of everybody.

"You're not going into anybody's room," she said.

Bob let out a hearty chuckle.

"What are you going to do to stop me? Call security?"

London suddenly felt stymied. After all, Mr. Lapham had said that Bob was here to assist on "security matters."

But maybe I can still talk him out of it, she thought.

"How do you know Letitia's not in her room right now?"

"Because I just now saw her up on the Rondo deck, playing bridge with three women including your concierge—Amy Blassingame's her name, we introduced ourselves a little while ago."

London stifled a sigh of annoyance.

So Amy's playing bridge.

It sure didn't sound like she was doing her job.

Bob gave London a mock salute.

"And now, with or without your permission—"

"I'm coming with you," London blurted before he could turn to go.

"Huh?"

London could hardly believe her own words. But what choice did she have? If Bob was going to go poking into Letitia's stateroom, London figured she'd better supervise. She didn't want him probing around more than he had to, much less trashing the room while he conducted his search. Besides, she felt mounting suspicions about Letitia Hartzer. The woman clearly wasn't what she appeared to be.

"I'm coming with you," she said again.

Bob's face seemed expressionless behind those glasses. Then he shrugged.

"OK, then," he said. "Maybe you'll learn something. Let's get going."

As she followed him out of the lounge, London wondered what she was getting herself into.

CHAPTER TWENTY SEVEN

As they walked down the spiral stairs, London saw that Bob was tapping on his cell phone.

"What are you doing?" she said.

"Making sure the coast is clear," Bob said. "I'm texting Amy Blassingame to make sure Mrs. Hartzer stays where she is, playing bridge up there on the top deck. I'm telling her to text you and me right away if she leaves, especially if she seems to be headed back to her room."

With a grin, he pointed one finger to his head again.

London had to admit that keeping track of Letitia might not be a bad idea, although she wondered what Amy was going to make of Bob's message. Had he actually enlisted the help of the concierge in his investigation?

Bob's phone quickly buzzed.

"Amy says OK," he said, looking at the phone.

Apparently that meant Amy was in on the covert operation, but London didn't know whether to feel relieved or not.

When they arrived at the door, Bob whipped out his card and opened it.

London glanced up and down the hall, feeling more than a little like some sort of burglar.

Then she followed him into the room and switched on the overhead light.

Like all the staterooms here on the Romanze deck, this one was classified as "deluxe"—not as large or elegant as those above on the Menuetto deck, but larger than London's own "classic" below on the Allegro deck. All of these deluxe rooms had wide picture windows, and Letitia's currently offered a nice view of Salzburg. The white furnishings and turquoise carpet gave it all a touch of opulence.

London's eyes immediately fell on the stolen feathered pen in its stand on the dressing table.

"I've found something," she called out to Bob.

"So have I," Bob replied.

London walked across the room, where Bob had opened the drawer of the small table beside the bed. Sure enough, he took out the purloined saltshaker. London then noticed that a cushion on a nearby chair was slightly crooked. She picked it up and found a cloth napkin embroidered with the logo of a restaurant back in Budapest.

Bob lifted a cushion of another chair and found a little booklet of artworks clearly labeled, "PROPERTY OF THE *NACHTMUSIK* LIBRARY." Then London noticed a peculiar little bulge in one of a pair of bedroom slippers beside the bed. She picked up the slipper and found a little porcelain cream pitcher with a café's logo on it.

"Holy smokes," Bob growled. "This room must be crawling with stolen stuff."

So it would seem, London thought.

Bob headed over to a chest of drawers.

"We'd better search the room from top to bottom," he said, opening a drawer.

London felt a jolt of alarm.

One of the reasons she'd come with Bob was to make sure he didn't wreck the room.

"I'm not sure it's a good idea," she said, struggling to think how best to handle this very awkward situation.

She heard a familiar voice echo her words.

"I'm not sure it's a good idea either."

London spun around and saw Amy Blassingame standing in the doorway.

"Amy!" London exclaimed.

The concierge must have used her own key to enter so quietly that neither London nor Bob had noticed.

Amy crossed her arms and glared back and forth at London and Bob.

"We thought you were playing bridge," Bob said.

"I was," Amy said to Bob. "But your text message mentioned London, and I knew the two of you must be up to something. And since you wanted me to keep an eye on Letitia, it was pretty easy to guess where I might find you. This isn't the first time I've caught London poking around someone else's room."

London stifled a groan of despair. It was true that Amy had burst in on her once before when she'd been searching a passenger's room, but back then London had been looking for clues to the woman's murder.

London resisted the temptation to point out the rather serious mistakes that Amy had made in regard to that situation.

"Amy, *please* get back up to the game and keep an eye on Letitia," she said.

"Why should I do that?" Amy said. "Why do you always try to keep me in the dark about what's going on? And why are the two of you sneaking around Letitia's room, anyway?"

"I, for one, am doing my job," Bob grumbled. "And my job is investigating criminal activity aboard the *Nachtmusik*. London here is along for the ride, I guess. Or for the lesson."

London felt a flash of anger.

Along for the lesson!

Now she really wished she'd found a way to talk him out of this whole cloak-and-dagger operation.

Right now, he was showing Amy the silver saltshaker.

"Does this look familiar?" he asked.

Amy's eyes widened.

"Is this from the Habsburg Restaurant?" she said.

"You bet it is," Bob said.

Gesturing toward the other objects, London said, "And she stole that pen from Mozart's Birthplace. And she stole that napkin from a restaurant back in Budapest, and that cream pitcher from a café somewhere. In fact, this lady is an international thief."

Amy looked simply amazed.

"But ... how did you know to look here?" she asked.

"Hah!" Bob said, pointing to his forehead again. "A crack investigator like yours truly doesn't miss a trick. My synaptic superconducting ultra-fast feedback loop of a brain is in full gear."

Amy simply stared at him as if she had no idea what he was talking about.

London explained, "He snapped a picture of Letitia stealing the saltshaker."

"Oh," Amy said. "Do you think she stole the musician dolls too?"

Bob drew back a little.

"How did you know about the dolls?" he asked.

"I don't miss a trick either, Mr. Turner," Amy said with a scoff. "I keep my ear to the gossip mill. Everybody's talking about two things—the murdered man and the missing dolls."

Bob shrugged.

155

"And if you'll just let me do my job," he said, "I'll solve both of those mysteries before I leave this room."

Amy gasped.

"Do you mean you think Letitia …?" she began.

It was Bob's turn to scoff.

"A good detective doesn't say what he's thinking until he's come to an ironclad conclusion. But if you'd like to make yourself useful, you can help find the missing dolls—and maybe something more sinister while we're at it."

To London's alarm, Amy now seemed eager to pitch in. With a nod, she turned and walked over to a closet door, pulled it open, and started probing among the shoes on a rack.

"Guys, I really don't think this is a good idea," London said to them. "Let's at least talk to Letitia and let her tell us her side of the story."

"Her side of the story? Hah!" Amy snorted, rifling among the clothes in the closet. "The woman is obviously an all-out klepto—and maybe something a whole lot worse, if Mr. Turner is right."

London tried to calm herself with a long slow breath.

Now I've got two loose cannons to deal with, she thought.

But what was she going to do about it?

She only knew one thing for certain—that Letitia Hartzer was at the very least a thief.

Maybe I should call the police, she thought.

But she quickly thought better of it. Crimes that took place aboard the *Nachtmusik* weren't within the jurisdiction of the Salzburg police. And as long as *Polizeidirektor* Tanneberger suspected anyone in the tour group—including London—of murder, bringing up the stolen objects would only make things worse. It was bad enough that the *Nachtmusik* was already going to be delayed yet again. She wouldn't want to throw the whole tour in doubt if these little items were the extent of Letitia's misdeeds.

Before she could think everything through, the room door opened again.

Turning to face the new intruder, London was stunned to find herself face to face with Letitia Hartzer herself.

"Letitia, we've got to talk," London said.

But Letitia didn't seem to hear her. The stout woman's face had gone white as a sheet.

156

With a slight cry, she fell face first to the floor.

CHAPTER TWENTY EIGHT

Letitia Hartzer was a big woman, and her fall was hard and loud.

As Amy let out a shriek, London rushed to check on the stout, prone figure.

"Is she dead?" Amy cried, wringing her hands.

For a moment, London wondered that herself. But when she knelt down to put her finger to Letitia's neck to check for a pulse, the woman let out a groan and brushed her hand aside. London breathed a sigh of relief.

"No, she just seems to have fainted," she said.

Amy shrugged and said, "Well, I guess the bridge game is definitely off."

"Come on, give me a hand with her," London said.

It took all three of them—London, Amy, and Bob—to get Letitia slowly to her feet and onto the bed, where she lay stretched out and murmuring semiconsciously.

"I can't believe this is happening ... I can't believe this is happening ... I can't believe this is happening ..."

I'm having some trouble believing it myself, London thought.

Suddenly Letitia sat bolt upright and pointed to the saltshaker.

"That's not mine!" she exclaimed.

Then she pointed to the pen and the napkin and the book.

"And those things aren't mine either!" she said.

"No kidding," Amy said. "So what are they doing in your room?"

"I—I have no idea," Letitia stammered. "Somebody must have put them here. Somebody must ... want to do me harm."

With a dramatic flourish, Bob produced his cell phone with the picture of Letitia stealing the saltshaker.

"Perhaps *this* will refresh your memory," he told her.

At the sight of the picture, Letitia let out a moan of anguish, her voice faded, her eyes rolled back in her head, and she lay back down again. London suspected that this second fainting spell was at least partly feigned.

"I can't believe this is happening," she murmured again.

158

In the meantime, a small group of people had clustered in the hallway and were peering curiously into the room.

Great, London thought. *Everybody on the boat must have heard Amy scream.*

Bob walked over to the door and waved the spectators away with a growl.

"There's nothing to see here, folks. Just routine investigative stuff."

Then he shut the door and strode back to his companions, who were who were still hovering by the bed.

London pulled up a chair to sit at the side of the woman. She made her voice as mild and nonthreatening as she could.

"Letitia, there's no point in lying to us," London said. "We know what you did."

"You're not going to call the police?" Letitia asked.

"Huh," Bob grunted. "I say we throw you in the brig."

"We don't have a brig," Amy told him.

"No brig?" Bob snapped. "What the heck kind of a ship is this? What are we supposed to do if there's a mutiny?"

A mutiny? London thought.

She quickly decided, *Don't ask.*

In answer to Letitia's question, London said, "No, we're not going to call the police. But we do have to make all this right somehow. And it would help if you explained what this is all about."

Letitia sat up slowly and sighed.

"What's there to explain?" she said. "I like souvenirs."

Amy scoffed, "Can't you afford to buy them like everyone else?"

"Of course," Letitia said. "But they just don't seem as … well, special that way. As keepsakes, I mean. This way they bring back more memories."

London, Amy, and Bob looked at each other with perplexity.

"So you do this sort of thing whenever you travel?" Amy asked.

Letitia nodded.

London's mind boggled at the thought. Letitia seemed to be a seasoned traveler. How many stolen items must she have on display at home? London wondered if maybe her stash would dwarf the legitimately obtained collection in Kirby Oswinkle's room.

"How much other stolen stuff have you got around here?" Bob asked gruffly.

Letitia took a quick look around.

159

"You've found all of it, I think."

"You *think*?" Amy asked incredulously.

Bob pointed to his forehead again.

"You can't fool me, lady," he said. "Not with all these super synapses of mine working in overdrive like they're doing right now. You've got two more stolen objects, and we both know it."

"I don't know what you mean," Letitia said.

"I'm talking about a music conductor and a drummer," Bob said, jabbing his finger at her.

Letitia gasped aloud.

"You think I'm the one who stole *those*?" she demanded.

"What else are we supposed to think?" Amy asked.

Bob was pacing now, and there was a note of rising triumph in his voice.

"Oh, you were clever, ma'am. I've got to admit you were clever. You pretended someone had stolen your little trumpet player. And if it hadn't been found, you might have gotten away with this whole haul. But Sir Reggie the wonder dog thwarted your little scheme, didn't he? He found the trumpeter where you'd hidden it—under the table where the other musicians were on display."

Letitia's eyes widened with disbelief.

"That doesn't even make any sense!" she protested.

No, it really doesn't, London thought.

The idea of Letitia stealing her own trumpet player as some kind of distraction seemed unlikely enough. But if she had snatched it, she'd surely have found a better hiding place for it than right under the table where somebody was sure to find it. London felt perfectly sure that it had been knocked off and kicked under the table purely by accident.

But Bob seemed very sure of his conclusions.

"Are you going to come clean and produce the stolen dolls or what?" he growled.

"I can't produce something I don't have," Letitia said.

"Then you leave us no choice, ma'am," Bob said. "We've got to search the room. We'll turn everything upside down if we have to."

London realized she had to put her foot down before this whole situation got out of hand.

"You'll do nothing of the kind, Bob," she said in an authoritative voice that startled even herself. "We'll find a better way to resolve this situation."

160

Bob looked at her with surprise and said nothing.

Meanwhile, Letitia seemed to be regaining her composure.

"The very idea, that I would steal the musicians!" she said huffily. "What kind of person do you think I am, anyway?"

"A thief, for one thing," Amy said.

"Well, that's an infelicitous word for it," Letitia said. "In any case, I would never ever take anybody's personal possessions. I just take things that … well, don't belong to anyone in particular."

"From a museum, for example?" Amy asked.

"Or a café?" London said.

"That's right," Letitia said. "Institutions. Businesses."

The group fell quiet for a moment.

Finally Bob spoke in an almost admiring tone.

"A thief with a code. I've got to say I respect that."

"Thank you, sir," Letitia said. "Although I wish you'd all stop using such ugly language—thief, stealing, all that kind of thing."

Another silence fell. Nobody, including London, seemed to know what to say.

Then Bob rallied himself and spoke again.

"OK, then, ma'am. I'll take you at your word—about the stolen dolls, I mean."

He jabbed his finger at Letitia again.

"But there's still a murder to solve. And what do you have to say about that?"

Letitia's mouth dropped open with disbelief.

"Absolutely nothing, of course," she said.

"Hah!" Bob said. "I'm not so sure about that! But I'll get to the bottom of things. You can count on that."

London realized that Bob actually looked rather tired.

Maybe he needs another nap, she thought.

As the security man strode toward the door, London got up from her chair and tugged at his arm.

She whispered to him, "Bob, don't say anything about this to anyone, OK?"

Bob swiveled his mirrored glasses toward her.

"Not a chance," he muttered. "Do you think I'm stupid? It would only muddy the waters of my investigation."

He turned away and strode out of the room, shutting the door behind him.

161

Letitia looked back and forth at London and Amy.

"Does that awful man really suspect me of murder?" she asked.

"So it would seem," Amy said.

"But why?"

Amy shrugged as if she had no idea.

As for London, she had some notion of what Bob might be thinking. She herself had briefly entertained the idea that the tour guide might have caught Letitia stealing the pen, leading to a fatal altercation. But now that she sat here in the same room with this distressed woman, the idea seemed completely absurd.

"So what are you going to do now?" Letitia asked miserably.

"I'm not sure," London said. "What do you think we should do?"

A silence fell among the three of them.

Finally London said, "Letitia, I'd like to put all this behind us. But I have to be sure—can you stop stealing things? Even little things like these?"

"Oh, yes, I promise," Letitia said almost tearfully.

That's a pretty big promise, London thought.

Still, she figured she had to take the woman at her word, at least for now.

London looked at Amy and said, "Can we agree to keep this unfortunate incident to ourselves?"

London sensed that Amy had to struggle with a decision for a moment.

The lady does love her gossip, London thought.

Finally Amy nodded and said, "I guess."

Then Amy began to gather the stolen objects in a single place on the central table.

"We'll have to take care of returning these to wherever they belong," she said. "Letitia, you'll need to tell me where you took them from."

London reached for the stolen booklet—a collection of photos of statues in Gyor.

"I'll take this one back to the library," she said.

With a slight gasp, Letitia got up from the bed.

"Oh—I forgot about one more thing," she said.

She opened a drawer and reached down among some clothing and took out a glass paperweight and handed it to Amy. London realized it was the same paperweight Bob had noticed her almost stealing on his

162

first day aboard. Apparently she'd gone back and grabbed it when no one was looking.

"This belongs on the reception desk," Letitia said, handing it to Amy.

"OK, now tell me about where the other things came from—and how we can give them back," Amy said.

As Letitia began to make her shamefaced accounting of stolen objects to Amy, London left the room with the booklet in hand. Not surprisingly, there was still a cluster of people in the hallway, anxious about the scream they'd heard earlier, and no doubt curious about Bob's sudden exit from the scene.

"What happened in there?" a woman asked as London shut the door behind her. "The security man wouldn't tell us a thing."

For a moment, London had no idea what to say. Apparently Bob had managed to brush by the group without comment. But it was London's job to keep passengers contented.

"Uh, nothing happened," she finally said.

"Nothing!" a man scoffed. "It sure didn't sound like nothing."

"I heard a scream," another woman said.

"It sounded like Amy Blassingame, our concierge," another man said.

"It *was* Amy," the first woman said. "I noticed her go in there just a few minutes ago. And I don't think she ever left. She must still be in there."

"So what happened to her?" the first man said.

"Is she OK?" the second woman said.

"Amy's fine," London said, relieved to be able to say something that was true. "Amy just had a little scare, that's all."

"What scared her?" one of the passengers asked.

"Was it a cockroach?" another suggested.

"Or a mouse?" yet another demanded.

"That must be it!" the first woman exclaimed. "Mice are the only things that would ever make *me* scream like that! There must be mice aboard this ship!"

London had to speak over the group's voices rumbling with alarm.

"There are no mice aboard the *Nachtmusik*," she said. "And no cockroaches either. Our staff takes good care to keep them away. And Amy's fine. It was just a misunderstanding, that's all. Please don't let yourselves worry about it."

The group just stared at her, still obviously unsatisfied.

London turned and headed toward *Nachtmusik*'s library to return the stolen booklet. As she walked away, she could feel eyes following her suspiciously. But since she'd just asked both Bob and Amy to keep Letitia's thefts a secret, she couldn't reveal the story of the drama inside that room.

Still, the stares unnerved her.

They don't trust me, she realized.

How could she do her job if passengers didn't believe what she said?

And to make matters worse ...

Polizeidirektor Tanneberger still hasn't eliminated me as a murder suspect.

CHAPTER TWENTY NINE

Although it seemed kind of furtive, London half-hoped she wouldn't find Emil in the library. The little booklet of artworks was clearly marked PROPERTY OF THE *NACHTMUSIK* LIBRARY, and she didn't want to have to explain to Emil why she had it. She wasn't ready to start spreading the news that Letitia Hartzer had stolen the booklet and a bunch of other items as well.

But when she reached the Menuetto deck and went straight to the library, London was surprised to see that the door was closed. The library was usually open to anyone who wanted to use it except when Emil was giving a lecture, and she knew nothing was scheduled there at this hour.

Then she heard music playing inside. Emil must be in there.

She knocked on the door and there was no response. Then she knocked again and called out his name.

She heard Emil's voice say, "Come in."

London opened the door and stepped inside. There was Emil, leaning back in a swivel chair. His fingers were steepled together and his eyes were closed. He appeared to be immersed in the music—so much so that he seemed indifferent to London's presence.

London immediately recognized the music. An operatic soprano was singing the Queen of the Night's aria from Mozart's *The Magic Flute*—the very aria that Letitia had fumbled while Olaf Moritz had accompanied her on the antique clavichord in Mozart's Birthplace.

"Emil—" London began.

He silenced her with a wave of his hand. His eyes still closed, he nodded with pleasure as the soprano's voice rose higher and higher.

Since it was obvious that he didn't want her company at the moment, London thought briefly about just putting the booklet down on the table and leaving.

"Such celestial ladders of arpeggios!" he murmured. "How effortlessly, how intrepidly this singer climbs them! How she hits that rare dangerously high F again and again, as if it were as easy as breathing!"

165

London sat down in a nearby chair and listened, finding herself enjoying the aria herself. When it ended, Emil opened his eyes and turned it off, still not looking at London. He spoke softly, as if to himself.

"I have been listening to this aria again and again since yesterday—*"Der Hölle Rache kocht in meinem Herzen."*

Hell's vengeance boils in my heart, thought London, translating the title in her mind.

"I have needed to hear it many times," Emil said, "just to get that woman's hideous voice out of my mind. To tell the truth, I was relieved that she could not get through it. We were spared the torment of hearing such great music defiled."

London was a little startled by the quiet intensity of Emil's words. She hadn't realized how bitterly he'd reacted to Letitia's failed effort to sing this aria.

"She said she was able to sing it in college," London commented.

"She was able to make a mockery of it, more likely," Emil said with a scoff. "One is either born to sing this role or is not. It is either in a singer's blood, or it is not. That woman is too ... *common* to make any such attempt."

Not for the first time during the last few days, London was shocked by his judgmental, snobbish tone. She flashed back to how he'd lashed out at Bob earlier today.

"You have got no case against me, you meddling fool."

But at least he'd had a reason to be annoyed with Bob, who'd been treating him like a murder suspect. His hostility toward people like Letitia seemed like a different matter—as if he considered himself superior to everyone around him.

Remembering her reason for coming here, London set the booklet of Gyor statues on the table in front of him.

"I brought this back," she said, hoping not to have to explain any further.

He scowled at the book, then at her.

"I noticed yesterday that it was missing. Did you ... borrow it?"

London gulped a little.

"Not exactly," she said.

"Where has it been, then?" Emil asked.

London hesitated.

"A passenger ... borrowed it," London said.

166

She blurted out the little falsehood before she realized it. Letitia had clearly meant to keep the booklet as a souvenir.

But what was I supposed to say? she wondered.

A slight smirk crossed Emil's lips.

"It was *borrowed*, eh?" he said. "On a ship where little musician dolls go mysteriously missing? I somehow doubt that."

London felt her own anger rising.

"I don't really owe you an explanation," she told him. "But maybe you owe *me* one."

"How so?" Emil said with a tilt of his head.

"The way you've been behaving lately—you're ..."

"I am what? Not like my usual self? And how would you know such a thing? We only met rather recently, after all."

London stared at him speechless for a moment.

"I may not know you very well," she said slowly, "but I do know that there are things I like about you. I like your keen intelligence, your knowledge of so many things, and how generously you share your knowledge with other people. I like your professionalism and ... well, your manners, your sophistication, your gracefulness. I like the way you dance. I like how you helped solve Mrs. Klimowski's murder. And most of the time I like how you behave toward other people."

"But not always?" Emil said.

London felt as though she'd said too much.

She also felt dangerously close to admitting that she was a bit infatuated with him.

"I'll just go," she said, starting to rise from her chair.

"No, not yet," Emil said. "We must ... 'clear the air,' I believe is the English expression. We will be working together professionally during the rest of this voyage. If you believe me to have any defects of character, now is the time to tell me."

Defects of character?

The phrase struck London as stiff and peculiar. She almost turned and left without another word. But she had to admit, Emil was right—it was time for her to be honest.

"You take things so personally," she said. "Why does it matter to you so much whether poor Letitia can sing a Mozart aria or not? Why do you have to keep brooding about it a whole day later?"

"I believe I just explained—I hate to see works of genius degraded."

"No, there's more to it than that."

Emil's lips twisted into a trace of a smile.

"Vanity, perhaps?" he said.

London took a deep breath, then plunged ahead.

"Yes, vanity's a good word for it. Back in Vienna, I saw you bristle with anger when Cyrus Bannister told the truth about whether Salieri really killed Mozart. You felt upstaged by him. You didn't want to share the spotlight."

Emil seemed almost to enjoy what he was hearing.

"Go on," he said.

"You also got angry with Olaf and Cyrus both when they contradicted you about whether Mozart wrote the Austrian national anthem—"

"I have done some research since then," Emil said. "It appears that the matter is up for scholarly debate. But it is highly possible—perhaps even probable—that I was right."

"That's not the point," London said.

"Then what is?"

London realized that Emil looked genuinely baffled.

What exactly am I trying to say?

She searched her thoughts and recent memories.

"I was surprised at how angry you got when you found out someone else would be leading the tour today," she said.

"You mean Olaf Moritz," Emil said.

"That's right. And even after you met him, and he started leading us on a tour, you kept right on resenting him—as if the whole situation was his fault, as if it was his idea to do the tour instead of you. Your anger against him was ..."

"Palpable?" Emil said.

"That's right. Even after he was dead, you seemed to think ill of him."

Emil let out a sardonic chuckle.

"I cannot say I have ever shared this notion that the dead deserve some special consideration, some immunity from criticism. How does death change who people were and how we should treat them? It quite escapes me."

He leaned forward in his chair, his dark eyes fastened intently on hers.

"Let us get right to the point and talk about your real concern. You

168

wonder if I am the one who killed Herr Moritz."

London stifled a gasp.

"I didn't say that," she said.

"But do you deny that you think it? Why would you not think it? I know a similar suspicion crossed your mind when Mrs. Klimowski was killed. And regarding Olaf Moritz, you would not be the only one to suspect me. That *Polizeidirektor* has got his eye on me, at least. So has our oaf of a security man, Bob Turner. Tell me if I am wrong."

London stood there speechless.

She wanted to tell Emil that she suspected no such thing.

But would it be true? she wondered.

Emil frowned at her darkly.

"So now I know the truth. You think I am—or might be—a murderer."

"Emil—"

"I think our little chat should end here. Kindly leave me alone."

Emil touched the button for his music player, and the aria started again. He sat back again with his fingers steepled and his eyes closed.

London felt a chill all over.

Her head was flooding with uncertainties, but she did feel sure of one thing.

Emil is right.

We don't have anything more to say to each other.

She left the library and shut the door behind her. She leaned against the door for a moment, slightly dizzy and breathless with anxiety. What was she supposed to make of Emil's behavior? Was it even dimly possible that ...?

No, it just can't be, she decided.

Emil was no murderer. She just couldn't believe that about him. He was simply a difficult man who let his prickliness and vanity get in the way of his charm. She felt more than eager to put him out of her mind, so she was grateful to be distracted by the demands of her job.

She hurried about, checking to make sure the night's activities were running smoothly—an improv comedy class, a meeting of a creative writing group, another performance of the choral group, and a game of charades. Then she headed back to her stateroom for the night.

She found Sir Reggie waiting for her inside the room.

"I haven't seen you for a while, buddy," she said, putting out some dog food and fresh water. "I hope your day wound up better than mine did."

As Sir Reggie started eating eagerly, London remarked to the animal, "Now that I think of it, I haven't had anything to eat myself since breakfast. I think I'll order in a sandwich. Would you like me to order some of Bryce's special dog treats as well?"

Sir Reggie let out a happy yap. London texted the food order to the kitchen. Then she went to her bathroom to take a long, hot shower.

The food was waiting for her when she got out of the bathroom, and although it was a fine sandwich, London was too exhausted to appreciate it completely. However, Sir Reggie obviously enjoyed his treats.

When she finally climbed into bed. Sir Reggie snuggled alongside her and let out an inquisitive little whine.

"So you want to hear about the rest of my day?" London said.

Sir Reggie yapped in agreement.

"OK, I'll tell you all about it ..."

As usual, Sir Reggie was an attentive listener. Also as usual, it felt good talking things out to him. It helped clear her thoughts, but also brought her back to the mysteries still at hand—the missing doll figures, the unsolved murder, and ...

Where is Mom?

CHAPTER THIRTY

The next morning, London was up and struggling to get ready for a new day when her cell phone rang. She shook off the last bits of dreams she couldn't quite remember and fumbled around for her phone.

The voice she heard was Captain Hays's, and he also sounded a bit addled.

"Eh, London, I wonder if you could come to my quarters right now."

London checked her watch. As usual, she had gotten up very early, and she was a bit surprised to be summoned by the captain at this hour.

"Of course, Captain Hays," she said. "May I ask what this is about?"

The captain said nothing for a moment. In the background, London could hear a familiar voice talking rather loudly, apparently to someone else.

It was Bob Turner. What would he be doing in the captain's quarters at this hour?

The captain explained, "Well, *Polizeidirektor* Tanneberger stopped by bright and early to discuss the murder case. Bob Turner has been filling us in on his progress with his own, eh, investigation."

Investigation? London thought.

She found it hard to think of whatever Bob was doing as an actual investigation. And from the captain's tone of voice, she suspected he felt the same way. London couldn't imagine what Bob might have been saying or what the *Polizeidirektor* himself might be making of it all.

Captain Hays continued, "*Polizeidirektor* Tanneberger says he'd like to see you too."

"I'll be right there," London said. She had a feeling she'd better get there before Bob wore out Tanneberger's patience, or worse, got the murder investigation headed off in some odd direction.

Fully awake now, she finished putting on a fresh uniform and went to take one last look at herself in her bathroom mirror. With a sigh, she dampened a comb and tried to bring a bit more order into her unruly auburn hair.

171

"This will have to do," she told Sir Reggie. "We'd better get going."

With the little terrier trotting alongside of her, London hurried down the passageway past the elevator and stairs to the captain's quarters. The door was open, and when she and Sir Reggie entered, she found Captain Hays seated at his desk, looking quite perplexed.

Looking rather confused himself, *Polizeidirektor* Tanneberger was sitting in a nearby chair. Bob paced back and forth in front of him, mirrored glasses in place, talking and gesticulating with animation. Bob seemed to be wrapping up whatever he'd been saying.

The conversation was in English, of course. Apparently the ship's security man wasn't able to converse in any other language.

"So as you can see, I've cracked the case wide open. All you have to do is make an arrest."

Nobody said anything at all for a long moment. London sat down, and Sir Reggie jumped up onto her lap.

Then Tanneberger stroked his white mustache and finally spoke.

"So you're saying this woman, Letitia ..."

"Letitia Hartzer," Bob said.

"Yes, Letitia Hartzer—you are saying that she had a motive to kill Olaf Moritz."

"I'm saying she actually *did* kill him," Bob replied enthusiastically. "There's not a doubt in my mind."

London shuddered at how sure of himself he sounded.

Tanneberger must think he's out of his mind, she thought.

The *Polizeidirektor* leaned a little to one side.

"And you think this because ... Herr Moritz caught her stealing a pen from Mozart's Birthplace."

"Exactly. She was afraid he'd call the police. And of course there's also the matter of the stolen musician dolls—"

Tanneberger interrupted with a wave of his hand. Bob had obviously told him about the dolls already, and he didn't want to hear about them all over again.

"So you've told me," Tanneberger said. "But the truth is ... I'm having trouble seeing the connection between the dolls and ... well, anything else, really."

Bob chuckled confidently.

"I'm not saying there aren't loose ends to tie up. But it's all connected. Everything's always connected. As a seasoned law

172

enforcement officer, I'm sure you know that as well as I do."

Judging from his expression, London sensed that Tanneberger "knew" no such thing. But he seemed too polite to say so.

London felt a need to contribute something to the discussion.

"*Polizeidirektor* Tanneberger," she said, "I'm very sorry about the theft of the pen. We've settled the matter with our passenger, and the pen will be returned to Mozart's Birthplace soon, if it hasn't been returned already."

Tanneberger nodded with approval. He looked relieved that at least some part of Bob Turner's tale had been resolved.

Then he said to Bob, "Herr Turner, yours is an ... interesting theory. But as you say, there are a few ... loose ends, and I cannot say that I feel ready to arrest the woman you speak of. Perhaps you could keep pursuing clues."

London was quite sure Tanneberger didn't believe for a second that Letitia Hartzer was the murderer. But if Bob Turner stayed busy playing detective on the *Nachtmusik*, the *Polizeidirektor* probably figured it would at least keep him out of the way of his investigation. Of course Bob would still be a loose cannon around the *Nachtmusik*, which wouldn't make London's situation any easier.

"You can count on me, sir," Bob agreed with an enthusiastic nod.

Tanneberger turned his attention to London.

"Fraulein Rose, yesterday you told me that you were at a café near the House for Mozart at about the time when Herr Moritz was killed. I believe you also mentioned that somebody could confirm your whereabouts."

"That's right," London said. "I was just sitting down with a young couple, Tina and Rudy Fiore, for a snack. But before I even got a chance to order, Tina noticed that her cell phone was missing, and I went back to the House for Mozart to look for it."

Tanneberger stared at her for a moment.

Something in his steady gaze chilled her. She sensed that he suspected her more than before.

I might be his only serious suspect, she realized.

But why? Did he have some sort of erroneous evidence that she didn't know about? She guessed probably not. But if he and his team hadn't turned up any leads or suspects on shore, of course his suspicions would lead straight back to her.

She wanted to ask him whether he had any other serious suspects, but she quickly decided it was best not to pry.

Finally Tanneberger said, "I'd like to talk to this couple—the Fiores—before I leave."

Captain Hays picked up his phone and said, "I'll call them and let them know you want to see them."

Tanneberger said to London, "I don't doubt that your companions will confirm your whereabouts. However, there's still the matter of the exact time of death. Unless you can prove you were not at the theater at the exact moment when Olaf Moritz was killed …"

"I wish I could prove I wasn't, sir," London said.

"If you think of anything that would do that, please let me know."

"I'll do that, sir."

London gulped hard and added, "Sir, I—I really didn't have any motive for killing Ms. Hartzer."

Tanneberger's expression darkened further.

"So you say," he replied.

London was on the verge of insisting that she was telling the truth.

No, that might only make things worse.

Meanwhile, the captain had finished his phone call and spoke to Tanneberger.

"I just talked to Tina Fiore. She and her husband are expecting you right now in their stateroom, which is right here on this level. I'll accompany you there and introduce you to them."

"*Danke,* Captain," Tanneberger said. "After I talk to them, I would like permission to stay aboard the *Nachtmusik* and talk to people however I find appropriate."

"Of course," the captain said.

Everybody left the captain's stateroom. Captain Hays led the *Polizeidirektor* down the passageway toward the passengers' quarters, and Bob, London, and Sir Reggie stopped in the little foyer in front of the elevators.

"So where are you off to now?" Bob asked London.

"To the restaurant to get some breakfast," London said. "What about you?"

Bob let out what was obviously meant to sound like an enigmatic chuckle.

"That's always the question, isn't it?" Bob said. "Where am I off to? What am I up to? There are people aboard this boat who would love to know the answer to that question. There sure are."

He turned the mirrored glasses down toward Sir Reggie and wagged his finger at him.

"As for you, pal—always be vigilant! That's the true secret of being a topnotch K-9 investigator! Vigilance!"

The elevator arrived and Bob dashed inside. London just stood there in the foyer and waved for him to go ahead on his own. As the doors closed, London shook her head with bemusement. Despite Bob's attempt to be inscrutable and mysterious, she didn't much care where he was off to or what he was up to …

As long as he doesn't cause any real trouble.

But *Polizeidirektor* Tanneberger was another matter. She didn't know what to expect from him.

As London and Sir Reggie started up the stairway, her cell phone rang.

When she took the call, all she could hear was some kind of loud, rhythmic, rumbling, crashing noise.

CHAPTER THIRTY ONE

London tried to shout over the noise on her cell phone, "Hello?"

No one spoke back right away. She struggled to identify the strange sounds coming from the phone.

Was that some kind of music?

Then she heard a voice speaking loudly over the noise.

"Ms. Rose, this is Carol Weaver."

London remembered that Carol and Steve Weaver were the middle-aged couple who had bought a couple of the musician dolls.

"Oh," London shouted back. "Are you all right?"

When Carol replied, London could detect agitation and alarm in the woman's voice, but could barely hear her over the noise.

She could only make out two words: "Please help!"

The call abruptly ended.

London checked the passenger list on her phone. The couple's stateroom was number 206, which was on the Romanze deck, and she and Reggie were already almost there on the stairway.

She dashed the rest of the way up and into the passageway, where she again heard the noise. With Sir Reggie alongside her, she hurried to their door and knocked.

Carol opened the door.

Now the sound blasted clearly enough that London realized what it was.

A heavy metal song was playing at an almost deafening level.

"Can you help us get rid of this?" Carol shouted.

London saw that Carol's husband, Steve, was poking desperately at the music console beside their bed. She walked over beside him.

"I just bumped it with my elbow," he said loudly. "I can't make it stop."

London looked at the console and saw that the button Steve had been frantically pushing was slightly crooked. London wiggled the button a bit. It was stuck, but after a little pressure and a twist, it popped back into place.

The music came to a merciful end.

"Oh, thank goodness!" Carol said.

London drew a breath of relief.

She smiled with satisfaction at being able to solve this problem in such a low-tech manner.

"What kind of music would you rather be listening to?" she asked.

Carol said, "Before this happened, we were listening to some nice Vivaldi."

London pushed the buttons for the appropriate channel at a lower sound level, and some pleasant Baroque music began to play.

London's ears were still ringing as Carol and Steve thanked her for her help.

"That's what I'm here for," she said. "Do you want me to send someone in to adjust that button?"

Steve looked embarrassed. "I'll be able to fix it myself if that happens again. I guess we both panicked."

"Just call me whenever you need anything at all," London said as she left the room.

As she walked toward the bow of the ship, London realized that solving that simple problem for the Weavers had felt good. That's what her job was supposed to be— keeping the passengers happy.

So what are you doing worrying about a murder instead? she asked herself.

After all, she always had plenty of work to do, and most of it was quite satisfying.

If only the cruise wasn't held up, she thought.

If only I wasn't a suspect.

Under the circumstances, she didn't have much choice but to worry about the murder. Even so, she decided to get a quick breakfast, then just go about her ordinary routine on the ship.

She noticed that Reggie was no longer with her and guessed that he'd fled the noise on account of his sensitive canine hearing.

Well, he has free run of the boat, she thought. *I guess he won't be joining me for breakfast.*

She went on into the ship's Habsburg Restaurant and sat down at an unoccupied table. Just like yesterday, she noticed some of the other passengers were eyeing her suspiciously. And was she becoming paranoid, or did she see a young couple whispering to one another as they watched her?

Again, London realized she was losing the trust of the very people whose happiness was her most important duty. She remembered, too, how Tanneberger had asked Captain Hays's permission to stay aboard the *Nachtmusik* and freely talk to its passengers.

About me, no doubt, London thought.

If rumors were starting to circulate about her, what might people tell him?

Her situation seemed to be going from troublesome to truly dire.

But what was she going to do about it?

And how was it going to affect her ability to do the job she loved?

She glanced toward the kitchen and saw Bryce smiling and waving at her from the serving window. He was obviously too busy to come out and chat with her. Even so, she found it nice to see someone looking at her in a thoroughly non-suspicious way.

Meanwhile, she felt as though her ears were still ringing. It wasn't just the out-of-control heavy metal music that was buzzing through her head. It was the troubling exchange of words she'd had just now with the *Polizeidirektor.*

He'd said he was going to ask Tina and Rudy Fiore to confirm that she'd been with them at the café when Olaf Moritz was killed.

But even if they could, Tanneberger made it clear that he was unlikely to be satisfied.

"Unless you can prove you were not at the theater at the exact moment when Olaf Moritz was killed ..."

But how could London possibly do that?

The waiter arrived, and she asked for some coffee before she ordered. But her eyes wouldn't focus on the menu. Her mind was wandering in all sorts of disturbing directions. For example, she remembered Emil's unsettling words and behavior when they'd talked last night.

"So now I know the truth," Emil had said. *"You think I am—or might be—a murderer."*

Ever since then, she'd been trying to convince herself that she thought nothing of the kind. But was that true? And if she did suspect Emil, shouldn't she report her concerns to *Polizeidirektor* Tanneberger?

No, she decided she couldn't let her suspicions run away with her. Surely Emil would never murder someone merely out of jealousy about conducting a tour, or over an issue as trivial as being corrected about who wrote the Austrian national anthem.

Which still left London with an important question ...

No matter how much she wanted to, could she really stop thinking about the murder and just go about her regular job?

Yesterday she'd felt sure that none of the people in her tour group had killed Olaf. She found herself feeling even more convinced of that right now. And yet Tanneberger was here aboard the *Nachtmusik* pursuing nonexistent clues pointing to London's own guilt.

And wasting valuable time, she thought.

As long as London hadn't managed to clear herself of suspicion, the killer was still at large—and possibly still dangerous.

London sighed. Her routine couldn't return to normal just yet.

I've got to do something. But where to begin?

Well, there was one thing she had never followed up on.

London took the folded piece of paper that Selma Hahn had given her yesterday out of her vest pocket. It had the name and phone number of Greta Mayr, the young maintenance woman who had been in the building when London had discovered Olaf Moritz's body.

London remembered how distraught Greta had been about the tour guide's death—which was hardly any surprise, since she seemed to have known the man.

London also remembered how emphatically Greta had insisted, *"I don't know anything at all."*

London hadn't quite believed her then, and wasn't sure she believed her now. But then, did it matter whether London believed her or not? The police had just started to interview Greta Mayr when London was heading back to the *Nachtmusik* with Emil and Tanneberger. Surely the police had found out everything Greta might know.

Or had they?

London picked up her cell phone and punched in the number.

When she got Greta on the phone, she said in German, "My name is London Rose. We met yesterday under ... terrible circumstances."

"Oh—yes," Greta said. "It was ... terrible."

"I was just wondering ..."

London hesitated.

"Greta, I've been very concerned about what happened to Olaf Moritz. The police have already asked me questions, and I know they've asked you questions as well ..."

"Yes, they have," Greta said, heaving a sigh.

"But if it's not too much to ask ... well, I was wondering if perhaps we could meet and talk about it."

"I don't think so," Greta said.

Of course not, London thought.

The woman was still traumatized. London didn't want to pressure her. But even so, she felt desperately in need of some answers. She quickly decided to be honest and to the point.

"Greta, the police seem to be thinking of me as a suspect."

She heard Greta let out a gasp.

"Oh—but I'm sure they are wrong," she said.

London breathed a little more easily, although she knew she shouldn't be surprised. Greta had seen London the moment after she had found the body. Naturally Greta had known what Tanneberger couldn't know—that London's distress had been genuine, and not that of a killer.

"I'm glad you think so," London said. "But I'm sure you understand, this is a problem for me. I work on a river tour boat, and our cruise is being delayed because of this, so it's also a problem for the company I work for. But more than anything else ... I don't want the police wasting their time and energy."

A silence fell.

London wondered whether Greta was giving her request some serious thought, or if she was just trying to think of a polite way to say no.

"Will you be at the House for Mozart today?" London asked.

"No. Frau Hahn—the director—gave me the day off."

London set down the menu she'd found herself too distracted to read.

"I haven't had breakfast yet, have you?"

"No."

"There's a nice little outdoor café right near the House of Mozart. Do you know it?"

"The *Altstadtcafé,* yes."

"Could you meet me there shortly?"

London held her breath for a moment waiting for a reply.

"Yes, I will," Greta said.

Then she abruptly ended the phone call.

London sat staring at the phone for a moment. Something in Greta's voice told her that the young custodian knew more than she had told the police.

And I've got to find out what it is, she decided.

Ignoring any inquisitive stares from other customers, London put the menu down and hurried out of the Habsburg Restaurant.

CHAPTER THIRTY TWO

The prospect of meeting with Greta Mayr recharged London's energy and sense of purpose.

Maybe I'll get to the bottom of this murder once and for all, she thought as she headed for the elevator. Resisting the temptation to just slip away without letting anyone know, she dutifully tapped a hasty text message to Amy, asking her to watch over things for a while.

Amy won't be happy, London realized.

But of course, Amy seldom seemed happy about anything these days.

When the elevator reached the Allegro deck, London hurried to her stateroom. She found Sir Reggie there, lapping from his water bowl.

The little terrier let out a friendly yap of greeting.

"So *there* you are," London said. "I was wondering where you'd run off to."

When she picked up her handbag and headed back toward the door, Sir Reggie dashed into the open closet.

"What are you doing?" London asked.

Sir Reggie reappeared with one of his leashes in his mouth.

London chuckled.

"I guess you can tell I'm going ashore," she said. "But I won't be gone long."

When London turned toward the stateroom door again, the dog scurried over and placed himself between London and the door. He sat there, looking at her expectantly, the leash still in his mouth.

London couldn't help but laugh.

"I don't know," she teased him. "You seem to be having plenty of fun on your own, now that you've got the run of the ship. You hardly bother with me anymore. I wouldn't want to bore you ..."

Sir Reggie let out a mild growl of protest.

"OK, if you insist," London said.

She stooped down and clipped the leash to his collar. When London and Sir Reggie left the stateroom, she paused for a moment in front of the door to Mr. Tedrow's stateroom. She felt sure that he was still in there, wearing pajamas and typing away at his novel. And of course, he had no idea about all the trouble that was unfolding around him. He was happily oblivious to everything except his own make-believe mystery.

It must be nice, she thought enviously.

She wished the mystery she was trying to solve wasn't so awfully real.

She and Sir Reggie took the elevator up one level, then descended the gangway off the boat into Salzburg. They followed the now-familiar route past the *Mozarts Geburtshaus* toward the House for Mozart.

The outdoor café where she'd briefly joined Tina and Rudy Fiore yesterday was just across the large, paved terrace outside the theater. Although Greta Mayr had agreed to meet London there today, she wasn't sitting at any of the tables.

I just hope she shows up, London thought, remembering how nervous Greta had sounded over the phone.

She sat down at a small table beneath a wide umbrella. Sir Reggie jumped up into her lap, but she lifted him over into one of the other chairs, where he lay down contentedly. When the waiter came to the table, she ordered the *Wiener Frühstück*—a simple "Viennese Breakfast" with coffee, rolls, jam and butter, and orange juice.

As she waited for both Greta and her food order to arrive, London took in the pleasant view of the pedestrian street lined with colorful vendor stalls and little shops. Clothes, food, flowers, crafts, and lots of other items were on display and it looked like both locals and tourists were cheerfully shopping.

A melancholy thought crossed her mind.

Mom had recently been here in Salzburg.

Not only that, but she'd stayed long enough to make friends—at least with Selma Hahn and her family. But now, like London herself, those friends missed her and wondered where she'd gone.

London's breakfast order arrived. She hesitated before eating, but it was really starting to seem as though Greta Mayr wasn't going to show up.

I might as well enjoy my breakfast, London decided.

She took a sip of the deliciously strong black coffee, broke open a soft, piping hot roll of *semmel*—"small bread."

Sir Reggie was sitting up in his chair and staring at her food, so she gave him a bit of buttered bread. Then she spread another piece with strawberry jam for herself. The fluffy, steaming bread and the sweet, tart flavor of the jam were a perfect combination with the soothing creaminess of the butter. It was an exquisite breakfast.

Then she wondered—might Mom have eaten in this very café while she'd been in Salzburg? Might she have sat at this very table, under this same umbrella?

And where is she now?

She'd told Selma that she was on her way to Germany.

But where did she go in Germany?

And why hadn't she stayed in touch with Selma and her family?

London remembered what Selma had said yesterday.

"She seemed very happy here in Salzburg. I got the feeling she was really thinking about settling down here at last."

As London looked around at the cheerful, bustling street, she could well understand why. She wished she and Mom could enjoy this lovely little city together.

Her thoughts were interrupted by the sight of a young woman making her way toward the café tables. Even though she was wearing a colorful dress instead of her maintenance uniform and her hair was more freely arranged, London thought it could be Greta Mayr.

The woman seemed to recognize London, then stopped and glanced around nervously. She looked as though she was having second thoughts about coming here and might go away.

"Greta!" London called out in German. "Please, come sit with me."

With faltering steps, Greta Mayr came and sat down in a chair across the table from London's table. When she saw Sir Reggie, she smiled and reached over to pet him.

"I already ordered," London said. "Please order something for yourself. I'll pay for it."

Greta Mayr picked up the menu and said, "Thanks, Fraulein … what was your last name again?"

"Rose. London Rose. Please call me London."

Greta nodded and peered at the menu, but London got the feeling that she was too preoccupied to really read it.

When the waiter came by, Greta said, "I haven't decided."

Greta again reached over and stroked Sir Reggie, who seemed to have gone to sleep in his chair.

Then she spoke so quietly that she seemed almost to be talking to

184

herself.

"I'm still not sure why you want to see me."

London swallowed hard.

"It's like I told you over the phone—I want to help the police eliminate me as a suspect. Not just for my own sake, but to make sure the investigation gets on track. I want to make sure the police's efforts are going in the right direction."

"How do you think I can help?" Greta asked, her eyes full of worry.

It was a good question. London wasn't sure just why she thought Greta might be able to answer some lurking questions, or even what those questions might be. But she remembered how horribly distraught she'd been when she'd found Olaf's body and how she'd cried out his name over and over.

"Olaf! Olaf! Olaf!"

Unlike London's own shock, Greta's reaction had seemed wrenchingly personal.

"What can you tell me about Olaf?" London asked.

A flicker of a warm, fond smile crossed Greta's face.

"Oh, he was very kind, and happy, and funny too."

London remembered Selma Hahn describing him in exactly the same words.

He must have been very likable, London thought.

Surely Greta knew quite a lot about him. But she was obviously very reluctant to talk. London wondered how she could draw her out.

"I only met him yesterday," London said, "but he was a wonderful tour guide. He knew all sorts of things. He must have been very smart. And knowledgeable. Especially about Mozart."

Greta seemed to be letting down her guard slightly.

"Oh, yes, he loved Mozart. And he loved living in the town where Mozart was born. He wanted the whole world to love Salzburg as much as he did. That's why he worked as a tour guide. And he loved music."

"I could tell," London said. "And he was talented. I heard him play a piece on Mozart's own clavichord at the Mozart birthplace."

Greta's smile widened.

She said, "He was so proud to have permission to play that clavichord. It gave him such a thrill just to touch those keys."

Greta added, "He was also a composer."

"Really?" London asked.

"Yes. I don't know much about music, but I really liked the pieces

185

he played for me. He even wrote a piece …"

Greta hesitated.

"Go on," London urged. "Please tell me."

"He … dedicated a piece to me. A whole piano sonata. I thought it was beautiful. I don't think he ever played it for anyone else, which seemed a shame. I suggested he show it to Wolfram Poehler, the pianist who was supposed to do a recital at the House for Mozart last night, and see if he might like to play it."

"Did he?" London asked.

"He said he did. But apparently Herr Poehler wasn't interested in it. I think Olaf's feelings might have been hurt."

London felt a surge of interest.

"Olaf must have cared a great deal about you," she said.

Greta gave London a startled glance, as if she'd said more than she'd meant to, and maybe more than she thought she should say. London sensed that she'd stumbled across an important issue. She wanted to keep Greta talking about it.

"Can you tell me about your relationship?" London said.

"There's not much to tell," Greta said. "We liked each other, and we were friends, but he told me he felt … and I felt too … well, I suppose we'd have become more than friends if it weren't for …"

Greta's eyes filled up with tears. London realized she'd better be careful not to pry too much. Besides, other questions were starting to occur to her.

"Greta, I take it you were the only employee working in the House of Mozart when it happened."

"That's right."

"Which means you and I were the only people in the building at the time."

London could see Greta bristle slightly, as if she were being accused.

"The police questioned me," she said. "I told them the truth. They believed me when I said I didn't kill Olaf. I could never have done such a thing."

London had no doubt that this was true. Greta was a slight woman, and she seemed to be perfectly gentle and kindly. London couldn't imagine her committing any kind of act of violence. The police officers who'd interviewed her surely felt the same way. Maybe they even knew her personally.

I make a much more likely suspect, she admitted to herself.

She leaned toward Greta across the table.

"What I'm asking is … was it very common for you to be working in the building alone? Don't you usually work with a partner or somebody like that?"

Greta shrugged slightly.

"Yes, usually I work with my supervisor, the maintenance chief."

"But he wasn't there at the time?"

"No."

"Where was he?"

Greta looked increasingly uncomfortable.

"I told the police yesterday," she said.

"What did you tell them?" London said.

"That he left the building a little while earlier."

"Did he say where he was going?"

"He said … he didn't feel well. He just wanted to go home."

London felt a strange tingle.

For the first time, she sensed that Greta was lying.

"What is your supervisor's name?" she asked.

"It doesn't matter."

"I wish you'd tell me—"

Greta abruptly stood up.

"I'm sorry," she said. "This was a mistake. I've got to go."

London stood up and stepped in her path.

"Greta, please—"

"No. I'm sorry I wasted your time."

Greta darted out of the café and quickly disappeared among the other pedestrians.

London felt stunned as sat back down. She looked over at Sir Reggie, who was sitting up and staring at London's breakfast plate. She gave the dog another piece of bread and confided in him, "That young woman seems to be desperately frightened."

But of what? she wondered, as Sir Reggie crunched happily on his snack.

London hadn't found out much from Greta—except that she and Olaf had been attracted to one another, and that the young custodian was very afraid of something she wouldn't even talk about. Now she sat wondering where to turn next to unravel the mystery behind the murder of Olaf Moritz.

187

"Greta did tell me one important thing," she remarked to Sir Reggie. "Someone else was also working in the House for Mozart on the day that Olaf died."

Sir Reggie had swallowed his bread and was staring at the half-eaten meal on London's plate.

With a tilt of his head, he seemed to be asking her silently, *"If you're not going to eat that, could I have it?"*

"Sorry, Sir Reggie," London said, patting him on the head. "We've got someplace to go."

London had lost her appetite now, and she was focused on that bit of information. Greta had said that her supervisor, the maintenance chief, was there that day. But when she'd asked Greta her supervisor's name ...

"It doesn't matter," Greta had said. And then she had suddenly left.

But it obviously did matter.

And London needed to find out why.

CHAPTER THIRTY THREE

London wondered whether Greta's supervisor might be working today. If so, she definitely wanted to ask him some questions. She left money for the bill and a good tip, and she and Reggie went out of the café and crossed the paved terrace to the House for Mozart. When they entered the glittering lobby, the building seemed eerily quiet.

Selma is probably up in her office, London thought.

Surely now the director would be willing to tell her something about the maintenance supervisor. But before they began to climb the gallery staircase, she was startled by a sound.

Music was coming from the auditorium.

London took a few steps in the direction of the music, then froze in her tracks.

A pianist was playing the joyful final movement of Mozart's *Eine Kleine Nachtmusik.* The spritely and light rondo always seemed to her like an exquisite Viennese pastry. It was, of course, the piece of music that the tour boat was named after. But it carried even more emotional significance for London.

Is that Mom playing? she couldn't help but wonder.

Her mother used to play this very piece on the piano at home, her expression glowing with delight at every note. She knew that Mom had been in Salzburg just a few months ago. Could she be here now, enjoying herself at the piano all alone in one of the world's great concert halls?

With Reggie at her side, London stepped into the vestibule and stood before one of the entrances to the auditorium.

Did she dare go through that door?

Feeling weak in her knees, she pushed the door open, and she and Reggie stepped into the cavernous space.

Her heart sank.

It wasn't Mom playing, but Wolfram Poehler, the same casually dressed pianist who had been here yesterday.

Of course, she told herself. *It was silly to think otherwise.*

Remembering that he'd cut his practicing short yesterday at the appearance of visitors, she thought she should probably leave. But she was too charmed by the music.

She and Sir Reggie stood silently in the aisle until Wolfram Poehler played the final chords of the rondo with a triumphant flourish. Then London couldn't help but break out in a round of applause. Reggie let out a yap of enthusiasm.

The pianist's boyish face turned toward them with a smile. He didn't seem surprised or annoyed to see London and her dog.

"It appears that there are two music lovers in the house," he said in German. "I'm glad you both liked it."

"Oh, very much," London said. She walked on down the aisle and sat in the row of seats in front of the stage. Sir Reggie jumped up in her lap.

"But I'm surprised to find you practicing here today," she said. "I thought your recital was supposed to be last night."

"It was—and it was canceled, of course," Poehler said with a sigh. "Such an awful thing to have happen in such a wonderful concert hall. I'm catching a train to Bonn tonight."

"Bonn—the birthplace of Beethoven," London remarked.

"That's right," Poehler said. "I'm scheduled to play the *Hammerklavier* in the *Beethovenhalle* there tomorrow night. It's going to be quite a thrill for me."

"And for your audience, I'm sure," London said smile. "I heard you practicing just a bit of that piece yesterday. It sounded amazing. I wish I could have heard your recital here."

"I wish I could have played it here," Poehler said with another sigh. "I couldn't resist stopping in this morning, just to enjoy this hall's marvelous ambience—and this excellent Steinway piano."

Casually and effortlessly, he began to play again.

And again, London smiled as recognized the piece.

It was Mozart's *Rondo alla Turca*—the irrepressibly sparkling and cheerful Turkish March. But then the music took off in into unexpected jazz rhythms and blues harmonies.

London chuckled with glee to hear one musical surprise after another.

When he finished the piece with the same aplomb as before, London burst into applause again, and Sir Reggie yapped several times.

"Not too irreverent for you two?" he asked with a laugh.

"Anything but," London said. "I'm sure Mozart himself would have

190

loved it."

"I'd like to think so. Mozart could be quite irreverent himself."

"Did you make up these variations yourself?"

"Oh, hardly," Poehler said. "I heard the great Yuja Wang play them in this very auditorium. The variations … well, they kind of stuck with me."

"You seem so young to be able to play so brilliantly," London said. "Were you some sort of prodigy?"

"Actually I'm something of a late beginner," Poehler replied. "I'm just now getting started on my concert career. But I do seem to pick up new sounds and techniques without much difficulty."

"I'm sure you'll become very famous," London said.

"So people keep telling me," Poehler said with a note of wistfulness in his voice. "I'm not sure how I'll feel about that. It already feels strange, just starting to get in the public eye. Strange, and more than a little scary. I like the way things are right now—just traveling around and giving recitals in really special concert halls, not a lot of flash or publicity. Just staying 'under the radar,' as you Americans put it—playing for people who want to hear me play. That's what I live for."

London was impressed by his attitude. It seemed rare and refreshing. She wondered how many talented musicians felt a similar reluctance to become celebrities.

Poehler turned away from the keyboard toward her.

"But I don't guess you stopped by just to listen to me practice," he said.

London was a bit startled by this insightful comment.

"No, I don't suppose I did," she admitted.

He smiled a knowing smile.

"I believe I recognize you," he said. "You were here with the tour group yesterday. And if you don't mind if I hazard a guess … you're the one who found Olaf's body."

London shuddered a little.

"That's right," she said.

"And you're looking for answers about his murder," Poehler added.

"Yes, I am," London said.

Poehler shook his head sadly.

"I'd like to find out some answers myself," he said. "The whole thing puzzles me. Poor Olaf."

"You say his name like you knew him," London said.

191

"Oh, not very well," Poehler said. "I arrived here a couple of days early for my recital. I love Salzburg, and if I may say so, I'm something of an aficionado of human nature. I like to get to know people wherever I go, and I seem to be good at drawing them out."

London felt a twinge of interest.

"What can you tell me about Olaf?" she said.

"He was a very nice man, quite clever, very interesting to talk to. Unfortunately ..."

Poehler shook his head sadly.

"He fancied himself a composer. The afternoon before yesterday, when I was practicing right here on this stage, he came and showed me his score for a piano sonata. He wanted to know if I'd play the piece he'd written."

"The sonata he dedicated to Greta," London said.

"Yes, Greta—the charming cleaning lady. He was quite in love with her. And he seemed sure she felt the same way about him."

Poehler chuckled sympathetically.

"Well, I sat here at this piano and sight read his whole sonata, played all four movements for him. Sadly, it wasn't very good. He had no talent at all for musical composition."

Poehler shrugged.

"I didn't tell him that straight out, of course. I congratulated him for his hard work and handed the score back to him."

A lull fell in their conversation. London was certainly grateful to have someone to talk to so openly about what had happened. She tried to process what she was hearing.

London pointed upward and said, "He fell—or rather was pushed—from the balcony up there. Does that seem odd to you? Why would he be in the balcony at the time?"

"Oh, I believe I can answer that question," Poehler said. "He told me he liked to sit up there when he had free time, enjoying the feel of this whole wonderful space."

Poehler gazed all around the hall with a rapt expression.

"I told him I feel the same way," he added. "Even the *silence* has a special quality in an auditorium like this. In fact, I expect to spend a few more hours today haunting this place—or rather letting it haunt *me*, work its magic on me."

He shrugged again and idly played a few notes on the keyboard.

"Anyway, anyone who knew him would have known they could

find him on that balcony, relaxed and unwary."

They stopped talking for a moment. The auditorium felt almost eerily quiet.

Finally London spoke cautiously.

"Herr Poehler, do you have any idea who might have killed Olaf?"

Poehler took a long, deep breath.

"Naturally, the police asked me questions," he said. "I wasn't here at the time, of course. After my practice, I'd gone out for a nice long walk along the *Sigmund-Haffner-Gasse*. I didn't find out what had happened until I came back and found the police here. I told them what little I knew. But now … well, I wonder if maybe I should have just kept my suspicions to myself."

London's breath caught.

Suspicions? she wondered.

Poehler continued, "Olaf had told me he'd finally gotten up the nerve to tell Fraulein Greta Mayr how he felt, and she'd said she felt the same way about him. He was like a giddy schoolboy, he said. The only trouble was …"

Poehler's voice faded.

"Maybe I shouldn't say," he said.

"Please. I want to know."

"He said she was afraid."

"Afraid of what?"

"Of her maintenance supervisor—Gunther Raab is his name."

London felt a jolt of excitement.

The very man I came here looking for, she thought.

Poehler continued, "Olaf said Raab was quite infatuated with Greta—obsessed with her, really, to the point of stalking her. She wasn't attracted to him, to put it mildly. She told Olaf that Gunther was intensely jealous—dangerously so, she thought. She didn't dare get into a relationship with Olaf on account of Raab."

"So you think Gunther Raab was the killer?" London asked.

"I don't know, but …"

He fell quiet again.

"I spoke with Gunther a little the day before yesterday. It wasn't a pleasant experience. I'd just finished practicing, and he'd just finished work for the day, so we left the building at the same time. As it happened, he lives in a four-story apartment building on the corner of Prinzenstrasse and Nibelungenstrasse, which is in the same direction as the hotel where I've been staying, so we walked and talked together."

Poehler shuddered.

"The whole way, he was badgering me about Greta, and whether *I* might be attracted to her, and whether she might be attracted to me, and how bad that would be for us both. Of course there was nothing of the kind going on between Greta and me, and I told him so, but I'm not sure I convinced him. I was relieved when we parted ways."

London felt a chill all over.

She asked, "Do you know whether Gunther Raab is here at work today?"

"Apparently not, I'm happy to say. Just a little while ago I was talking with Frau Hahn, the theater director. She was annoyed because Raab had left a message on her answering machine to say he quit his job. He didn't tell her why."

London's breath quickened, and so did her pulse. She remembered how terrified Greta had been at the mere mention of her supervisor. Gunther Raab sounded like a shadowy and even threatening character—perhaps, London thought, a truly dangerous man.

"It was nice talking to you, Herr Poehler," she said, her voice shaking a little at what she'd just heard. "I've got to go."

Sir Reggie hopped off her lap as she got up from her chair.

"Fraulein Rose, wait!" Poehler said, sounding suddenly worried. "You seem very agitated."

"Oh, I'm fine, Herr Poehler," she said. "Enjoy the rest of your day in Salzburg. I'm sure you'll give a great performance in Bonn."

Poehler peered at her with concern.

"Just tell me you're not going to do something rash."

"Don't worry," London said.

As she and Reggie left the auditorium and continued out of the building, London found herself thinking …

Herr Poehler really is a keen observer of people.

And maybe, she realized, he was right to worry that she was about to do something rash.

CHAPTER THIRTY FOUR

I hope I know what I'm getting myself into, London thought as she and Sir Reggie crossed the paved terrace in front of the House for Mozart.

Then she sighed at the very thought.

Of course she didn't know what she was getting into. She really had no idea. And the truth was, she was feeling more nervous and apprehensive by the moment.

With Sir Reggie trotting along beside her, London took out her cell phone and brought up a map of Salzburg. She quickly found the place where Poehler had said Gunther Raab lived, on the corner of Prinzenstrasse and Nibelungenstrasse. It didn't look very far away—a ten-minute walk at most.

As she headed in that direction, she found herself remembering what Mr. Lapham had said to her during their last phone conversation.

"I want no more of your amateur sleuthing, do you hear?"

And here she was, disobeying her boss's direct order.

Sorry, Mr. Lapham.

I can't seem to help it.

She figured the least she could do was exercise a little common sense. She really ought to alert *Polizeidirektor* Tanneberger of what she was up to. She found the card Tanneberger had given her earlier and punched in his number on her cell phone. She was immediately transferred to his answering service. She spoke at the sound of the recorded beep.

"Herr Tanneberger, I thought I should tell you ..."

She paused and asked herself—just what *did* she think she should tell him?

The truth, of course, she thought.

"I'm ashore right now," she said. "I've been talking to a couple of people about Olaf Moritz's murder. Perhaps you've checked him out already, but I think the theater's maintenance chief, Gunther Raab, may have had a motive to kill Herr Moritz. I thought I'd ask him some questions, and I'm on my way to his apartment right now.

She paused, wondering what else she should tell the *Polizeidirektor.* She couldn't think of anything.

"I will be in touch soon," she said, then ended the message.

As she and Sir Reggie continued on their way, London wondered just how Tanneberger was likely to react to her message. In her experiences of just the last few days, she'd learned that European law enforcement officials didn't much like it when civilians—especially foreign civilians—went off investigating on their own.

Was Tanneberger going to be furious with her?

Was she only worsening her already bad situation?

Maybe not, she thought. This morning Tanneberger had actually encouraged her to bring him any information that might clear her of suspicion. Wasn't that what she was trying to do right now?

She hoped he'd understand.

Their route took London and Sir Reggie through a pleasant residential neighborhood of upscale apartments with balconies decorated with flowers and nice patio furniture. Things got less stylish just a little farther along a narrow street, where the apartment buildings were simpler and less well-kept.

Finally she found the one she was looking for—a plain, blue, four-story apartment building that really could have used a new coat of paint.

Now what? she wondered, walking up the front stoop.

She scanned the list of residents posted beside the door and found Raab's name and apartment number. But when she tried the front door, she found that it was locked. Naturally, she realized, the entrance was locked for security. But would Raab buzz her in if she rang for him?

And if so, did she really want to meet him?

That's what I'm here for, she reminded herself.

She gathered her courage and pushed the button for his room and heard a gruff voice.

"*Hallo?*"

"Herr Raab?" London said in German.

"Who's asking?"

"My name is London Rose."

"What are you selling?"

"I'm not selling anything."

"You sound American."

"I am American. I just want to talk to you about ..."

196

London hesitated. If she told him the truth, maybe he'd refuse to have anything to do with her. But she couldn't think of any other approach.

"I want to talk to you about what happened to Olaf Moritz," she said.

"I told the police everything I know. What business is it of yours?"

"I found his body," London said.

A silence fell.

"Come on in," the voice said.

London swallowed hard. She almost wished she hadn't said that. It would have given her an excuse to just go away and try to forget about him.

Then came a loud buzz, and London was able to open the door. She and Sir Reggie walked into the building, where a narrow worn stairway awaited them.

She said to Sir Reggie, "Judging from his apartment number, he must be on the top floor. There's no elevator. Are you ready for a tough climb?"

Sir Reggie let out an affirmative yap.

But after a single flight, she saw that the little animal was having some trouble leaping from one tall step to the next.

London stopped and looked down at him.

"Maybe it's just as well," she said. "I don't want to get you into any trouble. You should wait right here until I come back."

Sir Reggie growled in protest. Obviously he was going to try to follow her, no matter how difficult the climb might be.

"OK, come on," London said, picking him up. "But if anything goes wrong, don't try to do anything heroic. Remember what happened last time I got you into a jam? You almost drowned. Keep calm and stay safe."

Carrying her little dog, she climbed the steep stairs all the way up to the fourth floor. London felt a bit breathless when they arrived at the last landing. But she suspected it was more from fear than the climb itself.

London found the right apartment. She hesitated anxiously, then knocked on the door.

A voice called out, "Come on in, it's unlocked."

London opened the door and carried Sir Reggie inside. She found herself in a cluttered one-room apartment with tattered furniture, a pile of dirty dishes in the kitchen area, and a single bed against a wall.

A tall pot-bellied middle-aged man wearing jeans and a torn T-shirt was packing a suitcase on the bed. He had massive biceps covered with tattoos. He stopped packing and turned toward London.

"You didn't tell me you had a dog," he said.

"I'm sorry. He can wait in the hallway."

"No, I like dogs. Have a seat."

Judging from the snarl in his voice and the nervous way he eyed Sir Reggie, London suspected that he really couldn't stand dogs. He just didn't want to seem weak by admitting that, especially to a woman. London took a seat beside the Formica-topped kitchen table. Reggie sat down in her lap.

London gestured toward the suitcase.

"Are you taking a trip somewhere?" she asked.

"Yes, I'm taking a well-earned vacation. Actually, I quit my job. I should have quit long ago. I figure I'll do a bit of traveling to celebrate my freedom before I get tied down with another job."

Raab sat down on the edge of the bed.

"So you found Olaf's body, huh?" he said.

"Yes," London said.

"And you want to talk with me about it."

"That's right."

"Well, that's fine with me, I suppose. I didn't get to see at his corpse. How did he look?"

London was startled.

"What do you mean, how did he look?" she asked.

"I mean when you found him. Did he look like he died instantly? Or did he look like he suffered?"

London was unnerved by the blunt morbidity of the question. She suppressed a shudder as she flashed back to the moment when she'd seen those unmoving, staring eyes in the darkened theater.

"I don't know," she said.

It was the truth, of course. She had no idea whether Olaf's death had been instantaneous or lingering. But Raab scoffed as if he didn't believe her.

"You don't know, do you?" he said. "Well, my guess is he didn't die right away, falling from the top balcony like that onto a row of theater seats. It probably took a few minutes. I'll bet he was in a lot of pain."

198

London was shocked by the sadistic glee in the large man's voice. She wished she could just walk out and leave right now. But she reminded herself of why she'd come here.

"Did you know Olaf personally, Herr Raab?" she asked.

"Yes, everybody knew Olaf. Good old Olaf. Everybody liked Olaf except me. I hated him. I was smart to hate him. I don't know why everybody else didn't hate him too. He was a blowhard, a loser, and a phony."

London felt a chill at the sheer animosity in his voice.

"What do you mean?" she asked.

"What do you *think* I mean? He acted superior to everybody, like he knew more than anybody else about everything there was to know. The whole reason he worked as a tour guide was so he could show off to people. He wasn't so smart, not really."

He let out a grim chuckle.

"He fancied himself a musician, thought he could really play the piano. I heard him play, I didn't think he was so good. Oh, and he thought he was going to be a great composer, like Beethoven or Mozart. Or at least he thought so until the day before yesterday."

"What happened then?" London asked.

"He showed a piece he wrote to Wolfram Poehler, that pianist everybody's talking about these days. I was backstage mopping the floor at the time. Poehler was trying to practice for his recital, and Olaf was making a nuisance of himself, trying to hand him the score, begging him to play just a few bars of it."

Raab laughed and added, "Poehler took one look at the piece and pushed it back at Olaf. Olaf tried to hand it to him again, and he pushed it away again. Olaf tried one more time, and Poehler wadded up the score and threw it on the floor. Olaf looked like someone had just killed his mother. He picked up the score and left."

London tried to make sense of what she was hearing.

This wasn't the way Wolfram Poehler had described the incident to her at all.

Raab is lying, she thought. *But why?*

Raab continued, "Well, that sure put Olaf in his place. He knew once and for all he'd never be any good as a composer. I even heard him say so. 'Now I know,' he muttered on his way out of the theater."

Raab shrugged and sneered.

"Anyway, I guess someone else must have hated him too. Enough to kill him. It wasn't me, though. I wasn't there. I was drinking lager with some of my chums at the Hopla Bar, just a short way from the theater. The cops checked out my alibi and my chums vouched for me. I'm not a suspect. But I'd like to shake the hand of whoever killed that useless guy."

So the police don't suspect him, London thought.

If so, she surely had no reason to suspect him either. But he was such a harsh man, she couldn't help dreading his very presence.

She found herself thinking about what Greta had told her about why Raab had suddenly left work that afternoon.

"He said ... he didn't feel well. He just wanted to go home."

She'd thought Greta was lying at the time, and now she was almost sure of it.

London squinted curiously at Raab.

"So you were at a bar drinking with friends when Olaf was killed," London observed cautiously.

"That's right."

"You left the theater earlier than usual to go there."

"That's right, I clocked out early."

"Why did you leave when you did?"

Raab threw his head back and laughed.

"Well, if you must know, I had a fight with my girlfriend."

His girlfriend! London thought.

"Do you mean Greta Mayr?" she said.

"Yes, that's who I mean. *Former* girlfriend, I should say. I broke up with her right then and there. She didn't take it well."

London wasn't sure whether he was lying outright or was engaged in some elaborate feat of self-deception. All she knew for sure was that Greta was not his "girlfriend"—she never had been and never would be.

"Why did you break up with her?" London asked.

"Because she's a flirt, that's why," Raab said bitterly. "She's too good-looking for her own good, and men are always after her, and she *likes* it. She likes the way men look at her, she likes the attention. She didn't appreciate the good thing she had with me. I'd told her time and time again the flirting had to stop, but she wouldn't listen. I finally had enough of it. I told her it was over."

London almost felt dizzy from the palpable lies Raab was telling. Of course he hadn't broken up with Greta. They'd never been a couple to begin with. But London felt sure of one thing—they really had gotten into an argument before he left the theater that day. And London also felt sure she knew what that argument was about.

"You were jealous of Olaf," she said.

The sneer faded from Raab's lips, and his eyes darkened.

"You don't know what you're talking about," he said.

London's fear was rising. It was a struggle to keep herself from running away.

Focus, she told herself. *Don't lose your nerve.*

"I think I do," she said. "Greta told you that Olaf was attracted to her, and she was attracted to him, and she said she wanted you to leave both of them alone so they could be together. How did that make you feel?"

London was stunned by the sudden roar that erupted from Olaf's throat.

He lunged from the bed and knocked her backward in her chair onto the floor. Sir Reggie yelped as he was thrown out of her lap.

London scrambled to get to her feet, her fear spreading through every fiber of her body, but one enormous powerful hand gripped her throat and shoved her back down.

"You sure do ask a lot of questions," Gunther Raab snarled.

CHAPTER THIRTY FIVE

London tried to scream, but she couldn't even breathe. She also couldn't move. The man holding her down was much too big and strong for her to escape his grip.

Then Raab let out a scream of pain, and the pressure on London's throat was gone. Still lying on her back amid what was left of the chair where she'd been sitting, she pulled herself up onto her elbows to see what was happening.

Raab was scrambling to his feet, holding one hand to his mouth. She was startled to see that the hand was bleeding.

She became aware of furious, ferocious barking and realized that her tough little Yorkshire Terrier had bitten her attacker, puncturing a pinky finger with his sharp teeth.

"Sir Reggie, no," London cried, terrified that at any moment the angry man would harm her little dog. But to her amazement, Raab backed away and climbed up on a chair, looking utterly terrified.

As Sir Reggie bounced around him barking and growling and snarling, London remembered sensing when she'd gotten here that Raab didn't much like dogs. Now she could see that he *really* didn't like dogs. Not even little ones.

"Get him away from me!" Raab shouted. "Get him away from me!"

London didn't feel inclined to do anything of the kind. The man seemed truly terrified, and the situation was vastly better than when Raab still had his hand around her throat.

But how long could Sir Reggie keep him at bay?

Suddenly there came a pounding on the door.

"Police!" called a familiar voice. "Open this door!"

Even Raab looked relieved to hear that voice.

"Help! Police! I'm being attacked!"

London rolled over and struggled to her feet, then staggered toward the door and opened it. *Polizeidirektor* Tanneberger strode inside, followed by two police officers.

Raab yelled at Tanneberger, "Help me! Get this animal away from me!"

Tanneberger crossed his arms and glared at the scene. He didn't even crack a smile, although London was sure she saw him catch his breath as if to contain his amusement. Then the *Polizeidirektor* turned and looked sternly at London.

"*Fraulein,* would you be so kind as to save this gentleman from this … vicious animal?" he said dryly.

London picked up the leash that had fallen to the floor and was now trailing behind Reggie.

"That's enough, Sir Reggie," she said, tugging on the leash. "He can't hurt me now."

With one last warning grumble, the dog fell silent and joined her at her side, looking quite happy with himself.

Tanneberger inspected the broken chair where London had been sitting when she had been attacked.

"Perhaps someone would like to tell me what's going on here," he demanded.

Raab climbed down off his chair and sat there panting.

"This woman burst into my apartment just now," he said, pointing at London. "She sicced her dog on me for no good reason at all. It actually bit me!"

He held out the wounded pinkie, which had stopped bleeding.

"Look what this animal did to me!" he said.

"So I see," Tanneberger said. "So this whole incident is the *fraulein's* fault?"

"Absolutely," Raab said.

"Why do I find that a bit hard to believe?" Tanneberger asked.

London found it easier to talk now.

"You know why I came here, sir," she said to Tanneberger. "I left you a message about it. Herr Raab let me into the apartment, and I asked him some questions, then suddenly he grabbed me by the throat and threw me and this chair to the floor. I thought he was going to strangle me."

London opened her collar to show Tanneberger the fresh red marks Raab had left on her neck. Tanneberger pulled out his cell phone and snapped some pictures of the marks, and then some of the broken chair and the open suitcase on the bed.

"Placed this man under arrest," he said to his colleagues.

Gunther Raab growled and struggled as the two policemen put him in handcuffs. London was afraid he might break away from them and escape down the stairs. But between the two of them, the officers had enough strength to subdue him, and they managed to lead him out of the apartment.

Tanneberger stood staring at London silently for a moment.

He's not happy with me, she realized.

"I suppose I owe you some kind of an explanation," she said.

"Oh, I think I can fill in a few of the facts," Tanneberger said, still without a trace of a smile. "As I believe you proved back in Gyor, you're really quite out of your mind. You have no idea how to just tend to your own business, and you have an almost uncanny way of getting yourself into trouble. Am I correct so far?"

"I'm afraid so," London said, looking sheepishly at the floor.

Tanneberger began to pace a little.

He continued, "Your ill-advised little investigation led you to believe that Gunther Raab killed Olaf Moritz. As it happens, my colleagues and I were verging on the same conclusion ourselves. But we had no proof of his guilt—certainly not enough evidence to make an arrest. So I let Raab believe he'd been cleared of suspicion to lull him into a false sense of security. I figured we could trip him up before long."

He stopped pacing and glared at her again.

"Then I received your phone message. It wasn't hard to guess what sort of danger you might be getting into. My men and I came here at once."

"I hope I didn't spoil your plans," London said.

Tanneberger let out a reluctant sigh.

"I hate to admit it, but the truth is probably quite to the contrary." He pointed to the open suitcase and continued, "It appears that Raab was more of a flight risk than we'd supposed. If you and your dog hadn't poked your snouts in where they didn't belong, he might well have slipped through our fingers before we could gather sufficient evidence to apprehend him."

He tapped on his cell phone and added, "That shouldn't be a problem now that I've got photographic evidence that he attacked you. We'll keep him in custody while we gather proof that he's the killer. I expect we'll be able to do that very shortly. Meanwhile, I need to take a statement from you concerning just what happened here."

The *Polizeidirektor* took out his cell phone to record London's statement. He kept nodding throughout her account.

"Yes, everything you say is consistent with what I'd already come to believe," he finally said. "Raab killed Olaf Moritz because he considered him a rival for Greta Mayr's affections. Hopefully we'll be able to determine soon whether the murder was premeditated or was a truly impulsive crime of passion. Meanwhile ..."

He scratched his chin as he looked at London.

"I suppose you must decide whether to press charges against Raab for attacking you. I'd much rather you didn't. The whole thing would most likely turn into an international incident, with the U.S. Embassy involved, and you'd have to stay right here in Salzburg for quite some time. I hope you don't take this the wrong way, Fraulein Rose, but ..."

He paused for a moment.

"I'd really like to see the last of you as soon as possible," he said.

Wagging his finger at Sir Reggie, Tanneberger added, "And that goes for this attack animal as well."

Sir Reggie let out an approving growl.

London couldn't help but chuckle a little.

"The feeling is absolutely mutual, sir," London said.

"Excellent," Tanneberger said.

*

Tanneberger called Captain Hays to tell him that the *Nachtmusik* was free to set sail as soon as was convenient. Then the *Landespolizeidirektor* gave London and Sir Reggie a lift back to the *Nachtmusik* in a police car.

London was feeling good as she and Sir Reggie walked across the barge and up the gangway to the ship. Despite the red marks on her neck, she hadn't really been injured, and now the man who had killed Olaf Moritz was in police custody. Best of all, the tour could continue on its way.

When she entered the reception area, she was glad to see three familiar faces—Cyrus Bannister, Amy Blassingame, and Bob Turner.

"I've got good news," she told them eagerly. "The murderer has been caught. We can leave for Regensburg as soon as the boat is ready and everybody is aboard."

"So we've heard," Cyrus said.

"The captain announced it just now," Amy added.

London wondered why all their expressions looked so ominous.

205

"We've got some news too," Bob said to London. "We've found out who has been stealing the musician dolls."

London gasped aloud.

"Who is it?" she asked.

For a moment Bob, Amy, and Cyrus all just stared at her.

"It's you," Bob finally said.

CHAPTER THIRTY SIX

London gaped back and forth between Bob Turner and Amy Blassingame. They both looked perfectly serious. Then she focused on Cyrus Bannister. As usual, he appeared to be darkly amused by the situation.

Finally, she couldn't help but laugh.

"This is a joke, right?" she sputtered.

Staring at London with a reproachful expression, Amy said, "If it is, it's not a very funny one."

"Well, I'd like to know how you came to such a ridiculous conclusion," London said.

"I wish it were ridiculous," Amy said. "You might have even gotten away with it if it weren't for our shrewd security man here. I'm certainly glad Mr. Lapham decided to bring him aboard. It was very wise of him."

Bob chuckled with satisfaction.

"It's like I told you before, missy—nobody can pull the wool over my eyes."

Tapping his forehead he added, "Like a steel trap, I tell you."

London was starting to feel impatient and annoyed.

"I think somebody had better explain to me what this is all about," she said.

"You're the one who should do the explaining," Amy said. "Honestly, London, I'd thought better of you."

London looked straight at Bob and said, "I really want to know how you got this crazy idea."

Bob jabbed his finger at her.

"Are you going to deny that you went to the Weavers' stateroom this morning?"

What's that got to do with anything? London wondered.

"As a matter of fact, I did," London said. "Steve and Carol had a small musical emergency. It was kind of comical, really. The sound system in the room got stuck playing heavy metal. I got it to play Baroque music again, the way they wanted."

Bob nodded and said, "And are you going to deny that you were the only person in that room today aside from the Weavers?"

London struggled for a moment to make sense of his question.

"How could I even *know* whether I was the only person in their room?" she asked. "It's not like I've been keeping watch over who comes and goes there."

Bob chuckled again.

"A clever answer," he said. "A very clever answer. But Steve and Carol Weaver told me the truth—that you were the only other person in their room today. Nobody even from the cleaning crew has been in there."

"Steve and Carol told you …?" London began.

"They came to me to report the theft of one of their musician dolls," Bob said.

"The little clarinetist," Amy added.

"And the first thing I asked was who else had been in their room," Bob said. "Mind you, missy, I've had my eyes on you for some time. Everything about your behavior suggests criminal tendencies—for example, the way you avoid making eye contact with me."

London glared at her own reflection in his glasses.

"How can anybody make eye contact with you as long as you're wearing those mirrors?" she asked.

"Another clever answer," Bob replied.

London's mouth dropped open.

"So you think I stole the doll?" she asked incredulously, still trying to get her head around what was happening.

"Mr. Turner here certainly thinks so," Cyrus Bannister said with a wry grin.

A small group of passengers was starting to cluster around, curious about the increasingly agitated discussion.

Great, London thought. *As if I didn't already have trust issues with the passengers.*

"Well, of course I *didn't* steal anything," London said. "All I did was fix their music selection. I didn't bother to even to take a look around their room. I didn't notice where they were keeping their musician dolls. I didn't even see them."

Bob drew himself up proudly.

"You can't escape pure deductive logic, missy," he said. "I've worked the truth out with the sort of reasoning that eludes people who

208

aren't deeply experienced in the investigative arts. You must have stolen the object in question. Otherwise, Steve or Carol must have stolen it themselves. And since they own it themselves, that's perfectly impossible."

The group of listeners murmured as if impressed by Bob's reasoning.

London herself wasn't impressed by it at all.

For his part, Bob was obviously basking in having an audience to play to.

Cyrus Bannister seemed to be delighted by the conflict.

"It's like the great Sherlock Holmes said," Bannister told them. "'When you have eliminated the impossible, whatever remains, however improbable, must be the truth.'"

Bob nodded firmly.

"That Sherlock Holmes was one smart guy," he said.

London glared at Cyrus. She was sure he didn't care who had or hadn't stolen the dolls. He was just here for his own entertainment. London felt like telling him to go away and mind his own business.

Bob continued, "However, I haven't quite wrapped up this 'Case of the Missing Musicians' just yet. I have yet to achieve the *pièce de résistance,* the *coup de grâce.* I have yet to produce the smoking gun itself."

"You mean the stolen objects," London said.

"That's right."

"Well, good luck finding them," London said. "I sure don't have any idea where to look. What are you planning to do, search me right here and now?"

Bob wagged his finger at her.

"A clever suggestion," he said. "Never let it be said that I underestimated your cunning. You're way too smart to be carrying those stolen goods around on your person. No, I've got a pretty good idea where you're keeping those dolls—at least a *general* idea."

It took a couple of seconds for Bob's meaning to sink in.

"You think they're hidden in my room?" she said.

Bob nodded.

"You don't plan on searching ..." London began.

"Why not?" Amy interrupted her. "If you didn't steal anything, you don't have anything to hide. And you didn't mind searching ..."

"Someone else's room," London said, finishing her thought. She didn't want Amy to blurt out Letitia's name in front of the group. And she didn't want to describe Bob's determination to search Letitia's room with or without her approval, or that she'd taken part in the search in order to try to keep things from getting out of control.

Now she felt the suspicious gaze of everybody around her—all except for Cyrus Bannister, who still just seemed amused at watching this ridiculous scene unfold.

London struggled to decide what to do now.

She could certainly refuse to allow Amy and Bob into her room.

But then she'd be stuck with a cloud of suspicion hanging over her, maybe for the rest of the voyage.

Then another thought crossed her mind.

I almost got strangled a little while ago.

It certainly made this problem seem pretty trivial, even if it included a search of her stateroom.

Stifling a sigh of annoyance, she said, "OK, come on down to my room. Just try not to make too much of a mess."

Leaving the gawking spectators behind, London, Sir Reggie, Amy, Bob, and Cyrus Bannister rode the elevator down to the Allegro deck. They all headed straight to London's room and went inside.

"Let me show you around," London said, hoping to control things by leading the search herself.

She went over to her closet and opened it.

"You don't see anything suspicious in here, do you?" she said.

Amy looked inside the closet skeptically.

"Maybe we should look through all the pockets. And inside the shoes."

"Oh, Amy," London said, rolling her eyes.

Suddenly she heard Bob's voice.

"Hel-lllo-o-o. What have we here?"

London and Amy turned and saw that Bob was crouching beside the bed. He stood up, triumphantly holding the missing clarinetist in one hand.

London gasped aloud. She couldn't believe her eyes. How could she explain what she was seeing? Had Bob been carrying the doll around himself? Had he stuck it under her bed to frame her?

That doesn't make any sense.

None of this makes any sense.

Sir Reggie ran up beside Bob and looked at the doll and let out an

210

enthusiastic yap.

The little dog plunged under the bed and came out with the missing conductor doll in his mouth. He put it down neatly in front of Bob.

Then Sir Reggie disappeared under the bed again and came out with the missing drummer. He set it down next to the conductor.

Then he turned to Bob, wagging his tail. Bob looked utterly confounded.

Before London could make any sense of what was going on, she heard a bellow of laughter. She turned and saw that the normally taciturn Cyrus Bannister was giving himself over to convulsive merriment.

"Can't you see what he's doing?" Cyrus roared. "He's arranging a little musical ensemble."

Cyrus stepped over to Bob and took the clarinetist out of his hand. He placed it on the floor, in line with the other musicians.

Sir Reggie wagged his tail with delight and crouched down near the dolls.

"There's your so-called thief," Cyrus laughed, pointing to Sir Reggie.

"I—I don't understand," Bob stammered.

But everything was beginning to make sense to London. The first stolen doll had been taken from Kirby Oswinkle's stateroom. She and Sir Reggie had been in there when Oswinkle complained about his thermostat. The second one had been taken from the Amadeus Lounge, where Sir Reggie had had ready access to them. And of course, he'd been with her when she'd gone to the Weavers' stateroom this morning. And Sir Reggie had left that stateroom before she did, apparently with the little doll in his mouth.

"You took them all," London said to her dog in dismay.

Bob looked bewildered.

"My K-9 partner?" Bob said. "A kleptomaniac?"

"Oh, hardly that," Cyrus said, still laughing. "Just an exceptionally smart little animal—smarter than present company, apparently, maybe even myself included. Smart enough to get bored easily. The poor little guy could really use some toys to play with."

London stared at Cyrus. She remembered that one of the first things he'd told her about himself was that he knew a lot about dogs.

"Toys," she whispered guiltily.

There had been no toys among the doggie supplies that his previous

211

owner had kept. During the short time Sir Reggie had been in her care, London hadn't thought of buying any. For that matter, when had she had any time to do any such shopping?

Cyrus was still laughing when he left London's stateroom. Amy gathered up the dolls to return them to their owners and left as well. Bob followed them out, scratching his head in perplexity, leaving London and Sir Reggie alone.

London sat down on the bed, and Sir Reggie jumped up next to her.

"I'm sorry, pal," she said, petting him. "I should have known you were bored. But wasn't helping me catch thieves and murderers exciting enough for you?"

Sir Reggie rolled over on his back so London could pet his stomach.

"You can't just go around taking things that don't belong to you. Do you understand?"

Sir Reggie let out a little whimper.

At that moment London's phone buzzed. Captain Hays was calling her.

"Hello there, London Rose. The *Polizeidirektor* called to say the murderer is in custody, and I made an announcement to that effect. He said that you helped in the apprehension of the culprit. But then he added something odd. 'See to it that she doesn't do anything like this again.' What did he mean by that?"

London chuckled.

"I guess you could say that Herr Tanneberger and I parted on ... well, ambivalent terms."

"Be that as it may, it's excellent news. The *Nachtmusik* can set sail as soon as all passengers are aboard and accounted for. A fair number of them are still out and around exploring Salzburg, but I'm sure they'll return shortly. We'll be on our way in a couple of hours or so. As always, thank you for helping to resolve this unfortunate business."

"I'm always glad to do whatever I can," London said.

As soon as they ended the call, Sir Reggie bounced off the bed and headed toward the doggie door.

"Sir Reggie ..." London called out to him.

He turned toward her expectantly.

"Don't steal anything, OK?" she said.

He yapped—and was it London's imagination, or did he nod his head?

As he darted out through the doggie door, London let out a long overdue sigh. She felt worn out from a long, difficult day, but even so ...

I've got an errand to run.

CHAPTER THIRTY SEVEN

Although there wasn't much time to spare before the *Nachtmusik* would be leaving Salzburg, London knew she needed to make one more trip into town.

She was feeling guilty over the issue of dog toys.

Why, she wondered, weren't there any dog toys among all the things that Mrs. Klimowski had for him?

When London collected Sir Reggie's things from the previous owner's room, she'd found several leashes and collars, some set with stones that she thought might be real jewels. There were dog-sized sweaters and jackets. There were little bows that Sir Reggie wouldn't need now, since his hair was clipped into a comfortable short style. There was even a very welcome doggie-potty contraption that was still put to good use.

But there had been no toys. The only reason that London could think of for that omission was that the woman had considered Sir Reginald a toy himself, rather than a living creature. London had seldom owned pets of any kind since her family had moved around so much when she was a child, but she was embarrassed that she hadn't thought of the need for toys for her new companion.

The toys didn't have to be dog toys, she decided. They just had to be something a dog would like to play with. She remembered that some of the street stalls along the route to the House for Mozart carried children's toys. Surely something like that would do.

As London headed out of her stateroom, she took out her cell phone and typed another text message to Amy telling her she'd be leaving the boat for just a short while.

"Double-check to be sure is everyone comes aboard," she wrote.

As London left the ship and walked the now-familiar Salzburg streets between the dock and the House for Mozart, the events of this strange day haunted her mind. Although the issue over the stolen dolls had been alarming, it was trivial compared to the earlier attack from the vicious Gunther Raab.

She replayed that awful moment in her mind. She hadn't actually

214

accused Raab of the murder. She had only suggested that Greta had told him the truth about the mutual action between herself and Olaf.

"How did that make you feel?" she'd asked him.

That simple question seemed to have triggered his uncontrollable rage. Clearly, the man was insanely jealous and prone to violence— probably especially toward women, which was why Greta not only rejected him but was afraid of him.

Was he really trying to kill me? she wondered.

All London knew for sure was that she was grateful to both Sir Reggie and *Polizeidirektor* Tanneberger for coming to her aid.

When she arrived at the area with the stalls and shops, she was surprised to see a familiar figure perusing a stall with small cheap souvenir toys on display.

"Hello, Bob," she said. "I'm surprised to find you here."

The ship's security man turned toward her, looking a bit surprised himself.

"Hey, London. How're you doing?"

"I'm all right. We're setting sail for Regensburg shortly, you know. You'd better get back to the boat soon."

"Oh, I won't be ashore for long," Bob replied.

He looked down and shuffled his feet awkwardly.

"I guess I owe you an apology," he said.

London almost blurted that he had nothing to be sorry for.

But of course he did, and she thought that an apology would probably do both of them good.

Bob continued, "I misjudged you, thinking you stole those dolls. The truth is, I don't know how I got things so wrong. It all seemed so clear at the time. I hope my razor-sharp detective prowess isn't declining with age."

Then to London's amazement, he took off those mirrored sunglasses and looked straight at her. The expression in his dark brown eyes was quite sincere.

Bob held out a hand. "Anyway, I'm sorry."

London was truly touched now. Bob was showing a side of his personality that she hadn't seen before.

Maybe I could even get to like this guy, she thought.

"Apology accepted," London said, shaking his hand. "But what are you doing ashore?"

Bob put the mirrors back into place and fingered some of the

215

merchandise.

"I thought I'd better look for some toys for my K-9 friend. I misjudged him too, at least for a moment there. He's no klepto, he's just been bored, and we can't have that."

London smiled as she realized she and Bob were here on the same errand.

He continued, "Back on the ship I asked a couple of passengers where I might go looking around to find something for a dog to play with, and they suggested these stalls along here."

He picked up a rubber ball with *Willkommen in Salzburg* stamped on it.

"Dogs like to play with balls, don't they?" he said.

"So I hear," London agreed. "I'm sure that's exactly the sort of thing Sir Reggie needs."

"I'll buy it, then," Bob said eagerly. "I'll buy two of them."

"That's kind of you," London told him.

"Thanks. So what are *you* doing ashore?"

"As it happens, I came looking for dog toys too."

"Well, you needn't trouble yourself, since I'm taking care of that. I figure I'll walk around here just a little while and see if anything else jumps out at me. See you back at the boat."

As Bob paid for his purchase, London thought she would take his advice and just go back to the *Nachtmusik*. But when she took a last glance around the historic area, her eyes fell on the House for Mozart, just on the other side of the plaza where they were shopping.

She remembered what Wolfram Poehler had said to her earlier.

"I expect to spend a few more hours today haunting this place—or rather letting it haunt me, work its magic on me."

The gifted pianist could still be there, and she felt an urge to pay him one last quick visit.

"I'll leave you to your shopping," London said to Bob. "I think I'll stop by the House for Mozart for a few minutes."

"Enjoy yourself," Bob said, peering at some more toys.

As she walked away, he wagged his finger at her sternly and added, "Just make sure you're back aboard soon."

"You too," London replied, heading toward the theater.

Although it seemed perfectly irrelevant, she found herself remembering what Raab had said about the way Wolfram Poehler had rejected poor Olaf's sonata. According to Raab, Poehler had pushed the manuscript away a couple of times, then he wadded it up and threw it away.

But Poehler had described the moment very differently.

"I sat here at this piano and sight read his whole sonata, played all four movements for him."

The two stories didn't jibe at all. Either Raab or Poehler wasn't telling the truth. And London had little doubt that it was Raab who was lying.

But why?

She crossed the plaza and went through the theater's sparkling lobby. When she reached the auditorium and opened a door, she heard a familiar passage of Beethoven's *Hammerklavier* sonata being played.

He's still here, she thought hopefully.

But when she walked on into the dimly lit auditorium, she was surprised to see that the stage was not only dark but also empty. The grand piano was there, but nobody was playing it, and the keyboard cover was closed.

What on earth ... ? London wondered.

Now that she listened more closely, she realized that the music was soft and muffled and wafting. It seemed to be coming from both nowhere and everywhere.

She called out in German, "Is anybody here?"

London was almost startled out of her skin by a noisy, echoing click and a sudden burst of light. A single brilliant spotlight had been switched on to illuminate the piano, making it look much as it would look during a performance.

Then she heard a cheerful voice calling out from some unknown location.

"London Rose! What a surprise! I hadn't expected to see you again!"

For a moment London was baffled. Then she realized that the curtains were pulled open wider than usual, revealing some sort of structures on each side of the stage. She could see a shadowy figure peering down at her from high up on one of them.

"Herr Poehler?" she asked, craning her neck as she tried to see him better.

"Yes, I'm up here," he said in a welcoming voice. "Come on up and join me. You'll love the view."

Then he added with a chuckle, "Unless you're afraid of heights."

217

"I'm certainly not," London said with a laugh.

She climbed onto the stage and got a better look at the towering fire-escape-like structures. Each level appeared to be some sort of complex control booth without walls.

Poehler was perched on the uppermost level of the tower on London's right.

A ladder fastened against a wall extended up through the platforms. For a moment, London hesitated. While she wasn't afraid of heights, she wasn't used to sheer, steep climbs like this, especially in such dim light. But she summoned up her courage and began to climb.

This could be very interesting, she told herself. *A new experience.*

But as she climbed, she heard the final movement of Beethoven's *Hammerklavier* sonata begin playing. For some reason, the movement's tentative opening notes filled her with foreboding.

CHAPTER THIRTY EIGHT

When London reached the fourth level of the tower, she found Wolfram Poehler standing there, leaning against a railing and looking down at the stage. On the platform right beside him, a portable music player was still playing the final movement of the *Hammerklavier*, now a complex fugue. An open electrical box indicated what Poehler had used to shine the bright spotlight on the piano.

He smiled and pointed below.

"What did I tell you about the view?" he said.

London walked to the edge of the platform and stood beside him, leaning on the railing. Far below them, the grand piano looked surprisingly small as it stood pinned under the piercing beam of light. The whole theater seemed almost unreal, like some magically detailed and vivid model.

"I love it," London said in a hushed voice.

"I do too," Poehler said. "Mind you, the rest of the theater is wonderful too. I can spend hours exploring every nook and cranny of such a place. But standing up here gives me … a special kind of perspective, I guess."

He let out a self-effacing laugh.

"You know, being an up-and-coming classical music star can go to one's head. Critics rave, audiences give you standing ovations, and you start to get some pretty grandiose ideas about yourself. But when I look down at that piano, I can imagine seeing myself sitting there, and I look so small, so insignificant. It keeps me …"

He paused for a moment, then laughed again.

"I'm embarrassed to say it keeps me humble."

"I'm sure that's a good thing," London said.

"Oh, yes. It's very good. I even think it makes me a better musician."

London and Poehler stood looking wordlessly over the theater together as the recording of Beethoven's mighty sonata came to an end. Then the theater fell eerily silent.

"I haven't left this theater since I last saw you," Poehler finally

219

said. "When I go through one of my solitary spells, I'm afraid I lose touch with everyday life. Maybe you could tell me what's been going on since we saw each other last."

London took a long, slow breath.

Where do I begin? she wondered.

She figured she might as well get right to the point.

"The killer has been caught," she told him.

Poehler looked surprised.

"I'm so glad to hear that," he said. "Who was it?"

"Your suspicion of Gunther Raab turned out to be correct."

"So he killed poor Olaf out of jealousy over Greta," Poehler said with a sigh.

"That's right."

"How tragic. Can you tell me how it happened?"

London's mind boggled at the prospect of explaining the whole affair, especially the terrifying part she had played in Raab's capture.

"I guess … I'd rather not go into that, if you don't mind," she said.

"Of course," Poehler replied.

Another silence fell between them, and unbidden questions began to bubble up in London's brain—questions that she suspected only Wolfram Poehler could answer.

"Herr Poehler …"

"Call me Wolfram, please."

"Wolfram, would you tell me again about what happened when Olaf tried to get you interested in his sonata?"

Wolfram shrugged.

"Well, there's not much to tell. As I said before, I sight read all four movements. I wish I could say I liked the piece. Unfortunately, it just wasn't very good. I tried to be honest about it without being too harsh."

London felt a flutter of mounting anxiety.

"Gunther Raab told me …" she began.

She hesitated. Did she really want to get into all this? Did it even matter?

Deep in her gut, London felt that it *did* matter, even if she didn't understand why.

"Gunther Raab told me he was there when it happened."

She heard Wolfram breathe in sharply.

"He told you that, did he?" Wolfram said, his voice dropping a little. "What did he say happened?"

"That Olaf came up to you when you were practicing here in the auditorium and tried to hand you the score. He said you pushed it away twice, and that you finally wadded it up and threw it on the floor. What I can't understand is …"

London swallowed hard.

"Why would Gunther say such a thing?" she asked.

Wolfram turned toward London and locked eyes with her.

"What else did Gunther tell you?" Wolfram asked.

London's jaw clenched anxiously. She suddenly wished she hadn't broached the subject.

"Nothing," she said.

But she knew that her lie didn't sound convincing.

"What else did he say?" Wolfram demanded again.

London took a deep breath.

"He said he heard Olaf mutter something as he walked out of the theater. 'Now I know,' Olaf said."

Wolfram's eyes narrowed. He leaned toward London, his expression dark and grim.

"Did Gunther tell any of this to the police?" he asked.

London couldn't help but gasp. The question took her completely off guard.

"I have no idea what he's told the police."

This was, of course, absolutely true. But Wolfram took one step closer to her, and she tried to back away. The platform suddenly seemed much smaller than before, and much more crowded.

"My boat will be sailing soon," London said, trying to sound calmer than she felt. "I'd better go."

But Wolfram stepped between her and the ladder that led back down to the stage.

"I think you'd better tell me more," he said.

"About what?" London asked.

"About what Gunther knows. And what you know."

What do *I know?* she wondered.

"I'd really better go," she said again.

But Wolfram loomed more threateningly than before, and he showed no sign that he would let her pass. London's skin tingled at the thought of trying to lunge past him and clamber back down the ladder.

If she slipped … or if he pushed …

It would be a very long fall to the stage.

Her mind clicked madly away, trying to make sense of things, trying to at least to keep the conversation going.

She found herself remembering the little impromptu performance he'd given her earlier that day—especially his performance of the jazz variations of Mozart's *Rondo alla Turca*. She remembered what he'd said when she asked him if he'd made up those variations himself.

"I heard the great Yuja Wang play them in this very auditorium," he'd said.

And then he'd added ...

"The variations ... well, they kind of stuck with me."

A realization came over London.

He learned the variations by ear.

Just by listening to Yuja Wang perform the variations, he'd been able to play them perfectly, note for note and without a score.

But why did that matter? What did this ability say about him except that he was a uniquely gifted musician with amazingly keen ears, a quick and adept mind, and dazzlingly swift and skillful fingers?

Suddenly the truth crashed over London like an ocean wave.

"You can't read music," she whispered breathlessly.

Wolfram nodded slowly.

"I couldn't let Olaf tell anybody that," he said. "And I can't let you tell anybody either."

Now London knew that she was in serious danger. She still didn't dare try to push past Wolfram to the ladder. And what if she screamed? She didn't think anyone was there to hear her.

London could barely breathe now, but she had to keep talking.

"I don't understand why it matters," she told Wolfram. "This secret of yours, I mean. Why are you hiding it? Why don't you just share the truth with the world? It sounds to me like you have a wonderful gift."

"You don't know what my life has been like," Wolfram snarled. "I grew up orphaned and poor. I escaped my last foster home when I was fourteen, and I've been making my own way in the world ever since then."

"You must have been ... very brave," London said.

"Not brave. Just cunning. I've never had the luxury of any kind of education, least of all in music. But one day when I was a teenager, I sneaked into a piano recital and listened to a true virtuoso play a Beethoven sonata—the *Appassionata*. Afterward I hung around until no one else was in the auditorium and sat down at the piano and ..."

He shrugged.

"I played the *Appassionata* note by note. It was only then that I understood my uncanny ability—and my future. I listened to hundreds of performances and recordings, strengthened my hands and arms, taught myself to play masterpiece upon masterpiece. And neither you nor anyone else is going to spoil all that for me."

"But—but if it's important, can't you learn …?" London stammered.

"To read music? To play from a score? I've tried. I can't do it. Whatever bizarre providence gave me the ability to play like that also doomed me to musical illiteracy. It's like some kind of sick, sad joke. Whenever I look at a score, all I can see are lines and dots and letters."

"Lines and dots and letters," London repeated. "That's all you saw when Olaf tried to get you to play his sonata. And then you realized that he knew your secret …"

"No one must ever know," he replied in a voice that had become raspy with fury.

"But why?" London asked.

"Don't you understand? It would ruin me. I'd be jeered and scoffed at, regarded as some kind of freakish phenomenon rather than the inspired artist I know myself to be. The great concert halls of Europe would close their doors to me. I'd be forced to perform in clubs and dives like some trained sideshow circus animal under the mocking eyes of people who know nothing about great art. I won't let that happen. I'd rather take to the streets again, like I did when I was a boy."

London felt an unexpected spasm of pity for him.

"I won't tell anybody," she said, momentarily thinking she really meant it.

"You won't?" Wolfram asked with a cynical sneer. "You really have no intention of telling the police what you know—that I killed Olaf Moritz? Somehow I find that very hard to believe."

London shuddered to realize that he was absolutely right.

There was no way she could possibly keep his secret now.

Without another word, Wolfram seized her by both wrists and shoved her backward against the railing. He had a concert pianist's powerful grip, and his hands felt like a pair of iron vises. He deftly avoided London's feet as she kicked out desperately.

She was about to be pushed right over that railing to fall helplessly to the stage far below.

But then a man's voice called out, "Hey! What's going on up there?"

Wolfram let go of London's wrists and leaped back, away from her.

She turned and looked down. The stage light was reflecting off of a pair of mirrored glasses.

"Bob!" she yelled back. "A man is trying to kill me!"

Bob yelled, "Whoever you are, buddy, I wouldn't do that if I were you. I'm the law. And you're under arrest."

It seemed to London like a rather ridiculous thing to say. After all, Bob was a retired New York cop who had no jurisdiction anywhere, let alone here in Salzburg. Nevertheless, his very arrival might have just saved her life.

She heard Bob shout, "You just hold tight now. I'm on my way up there. I'm going to fix all this."

"There's a witness," London said to Wolfram, who was standing as if frozen in horror. "You'll never get away with it."

Wolfram's eyes widened as it dawned on him that London was right. With a roar of desperation, he wheeled and started down the ladder, obviously intending to make a run for it.

London realized, *Bob's on his way up that ladder!*

She staggered over to the opening and looked down. Wolfram was descending rung after rung with animal-like speed and dexterity. And sure enough, he collided with Bob not far from the bottom. The two men fell in a heap together to the floor.

"Bob!" London screamed.

She ran back to the railing to see what was happening.

Wolfram had gotten to his feet, but then Bob tackled him to the ground with surprising agility. As Wolfram tried to get up again, Bob punched him in the jaw.

The murderous musician collapsed to the stage with a groan.

London clambered down the ladder herself as quickly as she could. By the time she got to the bottom, Bob was stooping over Wolfram, who lay moaning semiconsciously on the stage. The former cop strapped the killer's wrists behind him with his belt.

"I guess I should start carrying handcuffs again," Bob said.

Then with a laugh, he added, "I just hope my pants stay up!"

Flooded with relief, London took out her cell phone.

"I'll call the police," she said.

"Good idea," Bob said. "But there's no real rush. This guy ain't going anywhere." Then with a sheepish grin he added, "What I came over here for was to show you something. Take a look in that bag over there."

London saw a paper shopping bag lying on the floor where Bob had apparently dropped it.

She picked it up and reached inside and felt something soft and furry.

She took the object out and saw that it was a cute little teddy bear wearing a T-shirt that said "Salzburg" on it.

Bob grinned as he stood over his captive.

"I bought Sir Reggie a teddy bear!" he told her proudly.

CHAPTER THIRTY NINE

Sitting in the Amadeus lounge at a small table with Bryce Yeaton, London finally felt like she was unwinding from the strange day. Sipping on one of Elsie's superb Manhattans was certainly helping.

The *Nachtmusik* was in motion now, leaving Salzburg behind and making its way back to the Danube River to continue the tour. The police had taken Wolfram Poehler into custody, and although poor Tanneberger had been dumbfounded to learn that he'd arrested the wrong man earlier that day, he had assured London that he would sort everything out.

The *Polizeidirektor* had seemed more eager than ever to see the last of London Rose, and she felt exactly the same way about him.

That's quite enough adventure for a while, she thought.

Glancing over at Bryce, she saw that he was amused by the activity at a table across the room. He was watching Cyrus Bannister play fetch with Sir Reggie, using a ball that Bob had bought in Salzburg. The teddy bear Bob had bought was seated on a chair right next to Cyrus. Most surprising of all, the usually sardonic man was laughing and obviously enjoying himself.

Then a familiar voice from a nearby group of people caught London's attention. She smiled as she caught bits and pieces of Bob Turner's account of how he'd single-handedly caught Olaf Moritz's murderer and just generally saved the day. From the way he told it, it was thanks to him that the *Nachtmusik* was now sailing back up the narrow Salzach and Inn rivers on its way back to the Danube. Thanks to him, the *Nachtmusik*'s voyage to Regensburg wouldn't be disrupted by further delays.

"Oh, I've got brains, all right," Bob was saying. "But you see, it's more than just a matter of brains. Pure ratiocination doesn't always cut the mustard, nosirree. It's also a matter of instincts. And sometimes a crack investigator is amazed even by his own instincts. He can't quite put into words how he comes to certain conclusions. But somehow he knows what he knows ..."

Bob was fairly holding court at a large table with Captain Hays,

Letitia Hartzer, Kirby Oswinkle, Steve and Carol Weaver, and Rudy and Tina Fiore. His listeners appeared to be spellbound, understandably curious about how Bob could have tracked down a killer he'd never met in a city where he'd never set foot before, in a country where he didn't speak the language—and just in time to save London from certain death by falling.

What London could overhear was quite fanciful. Bob had just followed his hunches, he kept saying, relying on raw intuition—a veritable gut-level sixth sense that led him right to the killer.

"That sounds like kind of a tall tale Bob is spinning over there," Bryce said to London. "Have you got any idea how much of it is true?"

London let out a hearty laugh.

"What's so funny?" Bryce said.

"Never mind," London said.

"Well, aren't you going to tell me?"

"What makes you think I even know how much of it is true?" London asked with an impish smile.

Bryce shook his head with a smile of his own.

"You're really not going to tell me exactly what happened, are you?" he said.

"Not a chance," London said.

Of course London knew perfectly well that Bob hadn't been trying to solve a mystery when he'd stumbled into the House for Mozart. Fortunately, London had told him where she was going, and the only reason he'd stopped by the theater was to show her the teddy bear he'd bought for Sir Reggie.

But she couldn't really accuse Bob of lying. He obviously believed every word he was saying.

Besides, it hardly matters, she thought.

For it was true enough that Bob had saved her life. Although he hardly seemed like a vigorous man, his police training had kicked in, and he'd successfully tackled and subdued Wolfram Poehler. It suited London fine for Bob to take credit for catching the killer. She knew he'd already called Jeremy Lapham to report his version of the story, which meant that Mr. Lapham surely felt like he'd made an excellent choice in hiring the former cop to work as a "security expert."

And that was all well and good as far as London was concerned. If Mr. Lapham had any idea of what London had been up to and the dangers she'd faced today, he'd undoubtedly give her a severe scolding for continuing to play "Nancy Drew."

Turning away from Bob's performance, London saw that Amy and Emil were sitting alone at a table apart from other customers. She couldn't hear their conversation, but she could see that Emil was doing all the talking—probably holding forth about his vast knowledge of European history. Amy was listening with a rapt expression.

Is romance in the air? London wondered.

She wasn't sure how she felt about that possibility. Her recent altercations with Emil had dampened her feelings of attraction toward him, so she was far from jealous.

London's thoughts were interrupted by the arrival of a waiter she recognized from the ship's restaurant. He placed a small dish with a silver compote in front of her, then lifted the compote to reveal a sweet-smelling and aesthetically pleasing serving of apple strudel.

"Compliments of the chef," the waiter said with a wink at Bryce.

London laughed.

"How nice of the chef to think of me," she said. "Be sure to thank him for me."

The waiter said to Bryce, "The lady says thank you for the dessert."

"I'm glad she's pleased," Bryce said.

London took a taste of the strudel, which she found almost unimaginably delicious.

"It's beyond perfect," she said to Bryce.

"Thank you for saying so," Bryce replied.

London had to remind herself firmly that she had decided she wasn't going to get romantically involved with Emil or Bryce, no matter how charming either of them became.

Just then she was surprised to see a familiar face coming into the lounge. It was none other than Stanley Tedrow, the solitary mystery writer. Instead of his usual pajamas, the elderly gentleman was rather dapperly dressed in a suit coat with a bow tie, and there was now a cheerful spring in his step. London had never seen him out of his room since he'd first boarded the *Nachtmusik* back in Budapest.

"Mr. Tedrow!" London called out.

He turned and saw London, smiled, and came over to the table where she was sitting with Bryce.

London made introductions.

"Bryce, Mr. Tedrow is a novelist and my next door neighbor. Mr. Tedrow, Bryce Yeaton is our head chef and also the ship's medic."

228

The two men exchanged an amiable handshake.

"What brings you out of your stateroom?" London asked.

"I've finished my novel!" Mr. Tedrow exclaimed. "I came here to celebrate with a drink!"

"You mustn't celebrate alone," Bryce said. "Pull up a chair and sit with us. I'll buy you a drink."

Mr. Tedrow thanked him, pulled up a chair, and ordered a double bourbon.

"So," Bryce said to him, "tell us about this book you just finished."

"Oh, no, I can't do that," Mr. Tedrow said impishly. "I must keep the story secret until publication. I don't want to spoil it for my readers. I simply can't be persuaded otherwise."

"Of course, I understand perfectly," Bryce said.

Then Mr. Tedrow blurted, "Well, since you insist—my story takes place aboard a Mississippi steamboat back in the nineteenth century. When a cabin boy is murdered, suspicion falls upon a colorful group of passengers ..."

London smiled and listened with interest, and she saw that Bryce was enjoying the story as well.

I just hope he doesn't give away the ending, London thought. *Maybe things are more exciting when you don't know what's coming up next.*

But what was coming up next?

What did the near future hold in store for her?

She found herself wondering—now that the *Nachtmusik* was on its way to Germany, was there even the slightest chance that she and Mom would find each other? It hardly seemed likely. Realistically, London could only assume that Mom had intentionally gone away for good all those years ago and didn't want to be found.

I'll just have to live with that, London thought.

But could she live with it?

Where are you, Mom? she thought.

Why did you go away?

In her heart, she knew she could never let go of those questions until she saw her mother again.

NOW AVAILABLE!

CRIME (AND LAGER)
(A European Voyage Cozy Mystery—Book 3)

"When you think that life cannot get better, Blake Pierce comes up with another masterpiece of thriller and mystery! This book is full of twists, and the end brings a surprising revelation. Strongly recommended for the permanent library of any reader who enjoys a very well-written thriller."
--Books and Movie Reviews (re *Almost Gone*)

CRIME (AND LAGER) is book three in a charming new cozy mystery series by #1 bestselling author Blake Pierce, whose *Once Gone* has over 1,500 five-star reviews. The series begins with MURDER (AND BAKLAVA)—BOOK #1.

When London Rose, 33, is proposed to by her long-time boyfriend, she realizes she is facing a stable, predictable, pre-determined (and passionless) life. She freaks out and runs the other way—accepting instead a job across the Atlantic, as a tour-guide on a high-end European cruise line that travels through a country a day. London is searching for a more romantic, unscripted and exciting life that she feels sure exists out there somewhere.

London is elated: the European river towns are small, historic and charming. She gets to see a new port every night, gets to sample an endless array of new cuisine and meet a stream of interesting people. It is a traveler's dream, and it is anything but predictable.

In Book 3, CRIME (AND LAGER), the cruise takes them into Germany, into its historic towns and fabled beer festivals. But when a festival goer—a loud, arrogant local—turns up dead from drinking too much beer, suspicion falls on the touring passengers. The death is quickly ruled a murder, and London realizes her future—and that of the ship—hinges on her solving the crime.

Laugh-out-loud funny, romantic, endearing, rife with new sights, culture and food, CRIME (AND LAGER) offers a fun and suspenseful trip through the heart of Europe, anchored in an intriguing mystery that will keep you on the edge of your seat and guessing until the very last page.

Blake Pierce

Blake Pierce is the USA Today bestselling author of the RILEY PAIGE mystery series, which includes seventeen books. Blake Pierce is also the author of the MACKENZIE WHITE mystery series, comprising fourteen books; of the AVERY BLACK mystery series, comprising six books; of the KERI LOCKE mystery series, comprising five books; of the MAKING OF RILEY PAIGE mystery series, comprising six books; of the KATE WISE mystery series, comprising seven books; of the CHLOE FINE psychological suspense mystery, comprising six books; of the JESSE HUNT psychological suspense thriller series, comprising fourteen books (and counting); of the AU PAIR psychological suspense thriller series, comprising three books; of the ZOE PRIME mystery series, comprising four books (and counting); of the new ADELE SHARP mystery series, comprising six books (and counting); of the new EUROPEAN VOYAGE cozy mystery series, comprising six books (and counting); and of the new LAURA FROST FBI suspense thriller.

An avid reader and lifelong fan of the mystery and thriller genres, Blake loves to hear from you, so please feel free to visit www.blakepierceauthor.com to learn more and stay in touch.

BOOKS BY BLAKE PIERCE

LAURA FROST FBI SUSPENSE THRILLER
ALREADY GONE (Book #1)
ALREADY SEEN (Book #2)
ALREADY TRAPPED (Book #3)

EUROPEAN VOYAGE COZY MYSTERY SERIES
MURDER (AND BAKLAVA) (Book #1)
DEATH (AND APPLE STRUDEL) (Book #2)
CRIME (AND LAGER) (Book #3)
MISFORTUNE (AND GOUDA) (Book #4)
CALAMITY (AND A DANISH) (Book #5)
MAYHEM (AND HERRING) (Book #6)

ADELE SHARP MYSTERY SERIES
LEFT TO DIE (Book #1)
LEFT TO RUN (Book #2)
LEFT TO HIDE (Book #3)
LEFT TO KILL (Book #4)
LEFT TO MURDER (Book #5)
LEFT TO ENVY (Book #6)
LEFT TO LAPSE (Book #7)

THE AU PAIR SERIES
ALMOST GONE (Book#1)
ALMOST LOST (Book #2)
ALMOST DEAD (Book #3)

ZOE PRIME MYSTERY SERIES
FACE OF DEATH (Book#1)
FACE OF MURDER (Book #2)
FACE OF FEAR (Book #3)
FACE OF MADNESS (Book #4)
FACE OF FURY (Book #5)
FACE OF DARKNESS (Book #6)

A JESSIE HUNT PSYCHOLOGICAL SUSPENSE SERIES
THE PERFECT WIFE (Book #1)
THE PERFECT BLOCK (Book #2)
THE PERFECT HOUSE (Book #3)
THE PERFECT SMILE (Book #4)
THE PERFECT LIE (Book #5)
THE PERFECT LOOK (Book #6)
THE PERFECT AFFAIR (Book #7)
THE PERFECT ALIBI (Book #8)
THE PERFECT NEIGHBOR (Book #9)
THE PERFECT DISGUISE (Book #10)
THE PERFECT SECRET (Book #11)
THE PERFECT FAÇADE (Book #12)
THE PERFECT IMPRESSION (Book #13)
THE PERFECT DECEIT (Book #14)
THE PERFECT MISTRESS (Book #15)

CHLOE FINE PSYCHOLOGICAL SUSPENSE SERIES
NEXT DOOR (Book #1)
A NEIGHBOR'S LIE (Book #2)
CUL DE SAC (Book #3)
SILENT NEIGHBOR (Book #4)
HOMECOMING (Book #5)
TINTED WINDOWS (Book #6)

KATE WISE MYSTERY SERIES
IF SHE KNEW (Book #1)
IF SHE SAW (Book #2)
IF SHE RAN (Book #3)
IF SHE HID (Book #4)
IF SHE FLED (Book #5)
IF SHE FEARED (Book #6)
IF SHE HEARD (Book #7)

THE MAKING OF RILEY PAIGE SERIES
WATCHING (Book #1)
WAITING (Book #2)
LURING (Book #3)

TAKING (Book #4)
STALKING (Book #5)
KILLING (Book #6)

RILEY PAIGE MYSTERY SERIES
ONCE GONE (Book #1)
ONCE TAKEN (Book #2)
ONCE CRAVED (Book #3)
ONCE LURED (Book #4)
ONCE HUNTED (Book #5)
ONCE PINED (Book #6)
ONCE FORSAKEN (Book #7)
ONCE COLD (Book #8)
ONCE STALKED (Book #9)
ONCE LOST (Book #10)
ONCE BURIED (Book #11)
ONCE BOUND (Book #12)
ONCE TRAPPED (Book #13)
ONCE DORMANT (Book #14)
ONCE SHUNNED (Book #15)
ONCE MISSED (Book #16)
ONCE CHOSEN (Book #17)

MACKENZIE WHITE MYSTERY SERIES
BEFORE HE KILLS (Book #1)
BEFORE HE SEES (Book #2)
BEFORE HE COVETS (Book #3)
BEFORE HE TAKES (Book #4)
BEFORE HE NEEDS (Book #5)
BEFORE HE FEELS (Book #6)
BEFORE HE SINS (Book #7)
BEFORE HE HUNTS (Book #8)
BEFORE HE PREYS (Book #9)
BEFORE HE LONGS (Book #10)
BEFORE HE LAPSES (Book #11)
BEFORE HE ENVIES (Book #12)
BEFORE HE STALKS (Book #13)
BEFORE HE HARMS (Book #14)

AVERY BLACK MYSTERY SERIES
CAUSE TO KILL (Book #1)
CAUSE TO RUN (Book #2)
CAUSE TO HIDE (Book #3)
CAUSE TO FEAR (Book #4)
CAUSE TO SAVE (Book #5)
CAUSE TO DREAD (Book #6)

KERI LOCKE MYSTERY SERIES
A TRACE OF DEATH (Book #1)
A TRACE OF MUDER (Book #2)
A TRACE OF VICE (Book #3)
A TRACE OF CRIME (Book #4)
A TRACE OF HOPE (Book #5)

Made in United States
Orlando, FL
12 October 2023

37810908R00146